WITH EYES WIDE OPEN

Miss Rebecca Shaw knew the truth about the
handsome, high-born Christopher Sinclair, who
had loved her and left her five years ago.

The honest, plainspoken Mr. Stanley Bartlett had
informed her of Christopher's life in London,
where he had scorned his wife and flaunted his
mistresses.

Rebecca could see for herself that Christopher,
single again, was in search of another moneyed
marriage and had set his sights on Rebecca's
pretty cousin, Harriet—as impressionable an
heiress as was ever fair game for a fortune
hunter.

This time Rebecca could not pretend that her
love was blind. This time she could only
pretend it was not there. . . .

*(For a list of other Signet Regency Romances
by Mary Balogh, please turn page. . . .)*

D1527673

The
Constant Heart

Mary Balogh

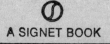

A SIGNET BOOK

NEW AMERICAN LIBRARY

NAL BOOKS ARE AVAILABLE AT QUANTITY DISCOUNTS WHEN USED
TO PROMOTE PRODUCTS OR SERVICES. FOR INFORMATION PLEASE
WRITE TO PREMIUM MARKETING DIVISION, NEW AMERICAN LIBRARY,
1633 BROADWAY, NEW YORK, NEW YORK 10019.

SIGNET TRADEMARK REG. U.S. PAT. OFF. AND FOREIGN COUNTRIES
REGISTERED TRADEMARK—MARCA REGISTRADA
HECHO EN CHICAGO, U.S.A.

SIGNET, SIGNET CLASSIC, MENTOR, ONYX, PLUME, MERIDIAN
and NAL BOOKS are published by NAL PENGUIN INC.,
1633 Broadway, New York, New York 10019

First Printing, July, 1987

1   2   3   4   5   6   7   8   9

PRINTED IN THE UNITED STATES OF AMERICA

*Love alters not with his brief hours and
    weeks,
But bears it out even to the edge of doom.*

WILLIAM SHAKESPEARE

• 1 •

"What I find most hurtful is their apparent lack of gratitude," the Reverend Philip Everett said. "It seems to me that the least they can do is be thankful for what we have done for them."

Rebecca Shaw smiled at him as she straightened the small pile of old books on the table in front of her. "You demand too much, Philip," she said placatingly. "You cannot really expect young boys to be grateful for being forced into a schoolroom to learn their letters when they might be out in the fields working with their fathers."

"Yet you and I have worked hard for more than a year to make all this possible," he said, gesturing vaguely at the room around them. He was standing squarely in front of the table, earnestly regarding his companion. "It seemed such a noble dream, Rebecca, to open a school for the village boys. Left to themselves, they would never have a chance for anything more in life than labor in the fields or perhaps employment in one of those dreadful new factories. We give them a chance of learning so that perhaps they can be employed as clerks at the very least. Do they not understand that?"

Rebecca rested her hands on top of the books and looked calmly at her betrothed. He had that crusading zeal in his eyes, the look that had always drawn her to him. It was there sometimes during his Sunday sermons, when he could transport his parishioners in spirit beyond the confines of their little world and all its humdrum activities and bring them closer to the meaning of it all. It was there when he had some fixed idea in his mind for service to mankind.

It was this zeal that still endeared him to Rebecca. Yet the purely feminine side of her nature had to admit she also took pleasure in his good looks. He was a tall young man, whose very upright bearing accentuated his height. He always dressed plainly in black. His only concession to vanity was the care he gave his thick blond hair, which was always clean and shining and which he always wore rather long. His complexion was fair and had a tendency to flush at the slightest emotion. He was flushed now.

"No," she said, "they probably do not understand, Philip. They are merely children. Most of them are incapable of looking to the future. All they know is that we are forcing them to sit in here when they could be outside helping in the fields or playing. Come, there is nothing so reprehensible in their attitude. We must have faith that what we are doing is right and will work out well in the end."

The Reverend Everett turned his head and looked around him. The building was not large—an oblong, single-roomed structure with whitewashed walls and dirt floor. Five rows of heavy wooden benches, nailed to the floor, filled much of the room. The roughly carpentered table behind which Rebecca stood occupied the remaining space. Small piles of books and papers were on the windowsills at the back of the room. A few watercolors, all apparently painted by the same hand of only limited talent, helped give the room a lived-in appearance.

He walked over to the doorway, from which the door had been pulled back to let in some fresh air, and gazed out to the bright world beyond. His hands were clasped behind him. "If the boys themselves cannot understand," he said, "at least I would expect their parents to do so. Do they not want something better for their children than what they have? Yet today you had only fourteen pupils. There should have been nineteen.''

Rebecca crossed to his side. She put a hand on his sleeve and looked up into his face. ''Have patience, Philip,'' she said. ''The idea of having their sons educated is new to them. Many of them find it hard to believe that learning to read will help their children to a better way of life. You have to sympathize with their caution, you know. Life does not offer these people much in the way of variety or advancement. They must be almost afraid to hope.''

''They will have no hope at all,'' he said, his arm unyielding beneath her touch, ''if they will not at least send the boys to school.''

''They will,'' she said, a smile on her face that he did not turn to see. ''Let us give it time. We must not lose hope, at all events, Philip. We have overcome too many obstacles to give up now. The money was truly a gift from heaven.''

''Yes,'' he agreed. ''I should have thought sooner of that wealthy acquaintance of mine in London. He told me years ago that I must call on him if ever I felt in need of funds for a worthwhile project.''

''I wish he could see the school,'' Rebecca said, looking with shining eyes back into the spartan little room. ''It is not much, Philip, but to have a building of our own and even books and paper and charcoal still seems like a dream come true. What I find most touching about your patron is that he insists on remaining anonymous. So many times the rich are charitable only so that others may see and praise their generosity.''

''I send reports to him regularly,'' the vicar said. ''He is pleased with what we have done and are doing.''

Rebecca squeezed his arm reassuringly before removing her hand and turning to take her bonnet and shawl from a hook on the wall behind the door. ''I must be getting home,'' she said. ''Maude will doubtless delay tea until I am there, and if I am late Harriet will be cross and make all our lives miserable for the rest of the day.''

Philip frowned. "I do not like the thought of your living with your uncle," he said. "Miss Shaw is by far too willful. She is all I abhor in people of wealth and privilege. And Lady Holmes, I fear, is too young and too weak to control her stepdaughter."

"One can hardly expect otherwise," Rebecca said cheerfully, tying the bow of her straw bonnet beneath her chin. "Harriet has been used to being mistress at Limeglade since she was ten years old. It is difficult for her to adjust to the presence of a new mistress and stepmother—especially when Maude is only three years her senior. But there is nothing malicious about either of them. And Uncle Humphrey has always done his best to make me feel that I belong in his home."

"I still cannot like it," Philip said. "I shall be thankful when we can wed and I can remove you to my own home."

Rebecca smiled fleetingly in his direction and crossed to the table to take up her reticule. She did not know exactly what Philip was waiting for, but ever since their betrothal almost a year before, he had spoken with some longing about their forthcoming marriage as if some definite obstacle stood in the way. He was not by any means a wealthy man, but then with his calling he was never like to be. The living in which he was established was a good one. The parsonage, which stood next to the church, was comfortable if not lavish in its furnishings. He had a wealthy patron, who was apparently willing to aid him in any charitable scheme he favored. There seemed no bar, then, to their nuptials.

Yet no definite arrangements had been made. When she stopped to think about it, Rebecca considered it rather strange. After all, neither of them was very young. Philip had recently turned thirty; she was six-and-twenty. But she did not think of it very frequently. She was quite content with life as it was at present. When Philip decided that it was time for them to marry, she would be ready. But she had no intention of pressing the issue with him.

"I shall see you tomorrow, then, Philip?" she asked cheerfully when she reached the door again. "I shall walk over to the parsonage as soon after luncheon as I may. Visiting the sick always takes a full afternoon."

"Yes," he said, "and I am always grateful for your help, Rebecca. Good day to you."

She left him standing in the doorway as she crossed the road to the country lane that led in the direction of her uncle's home. It would have been a three-mile walk, but she always took a shortcut through the pasture. She much preferred to walk than to call out the gig, though Uncle Humphrey constantly upbraided her for not using his conveyances. She would ruin her complexion with all the fresh air and exercise, he warned.

Rebecca smiled to herself. Uncle Humphrey had always been terrified of fresh air, and he rarely walked farther than from the dining room to his sitting room, or from his coach to his church pew. And his was not an attitude that had come only with advancing age. Indeed, he was barely fifty years old now. He had always been the same as far back as she could remember. Whenever he used to call at the parsonage to visit Papa, when Papa had been the vicar, he would always arrive in a closed carriage, summer and winter, and have to be escorted into the house by a footman, on whom he leaned heavily. Yet he must have been little more than thirty at the time she was remembering.

And his complexion always preoccupied Uncle Humphrey, too. He had continued to wear paint and powder on his face long after it became unfashionable for men to do so. The paint protected his face from the elements, he had explained to Papa at one time. And even now if she should happen to see him at night, his face would be heavily smeared with creams to prevent wrinkles. And indeed he was remarkably youthful looking for a man of his years. Somewhat portly, it was true, but he carried his weight proudly. He was an imposing, if a somewhat vain, figure of a man, Rebecca was forced to admit.

She had been living at Limeglade for five years now, ever since the death of Papa. Dear Papa! So deeply engrossed in the Lord's work that he had never seemed to have one thought to spare for the affairs of the world. He had been the younger brother of Uncle Humphrey, Lord Holmes, and therefore his life had been destined for the church ever since he was a young boy. But it was hard to imagine him in any other kind of life. On the death of his parents, he had inherited a sizable portion of both his mother's and his father's fortunes. Yet the money had all disappeared—not frittered away, but given freely to everyone who had asked his help, including several unworthies who had been less in need than he and his family.

Rebecca had been the sole member of her father's household after the death of her mother ten years before in the same smallpox epidemic that had carried off Aunt Sybil. She had accomplished the almost impossible—keeping house and feeding and clothing them both on almost no income. She had almost forgotten what money looked like. Yet she had been happy during most of those years. They had had a home and they had had friends. There had been no danger of starving. They were living the faith that they professed.

Yet when the Reverend Shaw had died, Rebecca was left quite destitute. She had been one-and-twenty at the time and would quite cheerfully have looked for employment as a governess. Uncle Humphrey had almost fainted away when she had made the suggestion on the afternoon following the funeral. He had indeed sat down heavily— yet gracefully—on the chair that was fortunately positioned just behind him, and fanned his face languidly with a lace-bordered handkerchief.

It was quite unfitting, he had said, for the niece of Lord Holmes of Limeglade to seek employment, albeit the job of governess was genteel work. His whole family would be disgraced. If she must insist on being useful—he had grimaced at the very thought—she must devote herself to being Harriet's companion. Harriet no longer enjoyed the company of her governess—penniless daughter of a mere country parson, poor soul—and needed someone of her own class and with her own good breeding.

Rebecca had hesitated. She hated to be beholden to her uncle. Her years with her father had made her value independence and had made her uneasy about privilege. Yet she was fond of her vain, foolish uncle and of his high-spirited daughter, despite her volatile temper. She had agreed to live with them on the condition that her allowance be small, only what she could feel she had earned as Harriet's companion. And she had continued to view herself more in the light of employee than relative, despite Harriet's apparent lack of interest in her company and despite Uncle Humphrey's frequent complaints about her plain attire and charitable works.

Things were different at Limeglade now, of course, with a new Lady Holmes. The baron had taken his daughter to London for a Season two years before, with the intention of finding her a husband suitable to his consequence. Harriet had returned unattached—though Rebecca had learned afterward by piecing together various hints and slips of the tongue that great scandal had been narrowly averted when she had been about to run off with a half-pay officer.

But the baron himself had brought home a new wife—a wide-eyed, rather frightened young girl who looked no older than Harriet, though in fact she was three years her senior. Rebecca had been horrified. Uncle Humphrey obviously doted on his prize and felt that he had conferred a great honor on her with his title, his wealth, and his imposing person. Yet it seemed glaringly clear to Rebecca that poor Maude had been the victim of ambitious parents. Several times she had caught an expression of distaste or even revulsion on the girl's face when she looked at her husband. She behaved with perfect correctness and showed him outward deference and even affection. But Rebecca was in no doubt that her new aunt was unhappy. Harriet did not help; she refused to recognize almost the very existence of the other woman.

Rebecca paused for a moment on the dirt road. Should she turn into the woods to her right and walk through them to the pasture? Or should she add an extra half mile to her journey by walking farther along the road until the pasture met it? The sunlight was so lovely—she glanced up to the clear blue sky. It would be a pity to plunge into shade and darkness. And she was really in no great hurry. She walked on.

She had resented Philip when he first came to the village. He had seemed a usurper—occupying Papa's pulpit, living in their house. She had forced herself to be civil to him and had gradually warmed to him as it became clear that he was almost as eager as Papa to minister to the needs of his parish. And she had had to admit that his sermons were easier to listen to than Papa's had ever been. She had resumed some of her old activities—visiting the sick and the elderly, distributing most of the money that her uncle insisted on giving her, decorating the church every week with flowers.

Without even realizing that it was happening, she had found that a friendship was developing between her and the vicar, over whose handsome person many a young female heart was sighing. Several times they had talked about the need of a school for the village boys. It had seemed like an impossible dream until one day he had told her that he had contacted an acquaintance of his, a gentleman from London, and had been offered a dizzyingly large sum of money with which to set up a school. The only problem was that they would not immediately be able to hire a teacher. The initial costs of a building and basic equipment would be too high. Rebecca had eagerly agreed to share the teaching responsibility with the Reverend Everett. It would mean teaching two days each week.

It had seemed almost natural a short time after that to receive Philip's undemonstrative proposal of marriage. She would be a good helpmeet, he had explained. Not wife. Not friend. Not lover. Just helpmeet. Yet Rebecca had cheerfully accepted. She was of an age when she must marry or resign herself to a life of spinsterhood. She was past the age for love. Her one experience with that emotion had brought enough pain and disillusionment to last a lieftime, anyway. She could do worse than be Philip's helpmeet. With him she would be living the life that she had always loved. And perhaps there would be a child or two. She would hate to think of going through life without experiencing motherhood.

She looked ahead along the road to see how far she still was from the shortcut across the pasture. As she did so, she became aware of two female figures approaching across the field to her left. The Misses Sinclair were also taking a shortcut from their father's house a mile away. They were waving to her and smiling.

"Well met, Miss Shaw," Ellen, the older girl, called. "We are on our way to the house."

"Indeed, it is a lovely day for a walk," Rebecca called, and stopped to wait for the two girls to catch up to her.

Primrose climbed the stile first and jumped into the roadway. Dimples showed in both cheeks. Rebecca had always been somewhat aghast at the younger sister's name. It was the sort of name that might sound very sweet for a tiny baby but quite inappropriate for a sixty-year-old dowager. Fortunately Primrose was a pretty and a happy girl and seemed to suit her name. She even favored, to a noticeable degree, dresses of yellow or lemon color. But she definitely did not suit the shortened name of Prim, which her family used.

"We are not going just for the walk," Primrose said now, suppressed excitement in her voice. "We have the most wonderful news to tell."

Her sister came hurtling down from the stile. "You shan't tell, Prim," she scolded. "It was agreed that I should tell since I am eighteen and the older. Mama and Papa said!"

"But that is just at the house," the younger girl complained. "You are to tell Harriet and Lord and Lady Holmes, Ellen. It is only fair that I tell now. It is only Miss Shaw after all."

Rebecca smiled at the unintentional slight. "An agreement is binding," she said. "I shall hear your news at the house."

"No," Ellen said, relenting now that her point had been won, "you can tell, Prim. But only here. Not a word at the house."

"Christopher is coming home!" the girl blurted, her extreme youth doubtless responsible for her inability to bolster her sense of importance by telling a story slowly.

Rebecca turned rather sharply in the direction of the pasture and led the way across the stile. "Indeed?" she said over her shoulder. "That is exciting news for you. It is many years since he was here last, is it not?" Six and a half years, to be exact, she thought.

"Almost seven," Primrose said. "I was only nine years old. I hardly remember his being here. He was away much of the time even then, you see, at university."

"Yes," Rebecca said, waiting for the girls to join her in the pasture, "it must be that long. How time does fly!"

"He never did come home even once when he was married to Angela," Primrose continued. "It always seemed strange. You would have thought she would have liked to see the place where he grew up, would you not? But they always stayed in London. We had to visit them there."

"It was lovely for us, though," Ellen said. "I hope that Christopher will not move permanently away from London now that he is a widower. It would be most provoking just when we are of an age to take part in the social activities there."

"He is coming for a visit," Primrose explained, "now that his year of mourning is over. He does not say how long he plans to stay. But Mama and Papa are over the moon, and Julian. I think he likes the idea of having a rich and fashionable brother to show off." She giggled. "And so do we. Christopher is most awfully handsome, Miss Shaw. We shall enjoy walking down the street in the village holding on to his arms. Shall we not, Ellen?''

''Maybe he will buy us some new bonnets and trinkets,'' the older girl said. ''It would be a shame if he did not. He is very rich, you know.''

Primrose, walking—or rather tripping along—beside Rebecca, looked up at her with a bright smile. ''You must have known Christopher when he lived here,'' she said. ''You are almost as old as he is, are you not?''

''He is three years my senior,'' Rebecca replied. ''And three years seems quite a wide span to children. I did not know him well when we were very young.'' She did not define what *very young* meant, but Primrose seemed satisfied with her answer.

''He was handsome even then,'' the younger girl said. ''I remember that at least. I'll wager all the girls were in love with him, were they not, Miss Shaw?''

Rebecca laughed. ''I daresay he had his fair share of admirers,'' she said. And she added lightly, ''It was a black day, indeed, for the female inhabitants of this county when he took himself off to London and decided never to return.''

''Well, fortunately he has decided to return again,'' Ellen said. ''The day after tomorrow, Miss Shaw. And he is single again. He surely will want another wife. He must have got used to the married state and will feel lonely without Angela. We think perhaps he will like Harriet. She is certainly lovelier than Angela was.''

He had said never, Rebecca was thinking. He had said he would never return. And never had turned out to be less than seven years. She supposed it was only natural that he would want to return to his parents' home at least for a visit when he had recently lost his wife and the child that she was unable to deliver before her death. It was understandable. But very unfair. She had thought that *never* meant not ever. She could have lived with that.

Primrose was nudging Ellen, and Ellen was giggling. "Is Mr. Bartlett at home this afternoon, Miss Shaw?" she asked finally. "Or has he gone out?"

I believe he and Lady Holmes were going driving in the phaeton together after luncheon," Rebecca replied, "but I think it likely that they have both returned for tea "

"Do you not consider him handsome, Miss Shaw?" Primrose asked. "Ellen does, though he is a little too short for my liking. I admire tall men. And I do not like men with red hair. Lady Holmes looks very well with it, but her brother would look better with brown hair, I believe."

"It is not red," Ellen protested. "It is auburn. Is it not, Miss Shaw?"

Rebecca considered. "Certainly Mr. Bartlett's hair is not as bright a red as his sister's," she said. "But is he not a little old for you, Ellen? I do believe he is at least of an age with me." She smiled in some amusement at the blushing Miss Sinclair.

"Well, you are not old, Miss Shaw," she said. "Besides, I have not said I have a *tendre* for him. Stop it, Prim," she said crossly as her sister nudged her again. "I have met him only once, when Lady Holmes brought him to call yesterday. And he had remarkably superior manners. Both Mama and Papa said so. Is he to stay long, Miss Shaw?"

"I really could not say," Rebecca replied.

Mr. Stanley Bartlett, Maude's older brother, had arrived quite unexpectedly three days before, followed by a valet and a veritable mountain of luggage. Nothing had been said in Rebecca's hearing about the expected duration of his visit. But no one was anxious to see him leave—thus far, at least. He was a man of considerable charm. He had that rare gift of being able to adapt his manner to all kinds of people so that all the varied members of the baron's household liked him, including Rebecca. His presence was a welcome addition to their family group and—if these girls were in any way typical—to the neighborhood.

"We are almost there," Ellen said, looking to the attractive yellow brick mansion ahead of them, its walls ivy-covered, its base surrounded by pink rhododendrons. "Now, remember, Prim, you are not to say a word. And you are not to jump up and down looking as if you were ready to burst. You are not to drop any hints at all."

• 2 •

Ellen was the first into the drawing room after the butler when they arrived at Limeglade. She was rewarded by the sight of both Lord and Lady Holmes as well as Mr. Bartlett and Harriet, all seated and obviously awaiting tea, though the tea tray had not yet been brought. She was less gratified by the sight of her brother, also seated.

She curtsied to all the occupants of the room and greeted each in turn. She turned to her brother last. "Julian," she said sharply, "you did not say at luncheon that you planned to ride over here. I suppose you galloped as hard as you could. And I suppose you have told already?"

Julian Sinclair, a tall, slim young man with a pleasant, eager face and thick, unruly brown hair, raised his eyes to the ceiling for a brief moment. "I knew I would not have had a moment's peace at home for a month if I had breathed a word," he replied. "No, the pleasure is all yours, Ellen."

"We thought you were never coming home, Rebecca," Harriet was saying crossly. "I met Julian while out riding and invited him back for tea, and we have both been waiting here for half an hour. Maude insisted that we wait for you, though I do not see why. You know when teatime is, and even if you are not here on time, you will not starve. You can eat when you come."

"The walk is too long, Rebecca, my dear," the baron added, looking at his niece with disapproval. "You would not be late for tea, you know, if you would just take the gig as I have advised you to do. Your cheeks are positively red, my dear. You will be fortunate if you do not do permanent damage to your complexion, or—worse—take a chill. Perhaps I should summon Dr. Gamble to look at you just in case?''

''But it is a good thing we did wait, Harriet,'' Lady Holmes said calmly. ''Now we can have tea with the Misses Sinclair too.''

''The rosy cheeks are vastly becoming to my mind,'' Mr. Bartlett said with a dazzling smile and an elegant bow in Rebecca's direction.

Rebecca smiled at everyone. ''I am certainly ready for a cup of tea,'' she said. ''And Miss Sinclair has brought some news that will be of interest to everyone.''

She sat down as everyone's attention turned to the elder Miss Sinclair.

Ellen was no more able than her sister had been to play with her audience and enjoy their attention for as long as possible before divulging the core of the matter. ''Christopher is coming home!'' she said, beaming first at Harriet, then at Maude, and finally at Lord Holmes. ''In two days' time he should be here.''

''Splendid!'' the baron said, showing a flattering degree of interest in the youthful Miss Sinclair. ''Shocking affair, that of his wife. Still in mourning, is he? A fine figure of a man he was when I saw him last. Fashionable. Top of the trees, you know. Liked to risk his health rather too much, perhaps—riding and boxing, you know. It is ironic that Mrs. Sinclair should be the one to pass on. One can never be too careful.'' He sighed deeply. ''He should have chosen his physician more carefully. One can never be too careful I always say. One should choose one's physician with as much care as one chooses one's tailor.'' He paused a moment. ''Perhaps even more carefully.''

Harriet waited impatiently for her father to finish his monologue. ''Christopher Sinclair is coming here?'' she said. ''Papa and I met him several times when we were in

town a few years ago. I hardly remembered him from
before he left here. But there he was a spendidly handsome
man. We would have entertained him more often if it had
not been for his wife. She was the daughter of a cit,'' she
added, the explanation directed toward Mr. Bartlett. ''Rather
a vulgar creature, I am afraid.'' She seemed suddenly to
realize that she was in the presence of the brother-in-law
and sisters-in-law of the late Mrs. Sinclair and had the
grace to flush. ''Of course,'' she added, ''one must not
speak ill of the departed.''

Fortunately two events occurred to cover her confusion.
The tea tray arrived and was carried over to Lady Holmes,
who proceeded to pour. And Mr. Bartlett took up the
conversation.

''Mr. Christopher Sinclair is your brother?'' he asked
Ellen, his eyebrows raised, one hand toying with the handle of his quizzing glass. ''I had no idea.''

''You know him?'' she said, all eager smiles and dimples.

''Why, yes, Miss Sinclair,'' he replied, ''I am acquainted with him. And was with his wife.'' He turned
with a reassuring smile to a still-flushed Harriet. ''It is true
that she did not share his breeding or his education, but
she did have other qualities that perhaps saved her from
being truly vulgar.'' He turned back to Ellen. ''I might
have known, of course, had I given the matter thought,
that he is of your family. He shares a remarkable hand-
someness with his brother and sisters.''

Ellen blushed and giggled, and even Primrose looked
gratified.

''Do you know my brother too, Lady Holmes?'' Julian
asked.

Maude looked up at him as she put down the teapot. ''I
am afraid not,'' she said. ''I spent only a short time in
London before my marriage. Stanley knows a vastly larger
number of people than I do.''

She turned her attention to Rebecca as the younger
people continued to talk about the expected arrival and all
the extra activities that the event was bound to bring.

"How was the school today, Rebecca?" she asked.

Rebecca shrugged and smiled rather ruefully. "There were only fourteen boys there," she said, "the fewest so far. But the weather is exceptionally good. I am sure there must be much work for them to do with their fathers."

"The Reverend Everett must be disappointed," Maude said sympathetically. "He sets great store by the success of the school, does he not?"

"Yes," Rebecca replied, "I am afraid he does. Poor Philip is so otherworldly himself and puts so much effort into all he does, that he expects an equal dedication from everyone. He cannot be contented with letting the school develop gradually. I keep telling him that it is a totally new idea for the people of the village and farms to be able to have their sons educated. They must be given time to get accustomed to the idea—a few years, perhaps."

"The Reverend Everett deserves success," Maude commented. "The welfare of others is always so much more important than his own well-being. I noticed last Sunday as I shook hands with him on leaving church that there was a patch on the hem of his surplice. I do admire him so."

"I call that affectatious," the baron added, having swung his attention from one conversation to the other. "The fellow does not need to walk around with a patched surplice. This is the richest living for miles around. It don't do for a clergyman to go around in rags. He makes the gentry look miserly. My brother never did that, Rebecca, dear, even though he had some peculiar notions."

Rebecca smiled. "I am sure Philip will never be reduced to wearing rags, Uncle Humphrey," she said. "But I do know that he cares little for personal vanity."

"It is a kind of vanity to wear patched clothes," the baron added sagely. "He likes other people to notice how godly he is. I still believe that the niece of Lord Holmes could have made a better match, Rebecca."

She smiled affectionately at him but did not reply. They had exhausted all there was to say on that topic long ago.

"May I come with you one day, Rebecca?" Maude

asked, looking almost beseechingly at the niece who was three years older than she. "I should like to see your school when the boys are there. I would not get in the way at all. In fact, I could perhaps be useful. You are by far more knowledgeable than I am. Yet you said yourself but last week that my French is better than yours. Perhaps I could teach a little?"

Rebecca opened her mouth to explain as tactfully as she could that she and Philip had decided not to include any language other than English in their school curriculum—at first, anyway. Not even Latin was to be taught. They had both agreed that the boys had a great deal to learn merely to read and write their own language correctly. However, the baron spoke before she did.

"There is no call for you to do any such thing, my love," he said to his wife. "It is bad enough to have my niece involved in such low pursuits. It would not do at all for Lady Holmes of Limeglade to involve herself in the running of a school for the vulgar. Such behavior would tarnish both your image and mine."

"But, my lord," Maude said, raising large eyes timidly to his, "it would give me something to do. Sometimes I feel so useless. The household runs so smoothly, and dear Harriet likes to do her part as she did before I came here. It is surely becoming for your wife to involve herself in charitable activities."

"I shall take you to visit the school one afternoon," the baron said, "and the boys can recite their lessons for us. That is charitable enough. But you will not teach. You have enough to do, my love, keeping yourself looking beautiful. You mustn't exert yourself doing much else. Work ruins the health and the complexion."

Maude's eyes had dropped to the tea in the cup she held with one hand. "I shall not go, then, my lord," she said quietly, "if you do not wish it."

Rebecca turned her attention away from this mild domestic dispute. She felt sorry for Maude. Her uncle's wife was a quiet and sensible girl. Yet she was married to a foolish and vain man thirty years her senior. He should have been much wiser than she, a father figure almost. Certainly he thought himself wiser. Consequently, he gave her very little freedom. It was not that he was a tyrannical or hardhearted man. Rather he was an aging man who was trying to prolong or recapture his own youth through a young wife. He cosseted her, protected her, and treated her more as a fragile doll than a woman. Having always been idle yet contented himself, he failed to understand that his wife was bored and restless.

It was a great shame that he refused to listen to her occasional pleas for more activity, Rebecca reflected. At least so far her suggestions had all been on the side of good. She had wished to create a flower garden to the south of the house, doing much of the work herself. The flower garden was now in existence, but Lady Holmes had not been permitted any part in its creation. She had wished to visit the sick, taking with her gifts of baking and needlework that she had made herself. She now did visit the sick one afternoon a month, conveyed in the baron's best closed traveling carriage. But she carried offerings that the servants had made. And now she wished to help at the school.

Perhaps if she became bored and frustrated enough, Lady Holmes would turn her attention to less desirable activities. Perhaps she would learn to ride recklessly or . . . Rebecca's imagination at the moment could provide no vice more terrible than that. But she did feel sorry for Maude. She knew that she herself would chafe terribly against such restrictions. At least with Philip she would be sure of always having plenty to do.

She let her eyes roam around the rest of the group gathered in the drawing room. Julian Sinclair, eager and boyish, was talking earnestly to Harriet. He fancied himself in love with her, perhaps really was so. They had grown up together, were only a year apart in age. He must know her well enough to know that she was moody: haughty one minute, all contrite affection the next; coldly aloof at one time, warmly impulsive at another. Yet he still sought her company, beseeched her with his eyes for something more than the offhand treatment he usually received from her.

Harriet, Rebecca suspected, still did not know what she wanted of life. She shared much of her father's vanity and foolishness. Yet against all reason, Rebecca was fond of her cousin. She had little reason to be. Harriet had scant patience for Rebecca's apparent lack of interest in her personal appearance and advancement and for her devotion to helping others.

She had once called Philip a pompous ass, but that had been immediately after she had been forced to listen to a sermon in which he had condemned the vanity of worldly possessions. She had been convinced that the sermon was directed against her because she was sitting conspicuously in her father's padded pew at the front of the church wearing a particularly frivolous new bonnet. She had apologized to Rebecca later the same day, saying that the sermon could not have been meant personally as the Reverend Everett's sermons were always prepared in advance and he could have had no way of knowing that she would be wearing a new bonnet on that particular Sunday.

However it was, Rebecca considered Julian's chances of winning Harriet slim. He was too young and unsure of himself to control her headstrong temperament. And he was of no social significance. The Sinclairs were of good lineage and were a long-established family in the county. But they had never been particularly wealthy or prominent in any other way. Their only claim to distinction at present was their relationship to Christopher Sinclair, who had made himself quite fabulously wealthy by contracting a marriage with the daughter of a cit, a man who had amassed a fortune in business and trade.

Rebecca had no wish to continue that train of thought. She turned her attention to Mr. Bartlett, who was entertaining the two Sinclair girls. He was smiling; his eyes were dancing. The two girls were listening to him, bright-

eyed and rapt. Rebecca found herself smiling too. Their
family circle had certainly brightened since the arrival of
Maude's brother, despite the fact that Maude herself had
not seemed overjoyed to see him when he arrived unexpectedly. Maude still seemed not to think of Limeglade as
her home. She seemed to have felt embarrassed that a
relative of hers would invite himself to stay with Lord
Holmes.

But he was a delightful man, Rebecca had decided. He
was not remarkably handsome. He was of medium height,
had auburn, wavy hair and eyebrows, and a pale complexion. His eyes were brown and set perhaps rather too close
together for perfection. But they were candid and smiling
eyes. His teeth were rather large for his face, or his mouth
was too wide. But they were white teeth and showed
frequently. He smiled a great deal.

He made friends very easily, a quality that Rebecca
admired in him. Soon after his arrival he was on the best
of terms with both the baron and Harriet, and thus any
resentment that his unexpected visit might have caused
was smoothed over. He made an effort to converse with
Rebecca, though he need not have done so. Her approval
was not necessary to his continued stay in the house. He
had expressed interest in the school and had even agreed
with her opinion that some form of education should be
offered to the girls of the village, too. Philip had never
been sympathetic to that idea. Mr. Bartlett had met Philip
and the Sinclairs and had been warmly welcomed by all.

Only Maude, strangely enough, seemed less than delighted
by his presence. But Rebecca could understand why. It
must be hard for a girl as quiet and shy as Maude to have a
brother like Mr. Bartlett, a man so much at his ease in
company. She had taken months to get to know and feel
comfortable with people whose approbation he had won
within days. It must seem unfair to her to know that they
were of the same family yet were so different in temperament.

The Misses Sinclair were the first to rise to leave. Julian
reluctantly followed their lead and got to his feet.

"Christopher will be here in two days' time," Ellen reminded the company. "I do not know how we will live through the rest of today and tomorrow. We will bring him to visit as soon as may be, Lady Holmes." She turned eagerly to Mr. Bartlett. "And you and he will have a chance to renew your acquaintance," she said.

Mr. Bartlett smiled and bowed.

After they had left, Lady Holmes rang the bell for the butler to remove the tea tray, and everyone sat down again.

"I am so pleased that Mr. Christopher Sinclair is coming here," said Harriet. "He is a very fashionable man, is he not, Papa?"

"Decidedly so, my dear," her father agreed. He had taken a jeweled snuffbox from the table beside him, placed a pinch on the back of his right hand, and sniffed delicately through each nostril in turn. Then he took a lace-bordered handkerchief from his pocket and waited with half-closed eyes and twitching nostrils for the sneeze to follow.

Having completed the action to his own satisfaction, he continued the conversation. "It will be interesting to hear what news he brings from town," he said. "It is so difficult here to be up to the minute on what styles and fabrics are currently in fashion. Mr. Bartlett, did you not tell me that black had become an almost acceptable color for evening wear? I can scarcely conceive of such a thing. Black!" He shuddered delicately.

"Beau Brummell started the fashion, my lord," Mr. Bartlett replied, "though at the time it seemed just a personal eccentricity. Yet now one sees the style with fair frequency. Of course, all men of any distinction of looks and bearing—like yourself, my lord, if I may be permitted to say so—still prefer more palatable colors."

The baron nodded affably to show that his guest was indeed permitted to say so.

"We must invite Mr. Sinclair to dinner within the week," Harriet said, as always oblivious to the fact that she was no longer mistress of the house. "But will that mean having to invite the whole family, Papa?"

"It will be a pleasure to have them all," Maude said. "It is some time since we gave a dinner party. Do you not agree, my lord?" she asked, glancing with hasty self-consciousness at her husband.

"Oh, quite so, quite so," he agreed.

"I hope Mr. Sinclair makes an effort to appear to advantage with his family," Mr. Bartlett added, smiling graciously at Harriet. "They are worthy and likable people."

Harriet raised her eyebrows and looked back at him, all attention. Rebecca, too, looked sharply across at him.

"Why would he not appear to advantage?" Harriet asked.

"Pardon me," Mr. Bartlett replied, serious for once. "There is nothing unacceptable in his manner by some London standards. If he is rather a spendthrift, one at least cannot say that he is so with anyone else's money than his own—now. And if he is something of a rake, one can say the same of many other men of rank in town."

Maude got to her feet and gathered together the embroidery that she had earlier set down beside her. "I am sure that Mr. Sinclair will know how to behave when he is here, Stanley," she said matter-of-factly. "Harriet, shall we go to my sitting room and make some plans for the dinner party?"

"Oh," replied Harriet, "I already have it all arranged in my mind, Maude. You do not need to worry about it."

"Then you shall tell me what you have planned," Maude said with quiet persistence, and she preceded her step-daughter from the room.

The baron too retired to his room in order to rest before beginning the exertions of evening dinner and a hand or two of cards in the drawing room afterward.

Rebecca also rose to leave the room. She planned to have a leisurely bath after the hours spent teaching in a warm schoolroom and the hot, dusty walk to and from the village.

"You must have known Mr. Christopher Sinclair before his marriage, Miss Shaw," Mr. Bartlett said in his friendly way. He was smiling at her. "Though I believe he must be considerably older than you."

"Only a few years, sir," Rebecca replied. "And, yes, I knew him. It is impossible in a small place like this not to know one's neighbors."

"Tell me," he said, looking at her candidly, "was he always such an unprincipled man? I must confess that now I have made the acquaintance of the Sinclairs, I find it difficult to understand how he has become the way he is. I suppose that in most families there has to be one black sheep."

Rebecca sat down again. "Unprincipled in what way?" she asked guardedly.

"Perhaps he was a close friend, Miss Shaw?" Mr. Bartlett added, looking at her searchingly. "I would not wish to ruin your memories of him."

Rebecca made a dismissive gesture with one hand. "It is many years since I have even seen him, sir," she said.

"I knew his wife," he said. "She was a friend. A delightful creature, though not by any means a beauty. And many people despised her because her father was in business and not, strictly speaking, a gentleman at all. Sinclair married her for her money, of course. And I would not stoop to blame him for that. Many a gentleman with pockets to let has been forced to do as much."

Rebecca lowered her eyes to the hands in her lap. Perhaps she ought not to be listening to this. It was none of her affair, after all. But she could not help herself. It is sometimes too delicious to hear evil of a person one has despised for many years. She had not been mistaken, then.

"I could certainly have forgiven him for marrying my friend for her money," Mr. Bartlett continued, "had he treated her with proper respect thereafter."

"And he did not?" Rebecca prompted, raising her eyes unwillingly to his.

"The Sinclairs seem a humble enough family," Mr.

Bartlett said. "And that makes it all the more surprising that Sinclair himself is so insufferably high in the instep. He treated her with the utmost contempt, Miss Shaw. He never took her about with him, and he flaunted his mistresses before her most shamefully."

"Poor lady," Rebecca murmured, feeling sympathy for the late Mrs. Sinclair for the first time.

"Perhaps the situation would not have been so tragic had she not doted so much on him," Mr. Bartlett continued. "She lived with the hope that perhaps the child would bring him closer to her. Her death was tragic, yet under the circumstances perhaps for the best. She would have been disappointed, I am sure." His tone had become almost vicious.

"I do not find your story impossible to credit, sir," Rebecca said, her voice strained. "Yet I believe it would be as well to keep it to yourself. I would not wish to see his family hurt."

"Indeed, ma'am," he assured her earnestly, "I would not dream of breathing a word to anyone else. I would not have said anything to you either, but you seem to me to be a lady of sense. And I fear that perhaps Sinclair will not, after all, behave as he ought here. He has lived for too long a life of self-indulgence and depravity. I wish to suggest, Miss Shaw, with all due respect, that you keep careful watch over your cousin. She is a lovely and impressionable young lady and wealthy enough, I believe, to attract a fortune hunter."

Rebecca's eyes widened. "Do you believe he would dare?" she asked. "I cannot think it."

"And I trust you are right," he said earnestly. "But I felt it my duty to speak. I would not be able to forgive myself if anything happened because I had felt the matter too delicate to involve myself. Forgive me, Miss Shaw. My sister's family has in a sense become my own. I must be concerned for the welfare of its members. If Sinclair behaves as a gentleman ought, I shall be happy, though I may lose credit in your eyes."

"Not so, sir," Rebecca assured him. "I thank you for taking me into your confidence. You may be sure that I shall be properly concerned for Harriet's welfare when Mr. Sinclair arrives."

"Thank you, ma'am," he said, and his face relaxed into its accustomed smile. He took Rebecca's hand in his and raised it to his lips before turning and leaving the room.

• 3 •

Rebecca ascended to her room with lowered eyes and lagging steps. She could feel one of her infrequent headaches coming on. The day had been hot and busy. She rang immediately for a maid and directed that bathwater be brought to her dressing room. She ran a finger beneath the high neckline of her cotton dress and turned her head from side to side. But it was no good. There was no cool air to be felt.

She should not have stayed to listen to Mr. Bartlett. She should have told him quite firmly as soon as he began that the way Mr. Christopher Sinclair chose to run his life was none of her concern.

People were all the same, she supposed. Everyone liked to hear gossip, especially if it showed someone one knew in an unpleasant light. She always prided herself on her lack of interest in either listening to or spreading vicious rumors. Yet there were times when she could not resist. And she had heard so very little about Christopher in almost seven years. She had taken a malicious sort of pleasure in hearing what Mr. Bartlett had had to say, and really she could not entirely blame either him for speaking or herself for listening. He had spoken from the best of motives—his concern for Harriet and the Sinclair family. And she had listened for the same reasons.

But now that she had had time to digest what she had heard, she would far prefer not to have listened at all. She undid the buttons at the back of her dress, not waiting for a maid to assist her. It was a relief to slip the fabric off her shoulders and arms, light as the cotton material was.

She had wanted to forget Christopher. Once she had convinced herself that he had meant it when he said that he would never return, she had resolutely set herself to forgetting him. The self-discipline that she had built up during her childhood and youth as her father's daughter had aided her outwardly. She had not crumbled, and no one—not even Papa—had known the size of the battle raging within. But finally she had won that battle, too, though never perhaps quite to the extent she would have liked. Occasionally she would think to herself with some satisfaction that she had now forgotten Christopher. But she would immediately realize that the very thought proved her wrong.

She had had to concentrate on the negative side of his character that she had known only at the last, the side that she had never even suspected. She had always known, of course, that he was not perfect. Her earliest memories of him were of a mischievous plague of a boy, whose greatest delight seemed to be to tease the prim, rather shy daughter of the vicar. She could remember him at church, sitting with his family in the second pew, behind her and her mother. She had worn her hair in long braids as a child, and she had liked to toss the braids over the back of the seat, where they would not dig into her back. One Sunday morning she had been forced to sit through most of her father's lengthy sermon with her head tilted back at an unnatural angle while Christopher's knee had kept her braid held firmly against the back of the pew. She had been released finally, she remembered, a moment after hearing the sound of a swift slap immediately behind her.

And then there had been the time when Mrs. Sinclair had been visiting at the parsonage and the children had wandered outside. She remembered sitting on a tombstone in the churchyard, finally too terrified either to get down or to turn her head as Christopher stood in front of her, very seriously and sincerely describing the ghosts that came out of the graves at midnight. For many nights after that she had awoken Mama with her screams as she struggled out of some nightmare.

Rebecca was very thankful to peel off her remaining clothes when the water finally arrived and to climb into the bathtub and soak in the lukewarm suds. It had been just such a day when she had finally realized that both she and Christopher were growing up. She had always hero-worshiped him to a certain extent. He had always been a tall boy for his age and slim and—to her child's eyes—very handsome with his dark, straight hair and blue eyes. She could even remember the time when she was about twelve years old and had started to fantasize about his rescuing her from terrible dangers: fire-breathing dragons, vicious highwaymen, treacherous quicksand. He had always been mounted on a white stallion in those fantasies and he had always had a black cloak streaming behind him. And the fantasies had always ended at the moment of rescue.

The time she was thinking of was the summer when she was fourteen and he seventeen. The annual village fair had lasted the whole day and was ending in fast and furious fun as everyone danced on the village green. Rebecca, for the first time, had been allowed to stay up until eleven o'clock, but finally Mama had instructed her to go home to bed. The whole village was alight. There was no need for anyone to acompany her. But Christopher had fallen into step beside her, chatting in his amiable way as he walked her home. By that stage of their lives they had become firm friends.

They had taken a shortcut through the churchyard on the way to the parsonage and Christopher had tried to revive her old fear of the graves there. But she had tossed her head, which was feeling very grown up with its hair pinned up for the first time, and thrown him a look of contempt.

"Pooh, Christopher Sinclair," she had said, "you cannot scare me with such tales any longer. I am grown up now.''

"Are you, though, Becky?" he had said, looking side-long at her. "I'll wager you aren't.''

"I bet I am," she had retorted, turning belligerently toward him and placing her hands on her hips. "I am too a woman grown. I am allowed to wear my hair up and I have been allowed to stay up until eleven o'clock.''

"I'll wager you don't know how to kiss, though, Becky," he had teased. "You aren't a woman until you know how to kiss.''

She had been very thankful for the darkness that hid her hot flush of shock and embarrassment. "Nonsense, Christopher Sinclair," she had said with all the bored sophistication of a fourteen-year-old. "Of course I know how to kiss.''

"You will have to prove it then," he had jeered.

She had kept her hands on her hips, lifted her chin defiantly, puckered her lips, and squeezed her eyes tightly shut as she saw his face approaching.

If she really had known how to kiss, it would have been glaringly obvious to her that he certainly did not. But she had assumed that that bruising, grinding pressure of lips and teeth against lips and teeth was how it was supposed to be done. She never did ask herself whether she had liked it or not. When she had stopped running and had the door of the parsonage safely between herself and any possible pursuit by Christopher, she had been too deeply in love with him to consider anything more than the fact that he had kissed her, and she had proved to him that she was indeed a woman.

She had loved him mindlessly, passionately, for the following five years, until he had told her that he was going away and never coming back. And even beyond that she had loved him, painfully and against her will, until she had finally forced herself to forget. Or to tell herself that she had forgotten.

Rebecca slid down in the bathtub until her whole body

was submerged to the neck. She put her head back against the metal rim and closed her eyes. The cool water felt very good. She could feel all her muscles relaxing. Perhaps her headache would not develop after all. It was pointless to pursue these memories of Christopher now. It was all ancient history. He was clearly a very different man now from the one she had loved as a girl and very young woman.

Two days later, Rebecca was again walking home from a day at the school. The weather was still hot, though clouds had moved across the sky since she had left home that morning so that at least she did not have the glare of the sun to contend with.

She was not feeling cheerful. She and Philip had come very close to quarreling during the morning. It was not his day for teaching, but he had spent half an hour with her before luncheon.

She had been listening to the boys reading aloud. The performance was not an inspired one, but most of the pupils had managed to stumble their way through the words on the page. However, there was one boy who had not. There was scarcely a word he could recognize, and even Rebecca's promptings and encouragement to sound the words out syllable by syllable did not help. Philip had walked over to stand silently behind the boy, his hands clasped behind his back, his expression stern. The boy, feeling the vicar's presence there, had become nervous and confused. His stammerings had become totally incomprehensible.

And finally Philip had lost his temper. He had scolded the boy for inattention, for lack of effort, for stupidity, and for truancy. He had finally berated the lad with bitter sarcasm for his dirty fingernails and uncombed hair. A few minutes later Rebecca had given the boys a break and stood silently at her desk while they filed out, far more subdued than usual.

"They are incredibly ungrateful!" Philip had exploded

after the last one had left the building. ''Do they not care? Do they not realize what an opportunity is being presented them? I am bitterly disillusioned.''

''Philip,'' Rebecca had said gently, ''most of the boys have made marked progress. If you consider the fact that a mere few months ago they could not even distinguish one letter from another, you would realize the truth of what I say. But you must have noticed that Cyril cannot learn as fast as the others. He knows the letters, but he cannot put them together to create words.''

''If he attended school regularly,'' Philip had said coldly, ''perhaps he would not have fallen so far behind.''

''It is not that,'' Rebecca had protested. ''He has not missed so many days, Philip. He is incapable of learning as fast as the other boys. He needs a great deal of extra help and encouragement.''

''We are here to teach, Rebecca,'' he had said passionately, ''not to coddle and baby these village lads.''

The argument had ended abruptly as the pupils began to file back into the schoolroom. Philip had left soon after, and she had not seen him again. This was his afternoon for visiting the elderly and sometimes, she knew, he did not arrive home until well into the evening. Visiting the sick and elderly for Philip meant more than sitting at bedsides holding hands and saying prayers. Frequently it meant chopping wood or hauling water or even preparing a meal.

And remembering that fact as she walked along the country lane, still a good half mile from the stile that would lead her into the pasture and across to the house, Rebecca's heart softened. Philip could be a strange mixture of harshness and dedication. He certainly did not spare himself in his devotion to his parishioners. And even his harsher moments, she realized, resulted from his zeal. He wanted these village lads to learn, wanted them to have a better future than they could otherwise expect. Unfortunately, he did not always have enough patience to allow for anyone with less drive than himself. He meant well and that was the important fact for her to remember.

She had not been in high spirits, though, even before the altercation with Philip. Christopher was coming home today, was probably already with his family, in fact. Tomorrow or the next day he would visit at Limeglade or her uncle's family would visit the Sinclairs. If she was fortunate, she would miss that first meeting. But she could not avoid it forever. The two families lived only two miles apart and had always been on the most intimate of visiting terms.

Within the next week at the longest she would have to meet him again. And she had no wish to do so. The battle to forget him had been a long and hard one. But she had won eventually. Her life for the last several years had not been a wildly happy one, but it had been of moderate contentment. She had a comfortable home with relatives who treated her with affection even if not with demonstrative love. She was continuing the works of charity that had been dear to her father's heart. And she was betrothed to a man who embodied those ideals for which she lived. She did not want to be reminded of a time when she had desired more of life, a time when she had wanted passion and romantic love. And she did not want to be reminded of how Christopher had changed. She wanted to remember him, if at all, as he had been before.

Rebecca looked ahead to the stile, not far distant now. She quickened her step. A cup of tea would be very welcome at the end of the walk. She slowed down almost immediately, though, and moved over the side of the road until her dress was brushing against the hedgerow. She could hear the approach of a horse behind her and had no desire to be ridden down. She gazed ahead absently, her mind swinging back to Cyril and his obvious learning problem.

"G'day, ma'am," a deep masculine voice said as a horse drew level with her on the road.

Rebecca looked up, startled, into the politely smiling face of a large young man, whose high shirt points pressed into his cheeks as if trying to burst them. He was touching a riding crop to his hat. She smiled in quick relief. She had feared for one horrid moment that it might be Christopher.

"Good day, sir," she said, inclining her head to him, and he rode on.

She had not realized there were two horses until the second one drew level with her and the performance was repeated.

"Good day, ma'am," the second rider said.

"Good day, sir," Rebecca replied, and glanced up at the speaker.

Did time stand still? she wondered later. Probably not. It just seemed to have done so. He was instantly recognizable, though changed in the course of almost seven years. He looked as tall and straight in the saddle as he had always looked then. His hair was as dark and straight and as long. His eyes were as intensely blue, his nose as straight, his mouth as wide. Yet the years had taken away his boyish slimness and left a solid, well-muscled man in his place. And time had taken away the open, pleasant expression that he had habitually worn and replaced it with a controlled, almost stern look. His jaw looked a lot firmer than she remembered.

He lowered his riding whip from the brim of his top hat and drew his horse to a halt. "Hello, Becky," he said quietly, unsmilingly.

"Hello, Christopher," she replied. She had stopped walking without realizing it.

There seemed to be nothing else to say. Both looked for a moment as if sorry they had stopped.

"How are you?" he asked.

"Well, thank you," she replied. "And you, Christopher?"

He nodded. He had removed his hat, and Rebecca could see that his hair was as thick and shining as it had ever been.

"I am sorry about your bereavement," she said.

He nodded once more. "Thank you."

They looked at each other awkwardly again. "You are

living with your uncle now?" he said. "I was sorry to hear of your father's passing."

She smiled stiffly.

"Are you on your way home?" he asked. "You have still a long way to go. May I offer you a ride?"

"Oh, no, thank you," she said hastily. "I enjoy the walk across the pasture. Uncle Humphrey always urges me to take the gig."

There was another awkward pause. The first rider broke it. He had turned his horse back to find out what had delayed his companion.

"I say, Sinclair," he said, sweeping off his hat. "Meeting old acquaintances already?"

Christopher smiled, a rather tight grimace that did not quite reach his eyes. "Miss Shaw, may I present Mr. Lucas Carver?"

Mr. Carver leaned down from his horse and stretched out a hand to Rebecca. His shirt points dug even more dangerously into his cheeks, she noticed.

"Pleased t'make your acquaintance, Miss Shaw," he said.

Christopher had pulled himself together by the time Rebecca and Mr. Carver had exchanged civilities. "We must allow you to continue your walk, Becky," he said. "It is good to see you again."

She inclined her head to both men and watched them ride away from her before continuing on her way. She was over the stile and well across the pasture before she came out of her daze. She had met him again, had talked to him. And she had survived. Here she was walking home as if nothing out of the ordinary had happened.

She stopped suddenly and looked down at herself, aghast. What would he have seen? How had she appeared to Christopher after six and a half years? She had been a girl of nineteen last time he saw her. She was a woman of six-and-twenty now. She had changed, she knew. She was still only of medium height, still very slight in figure. She still wore clothes of simple, unfashionable style. But her face and her hair must have appeared very different to him. Her face had paled and thinned over the years. She had lost her youthful look and sparkle, she knew. Her gray eyes, when she looked at herself in the mirror, looked back at her calmly with the look of a woman who had experienced the vicissitudes of life and not been destroyed by them. Her fair hair was no longer worn in loose curls. Years ago she had grown it longer and confined it in a loose knot at the base of her neck.

She looked her age, she knew. And her appearance was eminently suited to her station. While she tried always to look neat, she did not feel it appropriate to aim for elegance or prettiness. She was betrothed to a village vicar and she taught at the village school. She was six-and-twenty years old. She was usually un-self-conscious about her appearance. Why would she care now? Why care that Christopher Sinclair had seen the changes? If Philip liked her the way she was, why worry about the opinion of any other man? After all, he had changed too. He was clearly now a man of nine-and-twenty rather than the very young man she had known.

The changes in him were all improvements, though, some inner part of her mind told her, unbidden. He had been a very good-looking boy. Now he was an unusually handsome man. And a selfish, unprincipled man, she must constantly remind herself.

Yes, he had been a very good-looking boy. She had always been aware of the fact. Being three years younger than he, she had always looked up to him as an older, heroic male. But perhaps she had been fully aware of his good looks and attractiveness only when he had come home after his first year at Oxford. He was nineteen, vastly self-assured, and inclined to patronize the sixteen-year-old daughter of the vicar. He had been friendly, had sought her out whenever circumstances brought them into the same company, and had talked to her a great deal. But perhaps the friendship at that time owed more to the fact that there were very few other people in the area close to his age than to any special preference for Rebecca.

That had had to wait another two years until he came home after his final year at university. Rebecca had acquired poise in the few years since the death of her mother. She had also recently become more conscious of her looks and had had her hair styled so that the length and heaviness that had pulled it straight were replaced by soft curls over her head and down her neck. She had fashioned herself some light muslin gowns for the summer instead of the usual cotton ones.

Christopher had noticed the changes immediately. He had looked at her with admiration when they met the day after his return home.

"Well," he had said, "aren't you the fine lady, Becky! You must be beating back the suitors from the door."

"Silly," she had replied, pleased. "Where would they come from in a place like this?"

He had grinned. "I must be thankful that we do not live in a large place," he had said. "Does this mean I have you all to myself?"

His voice had been teasing. And that manner had set the tone of their relationship through most of the summer. They had met a good deal during various visits, and they had frequently walked and ridden together. But there had been nothing more than a very casual friendship until the night of the annual village fair.

They had spent part of the day together but had drifted apart several times to pursue their own interests or to mingle with other acquaintances. It had been a hot day, so that by the time the dancing started in the evening everyone was feeling rather tired and very thankful for the coolness that came after sunset. The dance Rebecca had with Christopher had been a particularly strenuous one. They had been laughing but panting at the end of it.

"Come and walk with me, Becky," he had said, pulling her arm through his and really offering her no choice. "Mrs. Pugh has been eyeing me purposefully for the past

half hour. I shall feel obliged to ask her to dance if I stay.
I should much prefer to walk with you.''

"I am suitably flattered, sir," she had said with mock
primness.

"I should think so, too," he had assured her. "It is a
signal honor, you know, to be preferred to Mrs. Pugh.''

And they had talked on, exchanging light banter, while
they strolled along the village street and out onto the
country lane that led eventually both to her uncle's house
and to his own. They had not noticed leaving the lights of
the village behind because the moon was bright. Only
when there was a lull in the conversation had they become
aware that the sounds of the village too had receded into
the distance.

Christopher had looked down at her and smiled, and she
smiled back. The silence was suddenly oppressive. Conversation, which usually flowed between them without
thought, suddenly refused to come. And their steps slowed
until they stopped walking altogether.

"I should take you back home," he said, turning to face
her.

"Yes," she agreed.

But they had not moved. They continued to look at each
other. And then his mouth came down to cover hers in a
light and slow exploration. It was not the hard, tooth-
grinding kiss that she remembered from years before. He
did not touch any other part of her. And then he raised his
head and they looked at each other again.

"I have gone and done something very silly, Becky,"
he said, flashing her a grin. "I have fallen in love with
you. You will think me very foolish, will you not, old
friend? I have been fighting it all summer.''

"I don't think you are foolish, Christopher," she said,
gazing earnestly back at him. "I have loved you for a long
time.''

"No. Really, Becky?" He became serious again.

"Yes, really.''

He had laughed and then reached out to cup her face in

his hands. Neither of them said anything for a while as they gazed into each other's eyes and he traced the line of her lips with his thumbs. She smiled.

And then he had kissed her again, drawing her against him, moving his hands in gentle caress down her spine and around to her breasts, teasing her mouth open with his lips and tongue, and finally kissing her closed eyes, her temples, her chin, her throat. And this time, she knew, he did know how to kiss, and by instinct and by love, so did she.

They had drawn shakily apart after several minutes, though he still held her within the loose circle of his arms.

"Oh, God, Becky, I want you," he said shakily. "I must get you back home quickly, love. It is dangerous to be alone like this."

She had looked at him blankly, not quite comprehending his meaning. She was in love, and it had been her first real kiss. It had been enough in itself. At that early point in their courtship she had not felt any urgent need of anything else. It was only later that she realized that his own reaction indicated that he had had other women before her.

That night had been the beginning of an idyllic few months. They had already been friends. Now they were also deeply in love. And he talked of marriage almost from the start. He did not know how he would support her. His parents were not wealthy. In fact, they had made great sacrifices just to send him to university. And they had three other children, all considerably younger than he. He talked frequently about becoming a physician. It was not an occupation that would bring him great wealth or prestige, and some would consider it beneath the dignity of a gentleman, but it would suit his wish to serve humanity. He had been very idealistic in those days, and Rebecca had loved him all the more.

They had not announced their betrothal or even spoken to their families of their plans, though everyone must have suspected that they had an understanding. They did little enough to hide their love for each other. But Christopher had promised to spend Christmas with an old friend from

university. It was his chance to see something of London
and to make a final decision about his future. When he
came home again, he told her, they would announce their
betrothal and plan for a wedding in the summer.

He had been gone for longer than she expected. And it
had been an uneasy time for her. At first his letters came
frequently and were full of satisfying ardor. But after a
while they came more sporadically and finally stopped
altogether. At the same time the Sinclairs themselves seemed
to change. They stayed at home and kept to themselves
more. When they were seen, Mr. Sinclair, usually so
placid, looked grim, and his wife looked as if she wept
frequently. Later Rebecca concluded that they must have
known before she did.

Christopher came home in March. She had been given
no notice of his coming. He called at the parsonage on a
particularly raw and gray morning and asked her to walk
into the churchyard with him. There he came straight to
the point. He was betrothed to a lady from London. They
were to be married the following week. He was sorry for
any misunderstanding there had been between him and
Rebecca. He felt that he owed her an explanation in person. But he was to leave again for London that same day.
He wished her well.

Rebecca had not said a word until he turned and began
to stride away.

"Christopher," she called then, her mouth and whole
face feeling numb. "Why?"

He smiled then, an unpleasant expression, approaching
a sneer. "She is wealthy, Becky," he said. "Her father is
loaded with money."

"I do not understand, " Rebecca said. "Since when has
money mattered to you?"

The unpleasant smile still twisted his mouth. "Since I
met Angela," he said. "Good-bye, Becky. I shall never
come back here. You need not fear that you will ever have
to face your faithless lover again."

Rebecca was stumbling now in her haste to cross the

pasture and reach the safety of the house. Safety from what? From the memories? She had put those in their place long ago. And she would again. It could make no possible difference that he had broken his promise and come back again. He was a stranger to her now. And if she was to believe what Mr. Bartlett said of him, she had been well rid of him. He would not have been the husband that she had expected him to be.

She must not let him ruin the tranquillity of her life again. She would not let him do so!

• 4 •

For six days following that unexpected encounter with Christopher on the road home Rebecca avoided any close contact with him. She did see him at church on the following Sunday but succeeded in leaving at the end of the service without coming face-to-face with him. He and Mr. Carver were standing on the steps talking to Philip when she left, and she walked behind them down the steps to her uncle's closed carriage, for which she was unusually thankful. It had meant avoiding any greeting with Philip, an omission that he commented upon the next day, but she could not have faced speaking to him and seeing Christopher too turn toward her. He had looked disconcertingly solid and real standing with her betrothed, not quite as tall as Philip, but broader and more athletically built. She had turned her mind from the comparison.

She heard about him almost constantly, of course. The Sinclair sisters had brought him and Mr. Carver to Limeglade the day after their arrival, and Harriet and Uncle Humphrey had sung their praises for the rest of that day and all of the next. Mr. Sinclair was pronounced to be even more handsome and charming than he had been during their stay in London. Mr. Carver was judged a very genteel kind of man with manners that could not be faulted and a fashionable air. Lady Holmes, too, seemed pleased by the visit and talked with some pleasure about the dinner party that Harriet had planned and that she had approved.

Rebecca had not invited Mr. Bartlett's impressions of the visit. Indeed, she felt quite sorry that he had seen fit to confide in her on that previous occasion, though she knew he had done so not out of any malice, but out of concern for the safety of Harriet, whom he saw to be an impulsive and headstrong girl. However, he took the chair next to hers in the drawing room on the evening after the visit.

"You must be feeling sorry that you were from home this afternoon, Miss Shaw," he said quietly. "You would have found it interesting to compare your memories of Mr. Christopher Sinclair with the present reality."

She had not told anyone of her meeting with the two travelers on the previous afternoon.

"I must admit that I was pleasantly surprised," Mr. Bartlett continued. "He behaved with perfect correctness and displayed an admirable affection for his sisters. I sincerely hope that my fears were groundless. Perhaps the death of his wife aroused enough guilt in him to help reform his character. I hope, Miss Shaw, that you will not allow your behavior toward him to be influenced unduly by what I said on an earlier occasion. We should give him a chance, I believe."

"You need not fear that I shall treat Mr. Sinclair with anything less than strict courtesy," Rebecca assured him. "I do not expect to be much in his company, anyway, sir."

"No," he said, "I do not imagine, Miss Shaw, that you could do anyone the injustice of treating him coldly only because of what you had heard of him. I have not been blind, ma'am, to your gentleness and your concern for all people, the poor and unfortunate as well as the members of your family."

Rebecca blushed. "And were you previously acquainted with Mr. Carver?" she asked, embarrassed by the compliment, which he had uttered with such sincerity.

"He has long been a friend of Mr. Sinclair," he replied. "An amiable man. A follower rather than a leader. I believe you will find him friendly, Miss Shaw."

Rebecca did not join Lady Holmes and Harriet the next day when they took out the carriage and returned the visit. She was invited to do so by Maude, but she made an excuse to avoid the outing. She would wait for the dinner party, when her next meeting with Christopher Sinclair would be unavoidable.

Philip too had been invited to dine at Limeglade. Rebecca suspected the hand of Maude in that particular invitation. But she was glad. The presence of her betrothed would give her the moral support to face a difficult situation.

She was in the drawing room with her uncle and aunt when the Sinclairs arrived. Harriet, as usual, was late getting ready. Rebecca suspected that on this occasion she had deliberately decided to make an entrance when everyone was already present. Mr. Bartlett too had not yet put in an appearance.

The baron greeted his neighbors with his usual air of well-mannered condescension. Friendly as he was with the Sinclairs, they were always made to feel the social distance between the two families. He always made it subtly obvious that he was conferring a great honor by being on such familiar and intimate terms with them. Maude's greeting was warmer than her husband's despite her shy manner.

"Mrs. Sinclair," she said, "how delightful it is to see you at our house again. Indeed, you do not visit us near as often as I could wish."

"Well, your ladyship," that matron replied, "I always seem to be so cozy with my own company that I rarely think of going out. It must be the laziness that comes with advancing age. I always welcome visitors to my own home." She took the seat that Maude indicated, lowering her considerable bulk into the comfortable upholstery.

Lord Holmes meanwhile was talking to the gentlemen while Ellen and Primrose hovered in the vicinity of their elder brother, who was looking remarkably handsome in dark blue satin evening coat and knee breeches and silver waistcoat.

Primrose caught his arm and turned him in the direction of Rebecca. "Oh, Christopher," she said, "You have not yet met Miss Shaw. She knew you before you married Angela. And she said that all the girls used to be in love with you because you were so handsome." She giggled up into his face.

Rebecca flushed hotly and curtsied. "Good evening, sir," she said, resisting the temptation to deny hotly what Primrose had said.

"Brat!" Christopher said with a grin at his sister. "Miss Shaw is by far too well bred to have said any such thing. She might have told you with some truth, though, that she was a remarkably pretty girl who attracted her own share of admiration." He turned his attention to Rebecca and bowed. "Good evening, Miss Shaw. I hope you did not exhaust yourself with your walk the other afternoon?"

"Oh, you have met before then?" Primrose said, pulling a face.

Mr. Carver too turned in her direction at that point, much to Rebecca's relief. "G'd evening, Miss Shaw," he said with the same polite smile he had given her at their first meeting.

Her impression of him on that occasion, though, as a soft, fat man, was quite erroneous, she could see now. He was indeed an enormous man—a veritable giant, in fact. There was far more muscle than fat, though, filling out his lavender satin coat and gray knee breeches. His shirt points were as high and stiffly starched as those she remembered.

Harriet, Philip, and Mr. Bartlett all arrived in the drawing room at almost the same moment. Harriet's big entrance, if indeed she had planned such, was certainly ruined. But Rebecca was relieved that she was released from the necessity of making further conversation with Christopher. She had been a remarkably pretty girl, he had said to Primrose. It was a two-edged compliment. Had he really thought of her as unusually pretty? But what did his words suggest about her now? That she was a faded creature, so far beyond that time when she had been pretty that

Primrose had had to be told? Rebecca gave herself a mental shake and smiled at Mr. Bartlett, who had crossed the room to her side as Christopher turned to greet Harriet and Philip.

It was an interesting evening, Rebecca decided later. Philip led her in to dinner and it was a relief to be seated beside him, where she felt perfectly comfortable and could observe the behavior of those around her. She was interested to observe that Christopher studiously avoided any contact with Mr. Bartlett both during the meal and afterward. He behaved much as if the other man were not present at all. She had expected to see some evidence of discomfort or guilt in his manner, but there was nothing.

For his part, Mr. Bartlett had made the effort to bow gracefully in the direction of both Christopher and Mr. Carver when he entered the drawing room. When he was ignored, he crossed the room and talked to Rebecca until dinner was announced, smiling at her in a rather pained manner.

"I do hope no one else noticed the hostility of Sinclair's manner," he said. "I would not wish anything to spoil the pride Mr. and Mrs. Sinclair clearly feel in their son. I shall stay away from him, Miss Shaw, and then his lack of manners will not be observed by anyone else. I will concede that finding me here on close terms with his family and neighbors must be something of a shock to him."

Rebecca glanced, troubled, across to where Christopher was talking to Harriet, all courteous attention. Yes, it must be a shock for him to find someone who had known his wife and his treatment of her. "I think you are wise, sir," she said to Mr. Bartlett.

And Mr. Bartlett, to his credit, carried out his plan and seated himself as far away from his adversary as he could during dinner. Afterward, in the drawing room, he hastened to make up a table of cards with the baron, Mrs. Sinclair, and Ellen.

Rebecca could see throughout the evening that Mr. Bartlett well understood his man. He had been wise after all to speak to her. Christopher led Harriet in to dinner and sat beside her. They were seated across the table from Philip and her, yet the conversation never included all four. Occasionally Philip made the attempt to converse with them, and Christopher always answered him, keeping his eyes on Philip only. But always he turned back immediately to Harriet, to whom he devoted his whole attention.

Rebecca tried not to listen. She tried to give her attention to Philip on her right and Julian on her left. Yet she could not be unaware of the pair at the other side of the table. His manner was not as bright and eager as it had used to be. It was quieter and infinitely more charming. In one swift glance across at him while he was answering one of Philip's questions, she was again made aware of the firmness of his jaw and the sternness of his face. There was a new intensity in his blue eyes, she noticed, as he turned his gaze back to Harriet.

She had recognized him instantly on the road the day of his arrival, yet she was aware now that he was a different man from the one she had known and loved seven years before. This was a man one would not want as an enemy. There was something almost dangerous about him. And he was taken with Harriet; that was clear to see. There was nothing necessarily bad about that, of course. If he really fancied her, there was every chance that he would behave honorably. She was, after all, the daughter of an old family friend. She was also pretty and wealthy and of superior rank to his own.

But she was not at all sure that Harriet would be able to cope with a man of his obvious experience. For all her confidence and headstrong behavior, Harriet was really just an innocent, Rebecca believed. She could handle with ease the attentions of a boy like Julian. But could she handle the practiced dalliance of a man like Christopher Sinclair? Rebecca thought with misgiving about that failed elopement that she gathered Harriet had attempted during her stay in London. She was not sure that the girl had developed any greater maturity since that time.

Yes, she decided, Harriet would definitely need watching in the coming days and weeks.

The pair still stayed together when the gentlemen joined the ladies after dinner. He followed her to the pianoforte and turned the pages of the music while she played and sang to him. Her cousin was excited by his attention, Rebecca could see.

Her own attention was finally taken by Mr. Carver, who seated his bulk beside her and proceeded to engage her in conversation. "I understand that you have begun a school in the village, Miss Shaw," he said, his head twisted awkwardly against the high points of his collar.

"Yes, sir," she replied. "The Reverend Everett and I worked toward that goal for a long time. We consider it a worthwhile project."

"Oh, quite so, quite so," he said. "Reminds me of m'mother. Always up to something new. Last thing I heard, she had all the tenants' daughters coming to the house to learn needlework. We'll have a town full of dressmakers before we know it." He laughed, a great rumble of sound that seemed to come from deep inside him.

"I do admire her efforts," Rebecca said, smiling and warming to this young man. "I would so like to teach the girls of the village, too, but Philip is wary. I suppose it is better to move slowly and get the boys' school well established first."

"Well, I'd press the point if I were you, Miss Shaw," he said. "Never could understand why learning is considered unnecessary for females. I cannot abide a silly, empty-headed girl m'self."

"Oh," Rebecca said, turning to him and smiling mischievously. "I shall have to turn you loose on Philip, Mr. Carver."

"No," he said. "Would have to bring m'mother here to do that. Carries all before her like a tidal wave. That's what Sinclair always says, anyway. They get on like a house on fire, m'mother and Sinclair. Both strong-willed.

Fortunately for m'peace of mind, they agree on most topics.''

"Indeed?" Rebecca said with some skepticism. She could not somehow see Christopher sitting in the midst of tenants' daughters, applauding their efforts with the needle.

Philip was standing beside the table that held the tea tray, talking to Maude. She was flushed and looking up at him, great respect written large on her face. Somehow Maude had come to believe that Philip was next only to God in holiness. Almost every Sunday she spoke admiringly of his sermon; she credited him with having been the main promoter of the school; she praised his efforts to treat the poor and the sick with even more deference than he showed the gentry; and she noticed when his surplice was patched.

Rebecca could never understand why Philip seemed always to disapprove of Lady Holmes. It disturbed him that she had married the baron, though Rebecca had pointed out to him on more than one occasion that Maude had probably had no say whatsoever in the matter. He felt contempt for the fact that she always played the lady, riding everywhere in a carriage, sitting in a padded pew at church, playing at visiting the sick once a month. Again Rebecca had tried to defend her aunt. She really had no freedom to behave otherwise, she explained to him. Would he have Lady Holmes be a disobedient wife?

And Philip criticized Maude's lack of control over her stepdaughter. He made no allowances for the fact that Harriet was a mere three years younger than Maude, and that she was a girl who had always been allowed her own way. His disapproval showed now, Rebecca thought. He stood beside Maude, looking very handsome with his slim height and blond good looks. But he looked unyielding. He was talking to Maude, yes, and giving her his full attention. But there was no warmth, no charm in his manner.

Rebecca sighed inwardly, while holding the thread of her conversation with Mr. Carver. Marriage to Philip was not going to be a smooth and comfortable experience. He found it so hard to make allowances for people's weaknesses. He appeared to have none of his own. He really was a remarkably dedicated and hardworking man. He had a great deal of self-discipline. Perhaps it would have been to his advantage if he did have a weakness. It might make him more sympathetic to the shortcomings of others.

Julian and Primrose wandered over to the pianoforte to watch Harriet play, Julian leaning on the instrument and watching her face. It must have been his idea that they organize a dance, because he was the one who claimed Harriet first as a partner. The group playing cards was eagerly commanded to stop as the services of Mrs. Sinclair were required as accompanist. Anyway, the table would have had to be moved so that the carpet could be rolled back a sufficient amount to allow several couples to dance.

They all danced several country dances except Mr. Sinclair, who suffered from the gout, and Lord Holmes, who declared that such physical exertion would be bad for his health. Rebecca danced with Mr. Bartlett and with Philip. She had danced on a few previous occasions with her betrothed and had found him surprisingly graceful on his feet. She would almost have expected that he would disapprove of dancing, yet he considered it an acceptable social pastime.

Harriet was soon flushed with excitement. Christopher, Julian, and Mr. Bartlett had all vied for her hand as a partner. She turned to Mrs. Sinclair at the end of the third set.

"Do let us have a waltz," she said. "I have not waltzed since Papa and I were in London, and it is a quite divine dance."

"But I don't know how," Ellen and Primrose chorused almost in unison."

"No, really, Harriet," Julian protested. "Most of us here have never even seen the waltz. You would have to dance almost alone."

"I have heard that it is all the rage in London," Philip

said. "I must say it sounds like a quite improper dance. I consider it not quite appropriate to the present gathering, Miss Shaw."

"Nonsense!" that young lady retorted, tossing her head with disdain. "Everyone in London does it. Even Prinny. I wish to waltz. Mr. Sinclair, shall we show everyone how it is done?" She smiled dazzlingly at Christopher and held up her arms, inviting his partnership.

"Perhaps we should call on Lady Holmes to act as arbiter," he said, smiling at Harriet and then turning and bowing in the direction of Maude. "Will you permit waltzing in your drawing room, ma'am?"

Maude flushed. "Indeed, sir," she said, "I have never danced the waltz myself. I was in London for such a short time before my marriage that I never had a chance to be approved by the hostesses of Almack's. But I have seen it danced, and I consider it to be very graceful and proper. I should be honored to see it performed in our home."

Christopher smiled at her, and the smile reached right to his eyes and crinkled their corners. Rebecca felt her stomach lurch. For a moment he had looked exactly like the old Christopher—warm and friendly.

"Come then, Miss Shaw," he said, turning back to Harriet. And the expression was gone, Rebecca saw with relief. "Let us waltz and give a lesson to those who do not know the dance. And then everyone can take the floor and try it. How do you like the role of dance mistress?"

Mrs. Sinclair began to play a tune that fit the rhythm of the waltz and Christopher took one of Harriet's hands in his and clasped her waist with the other. She placed her free hand on his shoulder. Rebecca felt her cheeks flush hotly, and she stepped back so that she was partly shadowed by the giant figure of Mr. Carver. But she could not keep her eyes from the couple as they twirled gracefully around the very small dancing space that had been cleared. It was a graceful dance, and both partners moved with lightness and confidence. But it was also an intimate dance. She might have felt quite faint had it not been for Christopher's voice counting the rhythm, explaining the steps and the movements to his small audience.

"Now," he said as the music came to an end and he and Harriet laughingly acknowledged the applause around them, "it is time for everyone to try. There are only two points to remember: count in threes, preferably in time to the music, and try to keep your feet from beneath those of your partner."

He smiled and turned to Maude. "Will you try it, ma'am?" he asked. "I promise not to tell the patronesses."

While Maude protested and gave in to the temptation to try a dance she had always admired, Mr. Bartlett appropriated Harriet, Julian grabbed Ellen, and Mr. Carver turned to Rebecca.

"Would you care to try, Miss Shaw?" he asked. "I assure you I've done it before. Nothing to it, really."

Rebecca laughed nervously. "I am not at all sure I shall do well, sir," she said, "but I am willing to try."

There was much laughter as the dance proceeded. Mr. Bartlett and Harriet were the only couple who danced without apparent effort. But they were both experienced waltzers. Mr. Carver was an accomplished dancer, Rebecca found to her surprise. Despite his giant stature he moved with grace and provided a firm enough lead that she could follow him without tripping all over him. After the first minute she even found it easy to pick up the rhythm and to relax somewhat.

Julian and Ellen were having troubles. Scoldings from him and giggles from her finally erupted into a short quarrel when he trod heavily on her foot. Before the dance was half over, Primrose had replaced her sister in Julian's arms and they proceeded in relative peace.

Maude looked anxious, Rebecca noticed when she felt confident enough to glance around her from time to time. Her lips were moving; she was obviously still counting out her steps. Christopher was smiling down at her, his face softened again. When she glanced a second time, Maude was just stumbling at a turn, and he pulled her against his chest for a moment until she had regained her balance. He laughed into her dismayed face, but his own expression was gentle. Rebecca swallowed and turned her head sharply back toward her own partner.

Philip joined her when the set came to an end. "I am sorry you had to be subjected to that indignity," he said, looking down at her with concern.

"Indignity?" she said. "You do not really think the dance improper, Philip, do you?"

"Perhaps not at a London ball," he said. "But I cannot think that it is right at a country home. For you, especially, Rebecca, it was an embarrassment. You are to be the wife of a vicar."

"I was not embarrassed, Philip," she said, touching his arm lightly. "We are among friends here."

"I blame Lady Holmes," he said. "She could quite easily have refused to allow the dance in her home. Yet again she has given in to the will of her stepdaughter, when she should be setting the example."

Poor Maude, Rebecca thought. She could do nothing right in Philip's eyes.

"Oh, that would be quite splendid!" Harriet was saying in a voice that was almost a shriek. "We have not had a picnic for an age. Not this summer at any rate."

"We thought the river would be a suitable site," Mrs. Sinclair said. "If the weather stays as it has been for more than a week now, we will be glad of the shade of the trees."

"Everyone must come," Ellen added, her voice as penetrating as Harriet's. "We decided that this afternoon. It will be no fun at all if anyone is absent. Lady Holmes, you will be there? And Mr. Bartlett?" She blushed as she turned to that gentleman.

He bowed and smiled at her. "How could I resist an invitation from such a charming young lady?" he said. "I shall assuredly attend your picnic, Miss Sinclair. And I am sure I speak for my sister too. Maude?"

"Lady Holmes and I shall both honor the occasion,"

the baron said, taking his snuffbox from a pocket and preparing to take a pinch. "There is a pathway that will take my carriage, is there not, Sinclair?"

"And will you be there, Reverend?" Mrs. Sinclair asked. "I know that the day after tomorrow is not a schoolday, and I am sure that the sick can spare you for one afternoon."

Philip hesitated. But Christopher replied before he had a chance to give an answer.

"Ellen has said that everyone must attend," he said. "And really we have decided that we will accept no refusals." The words were said with a smile. His intense blue eyes were directed, inexplicably, at Rebecca.

"Indeed," Philip said, "I was not about to refuse. You are all my parishioners, after all, even if only temporarily for some of you. The Lord's work can be done as well on a festive occasion as on a serious one."

"Miss Shaw, you will come too?" Primrose asked anxiously. "I wish to show you my new horse. Everyone else has seen him."

"Yes," Rebecca said, "I never could resist a picnic. Food always tastes so much more delicious out of doors. And I never could resist a horse, either, Primrose. I would love to see it." She glanced against her will at Christopher, but he was no longer looking at her. That momentary meeting of their eyes had been purely accidental.

She had not wanted to be drawn into the social events that she had known would develop out of his return home. She had thought to plead other more pressing activities during the days and tiredness during the evenings. But Philip had accepted this particular invitation. And she was betrothed to him. What could she do but accept too? Were this evening and the afternoon of the picnic to set a pattern? Had Philip been finally accepted as a member of the family circle although they were still only betrothed? It was a development that she had desired for a long time. But now surely was the wrong time for it to happen.

She was glad when this particular evening came to an end. She did not look forward to having to spend more time in the company of Christopher Sinclair. It was hard to believe that this man, so very self-assured and attractive yet so very aloof, was the same person as the boy she had played with and befriended, the young man to whom she had given her heart and all her confidences. She had felt so very comfortable with him for many years. Now it was an ordeal to meet his glance for a moment; it was an effort to avoid the embarrassment that a meeting of the eyes involved. She wished again with bitter passion that he had kept his promise never to return.

• 5 •

"But which do you think I should wear, Rebecca?" Harriet asked. "If I wear the yellow, I shall doubtless find that Primrose has chosen the same color. Yet it is more becoming on me, I think, than the blue. It shows my dark hair to more advantage. Do you not agree?"

Harriet was standing in her cousin's dressing room, her arms outstretched, a yellow muslin gown over one arm and a blue over the other. Her brow was drawn into a frown.

"I like both gowns," Rebecca said, considering. "The yellow is more vivid, but the blue is very delicate. If I were you, Harriet, I should wear the one that will be the most comfortable. It is like to be a hot day and there will be much walking and sitting on the grass."

Harriet lowered her arms and walked over to the stool that stood in front of the dressing table. She sat down. "My new straw bonnet is decorated with cornflowers," she said. "I suppose I should wear the blue. It will match his eyes." She sighed.

Rebecca went back to the task she had been busy with when Harriet had arrived, unannounced, without so much as knocking at the door—as usual. She was repairing the hem of the pink and blue floral-patterned cotton dress she planned to wear to the picnic that afternoon. She knew that Harriet's rare visits to her room generally lasted quite a while. They usually happened when the girl wanted to talk, yet found that neither her father nor Maude would do as listeners.

"Is he not gorgeously handsome, Rebecca?" she said, gazing dreamily in the direction of the window. "And so mature. It is a trial to live in such a retired corner of the country, where one rarely sees anyone worth seeing. I am so glad he came home. Do you expect he will stay long?"

"I really have no idea," Rebecca said. "But you are right. It is pleasant for you to have more young company. Mr. Bartlett, Mr. Carver, Mr. Sinclair: goodness, Harriet, we will hardly recognize our quiet neighborhood."

"Mr. Carver is quite insignificant," Harriet said disdainfully. "I cannot imagine why Mr. Sinclair associates with him. I suppose it is the other way around. Mr. Carver must feel that his own image is enhanced by his association with his friend."

"I would not underestimate Mr. Carver if I were you," Rebecca said hastily. "He is a well-bred and sensible young man, in my opinion. People should not always be judged by their appearance, Harriet."

"Mr. Bartlett is charming," the girl said, "though not exactly handsome, would you say, Rebecca? I could wish he were taller. But, of course, it does not matter. Mr. Sinclair is here now, and I mean to have him."

"Gracious!" Rebecca exclaimed, looking up from her task, her needle suspended in midair. "You have hardly even met him yet, Harriet. How can you be so sure of such a thing?"

"Oh," Harriet said, "it does not take more than one meeting to learn that a gentleman is the most handsome man one has seen, Rebecca. I have always been determined to marry such a man. I want to be the envy of every other female when I marry."

"And nothing else matters?" Rebecca asked.

"Well, of course," her cousin replied, "if he is also rich and wellbred, then the connection becomes quite irresistible. Mr. Sinclair is all three. I can predict that Papa will be less than eager to allow the match. The Sinclairs

are not our equal in rank, you know. But Mr. Sinclair has
been away from here for years. No one looking at him
now would know that his family was of such little
consequence.''

Rebecca kept her head lowered to her work. She found
it appalling that Harriet could be so unconcerned about
character or companionship or any of the other require-
ments that she might look for in a good marriage. Good
looks and money were the only criteria by which she
would make her choice. In the coming days or weeks of
Christopher's visit, she would probably remain oblivious
to all the shortcomings of his character. Only after marriage, if she did achieve her aim, would she come face-to-
face with the cold man who would marry for money and
then ignore his wife while he carried on with his life of
personal gratification.

In many ways Harriet deserved to be left alone to reap
the rewards of her actions. Yet Rebecca hated to sit back
and allow it to happen. She had known Harriet long enough
to realize that her selfishness and thoughtlessness were
more the result of a weak and indulgent upbringing than of
a basic defect of character. The girl was capable of warm
feelings and impulsive acts of generosity. If only she were
fortunate enough to find the right husband, she might yet
be shaped into a caring and responsible woman. Or so
Rebecca liked to believe. Perhaps it was just an unlikely
dream. But she must try if she could to discourage the
flirtation that she was sure was about to develop between
Harriet and Christopher.

Perhaps Mr. Bartlett could be persuaded to give Harriet
some attention. There was even a faint chance that the girl
would respond to his advances. She appeared not to dislike
him, though his appearance admittedly showed to disad-
vantage when compared with Christopher's. It would be a
great deal to ask of Maude's brother. He might well find it
irksome to be forced into showing preference for one lady
when he appeared to enjoy socializing with a wide range
of people. She would not say anything to him immedi-

ately. But if she felt it necessary to divert Harriet's attention, then she would ask him. He appeared to care about the welfare of his sister's family.

Harriet had been sitting quietly for a while, staring off into space, one leg crossed over the other and swinging back and forth.

"He must be ready to take a new wife, do you not think, Rebecca?" she said. "He has been a widower for more than a year, and he must be feeling lonely. And this time, surely, he will be eager to take a bride of his own class and breeding. She was most shockingly vulgar, you know. And not at all pretty. Do you think I am pretty, Rebecca?"

"You know very well that you are," her cousin replied, looking up and smiling at her. "And very young, too, Harriet. I would not fix my choice with too much haste if I were you. You know that your papa has talked of taking you to London again for the Season next year. You will still be only nineteen."

"That is old!" Harriet said with some vehemence. "And I should not be a debutante. Everyone would wonder what was wrong with me that I had not found a husband during my first Season."

"Rather," Rebecca suggested, "they would see you as a discerning young lady who chose with care instead of snatching the first eligible male she cast her eyes on."

Harriet burst out laughing. "It is no use trying to argue with you, Rebecca," she said. "I should know by now. You always have an answer for everything. But it does not matter. I mean to have Mr. Christopher Sinclair. I shall take part in the Season next year as his wife. I can see us now. We will be the most handsome couple in the *ton*, I believe."

Rebecca smiled. "If you do not go and dress yourself in one of those gowns soon, Harriet," she suggested, "you are going to miss this picnic altogether. You know that it takes you at least twice as long as anyone else to get ready to go into company. And you will put your papa into a thundering mood if you are very late."

"Pooh," Harriet said, "he is always late himself." But she got to her feet and wandered in the direction of the door. "Do you think I should get married here where everyone we know will see me, or wait for a society wedding in London?" she asked.

"Harriet!" Rebecca exploded. "You are being quite ridiculous."

The girl grinned unexpectedly. "Mrs. Harriet Sinclair. Mrs. Christopher Sinclair. Do you not like the sound of it, Rebecca?"

"Harriet!"

No, Rebecca did not like the sound of it at all. In fact, she did not like many of the thoughts and feelings that had haunted her for the past several days. She had continued with her usual activities since her uncle and aunt's dinner party. She had taught; she had visited Mrs. Hopkins, who was confined with her eighth child and who had no one to help her with the other seven, all of whom were younger than twelve. Rebecca had tidied the house for her, washed and fed the children, and played with them until almost a whole day had passed without her realizing it.

On yet another day she had visited Cyril's home after school was over for the day. It had basically been a social call; she had taken with her some freshly baked muffins. But really she had been hoping to talk to the boy, to win his confidence away from the public setting of the schoolroom. He was a puny and timid twelve-year-old who did not respond well to attention in class, even if that attention were kindly meant.

She had been glad of her visit. Cyril, shy at first, even perhaps dismayed to see her, finally brought forward a rough wooden bench that he had carpentered himself. It was for his mother to rest her feet on during the evenings while she was doing the family darning, he explained. And Rebecca found that she was able to direct the conversation toward his problems at school.

"I could read for sure, maybe, miss," he had said

apologetically, "if the words would just stand still."

"Stand still?" she prompted gently.

"The other boys don't notice, miss," he said, "but them words dance about too quick for me."

"Do they, Cyril?" she asked, her attention focused fully on him. "Are all the books the same? Are some easier than others?"

"Them ones with the letters and pictures is easy," he said after thinking for a moment. "The letters is too big to move around. But in them other books, when the letters is squashed into words, they chases one another all over the paper."

Rebecca smiled. "I shall see if I can find you a book in which the words are large, Cyril," she said. "Then I wager you will read as well as any of us."

"Aw, miss," he had said, "I'm just dumb, like the reverend says."

Rebecca leaned forward and smiled at him. "I am going to prove both of you wrong, Cyril," she said.

It was true that in the day since that visit Rebecca's mind had been much preoccupied with the new problem she had discovered with the solving of the old one. Cyril obviously had very poor eyesight. She did not know why the truth had not struck her earlier. It was easy now to recall that the boy always held his book unnaturally close to his face. She had scolded him for doing so on more than one occasion. But it did not help to know the problem when the solution was not at all obvious. The boy needed eyeglasses. But how could poor farm laborers afford to buy eyeglasses for their son? And there was no money left in the school fund even if she could justify using it for such a purchase.

Really, though, Rebecca had to admit to her own chagrin, the bulk of her thoughts during those days had centered around Christopher and his unwelcome return to the neighborhood. She had always known deep down that she had never recovered fully from his defection. She had loved him for so long that he had become part of her very being. And it had all happened when she was young and impressionable. It had not been an adult experience that she might have shrugged off more easily. She had known as soon as she heard that he was coming home that old wounds would be opened, that she would not be immune to him.

Yet she had hoped. She had hoped that when she saw him she would find that her fears had been unfounded. It had been possible that both he and she would have changed so much that there would be nothing left of the old feelings. And doubtless that was true for him. She was aware that she must have changed almost beyond recognition both in looks and manner. But he was Christopher still. His looks had matured, but he still had the same upright, proud bearing. And those very blue eyes would always be Christopher's.

She had not got over him at all, in fact, and she was disgusted with herself when forced to admit the truth. She had been aware of him in a very physical sense during every moment of that dinner party. And she was shocked and horrified to realize that the feeling she had had on seeing him with Harriet was not so much concern for the reputation of her cousin as jealousy. Pure and simple jealousy! She wanted him bending over her at the pianoforte, exercising that charm of conversation on her.

She almost hated herself. She certainly hated him for breaking his promise and coming back again. He had treated her so badly, abandoning her like that, breaking their engagement—even though it had been unofficial—after all that had happened between them in those months after they discovered their love for each other. Surely he could have done one honorable thing and stayed away from her for the rest of their lives.

She wished desperately that she did not have to attend this picnic. Yet for some reason Philip wanted to go. In fact, he had talked with something like enthusiasm about the occasion when she saw him two days before. And he seemed to be impressed with Christopher. He talked almost admiringly about his sincerity and friendliness. It was surprising, really. Philip was usually so sensitive to snobbery and hypocrisy. And surely he should have been able to see both in his new acquaintance.

Rebecca finally finished the repair to the hem of her dress. She would have finished long before had she not kept falling into a dream, she scolded herself. She got resolutely to her feet and began to change her clothes for the afternoon's outing. It was really useless telling herself that she did not wish to go and would not do so if it were not for Philip's wishes. Of course she wished to go. How dreadful it would be not to be there but to be wondering every moment what was happening, imagining with whom he was walking and talking.

Rebecca stopped guiltily in the middle of performing the awkward task of buttoning her dress at the back. She had been thinking almost exclusively of Christopher in the last few days. Yet she was engaged to marry Philip. She must spend the afternoon concentrating on the friendship and mutual respect they had for each other. She would be foolish to let go of those things when she had nothing to gain by brooding over Christopher. Her feelings for him were purely regrets for a past that might have been. He was not now the sort of man whom she would wish to captivate even if that were possible.

Rebecca spent five whole minutes before the shelf of her closet in an agony of indecision over which of her very plain bonnets she should wear. She wished she had something just a little prettier or more frivolous. Perhaps she would be quite reckless and buy one for the annual fair in three weeks' time.

Rebecca was very glad to ride the mile to the river from the Sinclairs' house in the gig with Ellen and Primrose. She had driven over there with Lord Holmes, Maude, and Harriet in the closed carriage. And the baron had insisted that all the windows remain closed for fear of a draft. Rebecca had thought she would explode before the two-

mile distance had been covered. However, most members
of the party had driven or ridden to the picnic site while
Primrose was showing off her new horse. By the time they
returned to the house, only the gig, a very irate Ellen, and
Mr. Carver remained.

"Oh, do come along, Prim," Ellen called out crossly as
soon as they were within earshot. "We will miss all the
fun. You could have shown Miss Shaw your horse at some
other time."

"I am afraid the fault is mine, Ellen," Rebecca said
with a smile. "One look was not enough for me. I had to
go right into the stall and get to know the horse. He is a
beauty."

"All we will have missed," Mr. Carver said with a
smile, "is the work: lifting down baskets of food and
spreading blankets. I think it clever of you, Miss Primrose,
to have thought of that." He shook with quiet laughter so
that Rebecca feared for a moment that he might fall from
his horse's back.

Primrose giggled. "You and I will do our share of the
work later when it comes time to eat, Mr. Carver," she
said conspiratorially, and he actually winked at her from
above his high and sharp shirt points, Rebecca noticed
with some amusement.

They had indeed missed most of the fuss and bluster of
the arrival, they found when they caught up to the others
on the riverbank. Lord Holmes, it was true, was still on
his feet, instructing his coachman to move his blanket yet
again so that it would remain in the shadow of a large tree
even when the sun shifted its position. The site that had
originally been chosen for him, Mrs. Sinclair explained
sotto voce to Rebecca and her girls, had been well shaded
but too much exposed to the wind. And they all knew how
delicate his lordship's health was, poor soul.

"What wind, Mama?" Primrose asked tactlessly and
rather too loudly.

Harriet was impatient to walk. "I have always loved the
old stone bridge," she said wistfully, gazing upstream to

the single-arched structure over the river that made this particular site so picturesque. "There is such a delightful view from the center of it, and such a lovely walk through the trees on the opposite bank. Do let us take a walk."

She smiled generally around the group, though her eyes lingered rather longer on Christopher than on any of the others. She twirled the blue parasol that matched perfectly the blue of the cornflowers in her bonnet and complemented the paler blue of her light summer dress. She presented a very pretty picture against the swift-flowing waters of the river.

Christopher smiled. "I should be delighted to accompany you, ma'am," he said. "I am in the mood for exercise. Will you take my arm?"

Harriet smiled with delight, though the smile faded slightly when Mr. Bartlett got to his feet and turned to Ellen. "Shall we join them, Miss Sinclair?" he asked, bringing a blush to the girl's cheeks by bowing in courtly fashion before her and smiling warmly.

"Come on, Carver," Christopher said, grinning back at his friend, who was already reclining indolently beneath a tree. "It would do you good to take to your feet too. Give us a chance to convince you that the countryside has as much to offer in the way of entertainment as the city."

"I could be entertained just as well sitting b'neath this tree," Mr. Carver grumbled. But he pulled himself to his feet. He sighed and glanced wistfully in the direction of the blanket on which Julian sprawled, looking less than delighted with life, and turned to Rebecca. "Will you bear me company, Miss Shaw?" he asked. "You may take m'arm. I believe I can support you through the ordeal of a country walk." He shook with laughter again.

The six of them strolled toward the bridge, Harriet tugging rather impatiently at her companion's arm.

"I used to come here often when I was a child," she said as they began to cross over the river, "with Julian. We used to try to fish from the bridge until we realized that the water was too fast flowing to make it possible to catch any.''

"That was far more innocent than my favorite game when I was a boy," Christopher said with a smile. "We used to walk along the wall and try not to fall into the water. It is amazing that we never did. We might have ended up with worse injury than a soaking."

"Oh," Ellen said, "I remember when you caught me and Julian doing that, Christopher, and gave us a thundering scold. You threatened to tell Papa if you ever caught us at it again. You said it was very dangerous."

"And so it is," he said. "The stones on top of the wall are irregular and it is not too wide to start with. Add to that the fact that it is not flat but continuously curved to form the arch and you have a pretty tricky walking surface. All children are mad daredevils. I suppose we become too staid and dull as we grow up. You see, all of us are perfectly content to cross the bridge sedately on the roadway."

"Oh, I would do it," Harriet cried, twirling her parasol behind her head and smiling gaily at her companions. "Does anyone dare join me?"

Ellen giggled. "Not me any longer," she said. "I have learned wisdom with age. I always used to be petrified, anyway."

Christopher smiled engagingly at Harriet. "I must admit you would make a remarkably pretty picture walking across," he said. "But I cannot allow it."

"Ah," she said, smiling brilliantly and giving the parasol another twirl, "but I am not your sister, sir, and am not obliged to do as you say. Hold my parasol, please, Rebecca. I shall show you who is old and staid in this party."

Rebecca was seriously alarmed. She knew that once Harriet got an idea into her head, it was very difficult to dislodge it. "You really must not try, Harriet," she said. "Indeed, it is very dangerous. And remember that your papa is looking on. He will be very distressed if he sees what you are about."

"Pooh," Harriet said. "Papa will be proud of me."

Before the paralyzed gaze of her five companions, Harriet ran lightly back to the end of the bridge, where the wall was low enough for her to get up on it despite the hampering influence of her long skirt. She held out her arms to the sides to get her balance and began to place one foot after the other ahead of her up the uneven incline to the center of the arch. The onlookers dared not move or say a word once she had started for fear of startling her and pitching her into the fast-flowing waters below.

She walked even more slowly and carefully on the downward slope at the other side of the bridge. Twice she stopped altogether and had to make an effort to regain her balance. But after what seemed like an age to those watching, she finally reached the other side and jumped down into the roadway. She laughed with triumph and made an exaggerated curtsy to the five people still clustered at the beginning of the bridge.

"Miss Shaw," Christopher said, hurrying forward, "if you were my sister, I should give you the worst tongue lashing of your life. As it is, accept my compliments, ma'am. I am full of admiration."

His voice was rather grim, Rebecca noticed, although he spoke lightly and was smiling at her cousin. Rebecca felt almost limp with relief. She could cheerfully have shaken Harriet until her teeth rattled. Looking anxiously back to the spot on the bank where the other members of the party were gathered, she saw that they were all on their feet gazing at the bridge, including Uncle Humphrey.

"Now," Harriet called gaily, "who said something about us all being staid and dull? I see only five such people!"

"Now there is a young lady," Mr. Carver said to Rebecca, "who needs a firm hand. A heavy hand, perhaps. Don't she realize that Sinclair or Bartlett or I would have been obliged t'jump in after her if she had fallen in? Selfish little hussy!"

Rebecca was surprised at the vehemence of his attack.

But she held her peace. She felt that her cousin thoroughly deserved such censure.

"I think that was very foolish," Ellen said, looking up at Mr. Bartlett. "Harriet is the same age as I, but I consider myself too old for such foolishness."

He patted her hand, which was tucked through his arm. "Ah, yes, Miss Sinclair," he said. "You are a very sweet and sensible young lady. I would be shocked to see you behave like a daredevil. Of course," he added, raising his voice just a little, "there is something very charming about a lady who is willing to take a risk and dare the consequences. My compliments, Miss Shaw. I salute your bravery."

"Thank you, kind sir," she replied, favoring him with a deep curtsy again and a dazzling smile.

"Perhaps we should walk on for a way," Christopher suggested, "before it is time to turn back for tea. I hope the pathway through the trees here has not become overgrown. It was always a place of great beauty, especially in the autumn when the leaves are of all colors."

His head turned rather jerkily toward Rebecca as he said the last words, and their eyes met. He flushed; she was sure she had not imagined it. She had certainly done so herself. It was a painful walk. It had been from the beginning. In a way she had almost been glad of the distraction of Harriet's madness. The bridge and the path beyond it had been one of their favorite retreats during those months when they had been in love and planning a life together. They had used often to stand on the bridge, leaning on the stone wall and staring downstream.

She could remember sitting up there once while Christopher stood before her, one hand resting on the stones either side of her, his face on a level with hers. When he had started kissing her, she wrapped her arms around his neck. And she ended up shrieking while he laughed into her ear. He bent her backward so that she was suspended over the water, only her hold of his neck and his of her waist between her and certain disaster.

And they had walked often in the woods during that autumn, their arms around each other's waist, marveling at the incredible beauty of the trees, their footsteps hushed by the still-soft leaves underfoot. They had talked and talked, planning and dreaming of a future that was not to be. They grew closer together in those months so that at last it seemed that there were no barriers left between them. They laughed a great deal, too, though she could no longer remember what had been so amusing.

They had become physically more familiar with each other during that time, too. They had always walked close to each other when there was no one else nearby, and they had kissed frequently. These woods, where they were walking now, the chatter loud and gay, had been the perfect setting for stolen embraces. Not only kisses. He had frequently explored her back and her breasts while he kissed her; she had often let her hands roam over the muscles of his back and shoulders and chest. And she gradually came to share his urgency, that heat of desire which had always finally driven them apart, smiling ruefully at each other.

Could this be the same place? And could that man ahead of her, the one bending his head with a smile to hear what Harriet was saying, be the man with whom she had walked and shared those confidences and those intimacies? Rebecca was conscious of a dull ache inside, which she could not disguise even by persisting in the conversation with Mr. Carver.

She was glad at least that it was not autumn.

•6•

Harriet was taken to task as soon as the group of six returned to the rest of the picnickers—by Julian.

"Really, Harriet," he said, leaping to his feet as soon as he saw her approach and steering her by the elbow away from the others, "do you have windmills in your head? What was the point of that ridiculous exhibition you were putting on at the bridge?"

"I was walking across the wall," she said, staring at him haughtily and jerking her arm away from him, "if it is any of your business, Julian. Anyway, you have done it a hundred times yourself. I have seen you."

"When I was twelve years old and younger and knew no better," he said. "Really, Harriet, I thought you had more sense."

"You are behaving just like a mother hen!" she snapped, striding ahead of him to the river-bank, where their quarrel could be a little more private. "Thank you kindly, Julian, but I do not need you to tell me what I should or should not do."

"I suppose it is all done for Christopher's benefit," he said scornfully.

Harriet glared at him, snapping open her parasol and twirling it behind her head. "And what is that supposed to mean?" she asked.

"You are showing off, Harriet," Julian said sullenly.

"Don't think I have not noticed that you have set your cap at him."

"Well!" she exclaimed. "You sound like a jealous lover, Julian. What if I do enjoy your brother's company? He at least is fun to be with. He admired my courage earlier."

"I doubt it," Julian said, his face contemptuous. "He probably was playing the gentleman. I wouldn't doubt that he really considers you to be a silly chit."

"Well!" Harriet said again. "At least I know where I stand with you, Julian Sinclair. And you have been declaring undying love for me for the last two years." She lifted her chin and turned back to the group of people seated on the blankets.

"I do care," Julian said, looking miserable now. "I just hate to see you make a cake of yourself, Harriet, that is all."

She tossed her head but did not deign to reply. She strode across to sit beside her father. There she received another scold.

Rebecca was talking to Mrs. Sinclair. She had been planning to join Philip but changed destination when she realized that Christopher had the same idea. The two men now appeared to be in earnest conversation.

"And when are you planning to set the date of your wedding, Miss Shaw?" Mrs. Sinclair asked. "Mr. Sinclair and I have been expecting it all summer, but the best of the season is already past."

Rebecca smiled. "We still have not set a date, ma'am," she said.

"It is such a long time since there was a wedding of any note in the church," Mrs. Sinclair said with a sigh. "It would be such a treat to have another. We were very disappointed, you know, when Lord Holmes decided to marry his lady in London before bringing her home."

"You can be sure, ma'am," Rebecca said reassuringly, "that when we do set the date, you will be among the first to receive an invitation."

"Such a very proper young man," Mrs. Sinclair said, looking across at Philip with an affectionate smile. "He will make you a good husband, Miss Shaw. He is very like your poor dear papa except that he is perhaps a trifle more serious. Perhaps he will soften somewhat under your influence."

Rebecca too looked across at her betrothed. He *was* very serious. She rarely saw him smile. She could not imagine what he found to talk about so earnestly with Christopher. She wondered what Mrs. Sinclair's thoughts were about the past. Everyone had known that she and Christopher were seeing each other. Surely they must have suspected that the relationship was a serious one. Did they ever wonder what had happened? Of course, perhaps Christopher had explained the situation to them. Perhaps they knew more than she did.

Philip looked up at her while she was still staring in his direction. He beckoned and called to her above the hubbub of voices. Rebecca got reluctantly to her feet and moved over to where he sat with Christopher. Both men got to their feet as if they were in a formal drawing room rather than outdoors at a picnic.

"I have been telling Mr. Sinclair about the school," Philip explained to her as they all sat down on the blanket.

Rebecca's eyes strayed to Christopher's chin. "Oh?" she said.

"I like the sound of what you have been doing there, Miss Shaw," Christopher said. "It is quite a brave venture."

"I do not know about brave," she said, raising her eyes to his at last. "I think it only right. The poor should have as much right as we to an education."

He inclined his head. "And do you find that the boys learn easily?" he asked.

Rebecca felt irritated. The school was too important to her to become the topic of a polite conversation. What did he care about the school or about the boys? "Probably as easily as any boys anywhere," she said. "Those at Eton, for example."

He raised his eyebrows, and she was annoyed to see that he looked amused for a moment. "I am glad you feel strongly about it," he said. "But then I might have expected it. You always did feel passionately about the unfairness of class distinctions, I remember."

Rebecca stared back, unable to look away from those blue eyes, and unable to think of anything to say in reply.

"Mr. Sinclair would like to visit the school one day, Rebecca," Philip said. "I have suggested that he come tomorrow."

"No!" Rebecca said sharply. "Tomorrow is my day, Philip. I am sure Mr. Sinclair would far prefer to see you teach. You are more competent than I."

"I should like to be free to show him around," Philip said. "It really would be more convenient if you would do the teaching."

Rebecca looked back in dismay to Christopher. What right did he have to interfere with her activities this way? Was it such a great curiosity, a novel amusement, to be able to watch a village school in operation? She hated him for a moment.

"You will not be nervous, will you, Miss Shaw?" he asked. "I really am not a severe critic, you know. I am full of admiration for your efforts."

He had said something very similar to Harriet after she walked across the wall of the bridge, Rebecca thought indignantly.

She lifted her chin. "I shall look forward to seeing you tomorrow, sir," she said.

Philip's attention had strayed several times in the direction of the river. "Lady Holmes was very foolish to wear such thin slippers," he said at last. "The stones near the river are quite loose and jagged. How foolish some females are to sacrifice good sense and comfort to fashion."

"But one must admit that she looks most charming," Christopher added, also looking at Maude, who was standing alone at the river's edge looking down into the water.

"She has learned, you see, that greens look quite stunning on redheaded ladies."

"She needs someone's arm to lean on," Philip said irritably, "before one of those stones cuts through a slipper and lames her."

Christopher grinned. "I don't believe we can expect her husband to walk that far," he said, lowering his voice. "It looks as if you will have to play the gallant, Everett."

Philip hesitated but finally got to his feet and strode across the grass to the stones that bordered the riverbank, his back registering anger. Maude turned hastily when he drew close, and even at the distance from which she viewed them, Rebecca could see that she flushed as she looked up into his stern face. Poor Maude! She admired Philip, but she seemed to sense that he disapproved of her. She seemed almost afraid of him.

"Is your fiancé always so humorless, Becky?" Christopher asked quietly, and Rebecca turned back to him with a start, realizing suddenly that they were almost alone, set apart from any of the other groups.

"Humorless?" she repeated. "You mean that he is not constantly laughing and joking? I think such behavior would be inappropriate in a vicar, don't you?"

He did not answer immediately but regarded her with a half smile. "You are very much on the defensive," he said. "Do you still hate me, Becky? Have I not been forgiven?"

She looked back at him, her jaw clenched. "I really don't know what you are talking about," she said. "What reason do I have for being angry with you?"

He smiled, his mouth a little twisted. "No," he said, answering his own question, "I can see I have not. I did not expect to be. I cannot blame you, Becky. Ah, I see that finally Mama has signaled that it is time for the food. I thought she would never get to the point. Come. Let us go fill some plates."

He got to his feet and held out a hand to help Rebecca to hers. She could not refuse without being publicly rude to him. But it was an ordeal worse than any she had yet experienced in the days since she heard he was coming home. To see him and to hear him was bad enough. To touch him was unendurable—that slim yet surprisingly strong hand that had so often held hers in the past, so often touched and caressed her.

Rebecca snatched her hand from his as soon as she was on her feet, hoping that her blush was not as noticeable as it felt. Had she looked at him, she would have seen that all traces of his smile had disappeared and that the new set to his jaw, which she had noticed during their first meeting, was very apparent. But she did not look up. She walked hastily over to the open picnic baskets, helped herself to food without even considering what it was she took, and seated herself right in the middle of the noisy group that included Ellen, Primrose, Julian, Mr. Bartlett, and Harriet.

Rebecca had hoped that Christopher would come on his curiosity visit to the school early in the morning. She wanted the ordeal over with. She had had a very disturbed night, lying awake and tossing and turning for what seemed to be hours and then dreaming so vividly that she felt afterward that she might as well have lain awake all night.

It felt so strange to see Christopher again, to move in the same circles as he yet to feel uncomfortable. They had always been friends, even when they were children and his friendly feelings had been displayed largely through practical jokes. They had always been comfortable together. She could hardly bear to be in his company now and to feel a stranger. She had never really known him, of course. The Christopher she had thought she knew could never have broken all his promises to her in order to marry a stranger for her money. And that Christopher could not have neglected his wife and cruelly flaunted his mistresses before her.

Now, since his return, she was very much aware that she did not know him. She no longer felt, as she used to, that just by looking at him she knew what he thought and how he felt. Now looking at him was rather like looking at a shield. She did not know how he felt about being home; she did not know what his attitude toward Harriet was; she did not know if he felt contempt, regret, amusement, or sheer indifference for herself. And she had no idea of why he would wish to give up a morning of his time to watch untutored boys learn their lessons. Was he trying to impress Philip? Her?

There was another reason why she wanted him to come early. She usually began the day with arithmetic, having found that the boys' minds could handle numbers best when they were fresh. And all of the boys were progressing satisfactorily in that subject. Even Cyril could excel, since there was no reading involved. He was, in fact, one of her best pupils in mathematics. Being slow and meticulous, he was less likely than the others to make careless mistakes.

But the lesson in multiplication passed, and they had turned to their reading books before Philip finally pushed open the door and stood aside to let Christopher pass. Rebecca immediately felt herself flush. She curtsied, and then wished she had not done so. She felt very much like a lowly servant paying homage to a grand gentleman. He looked remarkably fine in buff riding breeches and olive-green superfine riding coat, snowy-white neckcloth arranged in intricate folds, black topboots still spotless and shiny after the ride from home.

He and Philip wandered to the back of the room and Rebecca resumed the lesson. The boys' reading abilities seemed even less competent than usual. She guessed that they were feeling self-conscious. She was constantly aware that Cyril's turn to read could not be ignored, though she did for a moment consider deliberately forgetting him.

The two men stood with their backs to the room for a few minutes while Philip was apparently showing the visitor the few books they possessed and the meager samples of the student work that they kept. But finally Christopher turned around and watched her as she listened to and helped each reader. He stood with his legs slightly apart, arms folded across his chest, looking totally out of place in the very modest setting of the schoolroom, thought Rebecca, though she did not once look directly at him.

Philip too turned around when Cyril began to read. Rebecca had found him a book in which the print was larger than in the others. She believed that under normal circumstances he might have read slightly better than usual. But these were not normal circumstances. The child glanced nervously around at Philip and in the process was also reminded that another strange and very formidable-looking stranger stood there, his whole attention on the class. His reading was quite incoherent. After a mere minute Rebecca told him gently to sit down and called the name of another boy. She was relieved that Philip said nothing.

The two men still lingered when she had dismissed school for the morning and the boys who lived too far from the village to go home for luncheon had taken their food outside. Rebecca stood at the table, straightening books that already stood in a neat pile.

"I am impressed, Miss Shaw," Christopher said, moving toward the front of the room. "You have done your work well. The boys are amazingly proficient in reading, considering the fact that they have been coming to school for only a few months."

"I am pleased with them," Rebecca said, looking unwillingly up into his face. "But Philip works very hard too."

He nodded. "You have commendable patience," he said, his eyes smiling at her. "You always did, I remember. You would do tasks for the elderly even when they were tedious enough to try the patience of a saint. I would be inclined to yell and fume if every time a boy came to the word *the* I had to tell him what it was."

"Yes," she said, "Ben cannot get over that stumbling block. But he so consistently improves in all other areas that I do not have the heart to get cross with him over that one problem."

Philip spoke, and they both turned toward him as if only then remembering his presence. "I really think we must tell Cyril's parents that they are wasting their time sending him here," he said. "He is our only real failure, Mr. Sinclair. The child does not even try, and it seems that one cannot force learning on anyone."

"Oh, no," Rebecca protested, "I think you are too harsh, Philip. It is true that he is not doing well in reading, but you must have noticed that he is more than satisfactory in arithmetic. And he does care. If he did not, he would not have become as nervous as he did this morning, knowing that you and Mr. Sinclair were listening to him. Anyway, Philip, I believe I have discovered his problem. I have been meaning to speak to you about it."

"Perhaps another time," Philip said. "We do not want to bore Mr. Sinclair with minor matters. Shall we go for luncheon, sir? My housekeeper will be expecting us."

"In a moment," Christopher said. "I should like to hear first what Cyril's problem is. I felt great sympathy for the lad, I must admit."

"He cannot see well," Rebecca said. "I visited his home a couple of days ago, and he told me the words will not stay still on the page when he reads."

"Ah," he said, "I believe you are probably right. The boy must be fitted for eyeglasses."

Rebecca stared at him blankly. Had his years in London removed him so far from reality? She could hardly keep the contempt from her voice when she spoke. "One might as well tell his parents to take him to the moon for a cure as advise them to buy him eyeglasses," she said. "They would have to work a lifetime to pay for them."

He looked searchingly back at her, an unreadable expression on his face. Then he nodded slightly but said nothing.

"My opinion is still the same," Philip said. "If the boy cannot see to read, there is really no point in his being here. He would be better off and less frustrated working with his father. I do believe, as I always have, that all our children should have the right to an education, but it would be foolish to insist that everyone participate.''

"Girls, for instance,'' Rebecca said with a smile. She did not really treat the topic as a joke, but she felt that the moment called for lightheartedness.

Christopher grinned unexpectedly, looking disturbingly like the old Christopher. "Do I detect a grievance, Be— Miss Shaw?'' he asked.

"Rebecca has several ideas that are very humane but quite impracticable,'' Philip said without a glimmer of a smile. "Shall we go for luncheon?''

The invitation did not include Rebecca. Philip had explained when they first became betrothed that no breath of scandal should ever attach itself to their persons. She had never so much as been over the doorstep of the parsonage since he had moved in. And even on this occasion Philip obviously deemed it improper to ask her to dine with two single gentlemen.

Rebecca was very thankful now, though, for her betrothed's strict notions of propriety.

Primrose and Julian Sinclair were in the drawing room drinking tea with Maude and Mr. Bartlett when Rebecca arrived home that afternoon. She was feeling unusually tired after the nervous tension of the morning and the long walk home through weather that had turned cold and blustery. She was thankful that brother and sister had come alone.

"How do you do, Miss Shaw?'' Primrose cried gaily. "I have ridden Peter all this way today. Papa said I was accustomed enough to riding him that I could take him some distance. Julian insisted on coming too just in case there was any trouble.'' She pulled a face and then giggled. "Though what he would have done if Peter had suddenly decided to bolt with me on his back I do not know.''

"I really had to make sure that she did not do anything foolish like trying to gallop across the fields,'' Julian explained as if his sister were not present. "Prim used to do that with old Mollie when she thought no one was looking. But then old Mollie's gallop was a mere trot by any normal standard."

"It is terrible to be the youngest in the family," Primrose said indignantly. "Everyone thinks I am still a baby to be protected instead of a seventeen-year-old young lady."

"Sorry, Prim," Julian said uncontritely, "but sometimes you play the part too convincingly."

"Well, Christopher can see that I am grown up anyway," Primrose said, and turned her attention to Maude and Rebecca, her eyes dancing. "He says that Ellen and I may have a Season next year," she said. "He will be in town again and he will see that we are admitted to all the important *ton* events. Even to Almack's."

"How splendid for you," Maude said warmly. "I am sure your brother will make sure that you have a wonderful come-out Season."

"Papa did think I would be too young," Primrose said. "I nearly died! But Mama reminded him that I will be eighteen soon after Christmas, and he has said I may go."

"Christopher wants to send me on a Grand Tour," Julian said. "It has always been my dream to travel, especially to Greece. But it just seems too extravagant. He is very insistent, though."

Maude smiled warmly and poured a second cup of tea for Rebecca. "You are very fortunate to have such a generous brother," she said. "I am glad Mr. Sinclair has come home so that we might make his acquaintance."

Rebecca was aware of Mr. Bartlett's eyes on her and looked up at him. He was frowning broodingly. "He is riding with Miss Shaw this afternoon?" he asked, shifting his glance to Julian.

Julian glowered. "Yes," he said. "She don't seem so interested in me since Christopher came home. Can't say I blame her really. He is top of the trees, I can see that."

"And so will you be soon enough," Maude said gently, "especially after your Grand Tour."

Mr. Carver and Ellen are with them," Primrose added. "They would not let me go with them because I would make an odd number. Or so Ellen said. I would have enjoyed going. Mr. Carver is so funny, though I do not believe he always means to be. Just seeing him laugh is enough to put me into convulsions."

Rebecca smiled. She could not help but agree.

"Have you had your invitations to the Langbourne ball, Lady Holmes?" Primrose asked. "I cannot imagine why I did not think of it until now. We were in a fever of excitement this morning. Ellen could not go last year because she had a chill, and this is the first time I have been included in the invitation. And they must have heard of Christopher and Mr. Carver being here because they are to go too."

"Sir Clive and Lady Ethel Langbourne always pride themselves on having as great a squeeze as possible for their annual ball," Maude said. "They must indeed have discovered the goings-on for miles around, for Stanley was included in our invitation. You have a card too, Rebecca. Did you not see it on the hall table?"

"No," Rebecca replied. "I must admit that I had only two thoughts as I came through the hallway, and those were to reach a comfortable chair and the teapot."

"You will be accepting the invitation I trust, Miss Shaw?" Mr. Bartlett asked with his charming smile.

"I really do not know," she said. "I went to sit with Ellen and Primrose last year, I remember."

"Ah, but there will be no one needing your services at home this year," he said, "and the gathering would certainly not be complete without your presence, you know."

"You really must come, Rebecca," Maude agreed. "I greatly admire you for all the useful work you do, but I really would like to see you enjoy yourself more. Do you think the Reverend Everett will be invited?"

"He was last year," Rebecca said, "though he was forced to send his apologies at the last moment in order to stay at a deathbed."

"Perhaps you will both be able to go this year," Maude said. "It will be good for you."

"I think we should be starting back, Prim," Julian said. "It looks as if it may rain before the day is out."

"Oh, Miss Shaw," Primrose said, jumping to her feet, "do come and see me on Peter's back. You will see how really splendid he is."

Rebecca got to her feet with a smile. "Lead the way," she said.

They were in the stable yard, Primrose and Julian already on horseback, when Harriet and Christopher came riding in. Rebecca was clasping her arms, rubbing them against the chill which the brisk wind was causing. Loud greetings were exchanged.

"What a glorious day for a ride!" Harriet said brightly. "Of course, we could have had a much brisker gallop if Mr. Carver had not been with us. He is quite staid."

Luke?" said Christopher, dismounting and holding up his arms to lift Harriet to the ground. "Not at all. He was just wise enough to know that the countryside over which we were riding was not suitable terrain for a gallop."

"Pooh," said Harriet. "I have been galloping over all the land hereabouts for years."

"Then you are very fortunate, young lady," Christopher said with a smile, "to still have a neck on which to balance your very pretty head."

Harriet tittered and smiled coquettishly into his face, which was very close to hers at that moment.

He released his hold on her waist and turned to Rebecca. "I'll wager Primrose dragged you out here to see her Peter, Miss Shaw," he said. "She seems to feel that there is no greater treat in life for other people than to be allowed to view her horse, especially with her perched on its back. But you are cold. You should have brought a shawl with you."

She smiled rather stiffly. "I shall go back inside in a moment," she said. "And indeed, I must agree with Primrose. Peter is well worth seeing."

He held her eyes for longer than seemed necessary. "You look tired after a day of teaching," he said, his eyes searching hers. "It must be an exhausting business. May I escort you inside?" He offered his arm.

"No!" she said breathlessly and hastily. "Indeed I am not as tired as all that, sir. The air feels good. I shall say good-day to you all." She turned and would have left the four of them standing there.

"Christopher," Primrose said suddenly, "Miss Shaw says that she is not sure if she will attend the Langbourne ball next week. Do you tell her she must. You are very good at bullying people."

"I wish I could bully you into a greater display of good manners, my girl," Christopher said as Rebecca clutched her arms harder in an agony of embarrassment. "I have no wish to coerce Miss Shaw into doing anything she does not desire to do."

"Oh," Harriet said. "You must come, Rebecca. You can be so stuffy sometimes, but you are only six-and-twenty. Really that is not so old. It will be a few years yet before you will be forced to sit with the chaperons."

"I really have not said I will not go," Rebecca said. "I have not even read my invitation yet, Harriet."

"I have no wish to coerce you," Christopher repeated, "but I do hope that you decide to come, Miss Shaw. Those of us who learned and performed the waltz here last week must show off our accomplishment at the ball."

His eyes, she saw when she looked directly at him over her shoulder, were positively dancing with merriment. Her stomach lurched. The old Christopher, some joke constantly on his lips.

"Go, Miss Shaw," he said, "before your hands and face match the blue of your dress."

Rebecca went.

· 7 ·

Rebecca returned a card accepting her invitation to the Langbourne ball. She had dithered long over the decision. She did not like to think it was true that she was becoming stuffy, and of course it was not necessarily true merely because Harriet had said so. But Rebecca had the feeling that it would be very easy for her to cut off all ties with her own class. And she had no real desire to do so. As a girl she had always enjoyed a party or ball or picnic. Indeed, Mama and Papa had done so too.

And she needed friends. She liked the poorer people of the neighborhood and enjoyed their company. But she was well aware that there was an invisible barrier between her and them that would always prevent them from becoming truly her friends. Her birth and her education set her apart from them. On the other hand, the people of her own class frequently annoyed her with their seeming unawareness that people around them constantly suffered from their poverty. Yet these were her people, the ones with whom she felt she belonged.

As a younger woman, Rebecca had succeeded in dividing her time to her own satisfaction, enjoying the pleasures that social life had to offer, yet using the bulk of her time to minister to the needs of her father and his poorer parishioners. Looking back now, she could see that the change had come with her rejection by Christopher. Social activities without him had lost their appeal, while serving others had helped dull the pain of her loss. The passing of Papa had completed the process, and she had had little to do with the various activities of her class in the years since.

It had not been a conscious choice. She had never rejected invitations out of hand. She had always considered them. But more often than not, she had found an excuse for not attending that had always sounded quite convincing to her. Yes, Harriet was right, she had decided at last. She had become staid, something of a killjoy. She would go to the ball, which was generally accepted as the most glittering event that the year had to offer in this part of the world.

Yet the decision had not been as easy as these thoughts might have made it. Christopher would be there, and he had expressed a hope that she would go too. Should she go and perhaps let him think that his words had prompted her into going? Should she allow him to think that his wishes still mattered to her? And did they? Could she convince herself that she was not now finding excuses to attend the ball because she did not want to admit to herself that it was the certainty of his presence that was drawing her there?

Philip was the one who finally helped her make up her mind. He had accepted his invitation, he told her when they were visiting the sick together one afternoon. It seemed only right that she should go too. Their relationship, which had seemed perfectly satisfactory to her in the months since they had become betrothed, suddenly seemed to be lifeless. Had things changed between them in the previous few weeks? Or had it always been like this, and she had only now become aware of the fact? Perhaps her memories of the way things had been with her and Christopher were making her realize the great contrast with her present engagement.

Yet she must never complain. Love and passion were unreliable. They did not stand the test of time. Her relationship with Philip was undemonstrative, but in that fact lay its very strength. They shared similar ideas, beliefs, and values. They were involved in similar work. They respected each other. She need never fear that he would abandon her as Christopher had done when he had tired of his love for her.

Thinking about Philip made Rebecca feel guilty. She did not believe that she had behaved differently toward him in the last few weeks, but she knew that she had felt differently. She had been feeling dissatisfaction. She had noticed things about him that really did not matter at all. He was not a lighthearted man; he did not smile or laugh a great deal; he did not spend time on activities or conversation that he felt did not relate to his work. Even attending functions like the Sinclair picnic and the Langbourne ball were duty to him.

But truly these things were unimportant. Philip was a man of great integrity, and he really did cater to the needs of his flock without regard to his own comfort. On the afternoon when he told her of his acceptance of his invitation to the ball, for example, he had also told her of a new scheme of his. It was to visit the elderly and the sick—people who were confined a great deal to their homes—in order to read to them. Some of them had never heard a story, except perhaps the type of folktale that parents told their children. Surely it would help relieve the tedium of their days if he could read to them for an hour a few times a week from the great works of literature.

It was a simple enough idea, yet it was typical of Philip. He listed several people whom he intended to serve in this way. And Rebecca, doing quick calculations in her head, realized that this new project would add many hours to his work schedule each week, and miles of extra travel.

She must return her thoughts to him. She must concentrate all her attention on his good qualities and ignore those things about him that were less attractive. After all, no one was perfect, and she hated to think of what would happen if he started to dwell upon her weaknesses. So she would attend the ball and devote herself to showing her esteem for him during the evening. It did not matter that Christopher would be there too. She must get used to seeing him without being affected by his presence. After all, he was the son of the Sinclairs. She was likely to see a great deal of him in the coming years.

She hoped to avoid meeting the visitors at the Sinclair home during the week before the ball, but it was not to be. The chilly, windy weather continued and seemed very likely to turn to rain as Rebecca walked home from school one afternoon. Her shawl did little to keep the wind from cutting through to the very marrow of her bones. Several times she felt an isolated spot of rain, and there was still almost half a mile to walk before she could turn off onto the shortcut through the pasture. For once she was definitely sorry that she had not accepted Uncle Humphrey's offer of the gig. He had been quite insistent that morning. She bent her head to the wind.

This time she did not hear the horses come up behind her until they were almost level with her. When she did hear them, she looked back anxiously, and sure enough, there they were again, Mr. Carver in the lead, and Christopher slightly behind him.

"Miss Shaw," Lucas Carver said in his usual amiable way. "You look like a damsel in distress, if ever I saw one. It's a pity damsels are not attacked by dragons in these days. The fire from its nostrils might warm us all up." He shook with mirth at his own joke.

"Everett should have brought you home," Christopher said. "Does he not have a conveyance?" His face and voice were quite severe. He also looked quite snug in his greatcoat.

"Philip was from home this afternoon," Rebecca said curtly. "He is a busy man."

"Too busy to look after the welfare of his betrothed?" Christopher asked, one eyebrow raised.

Had Mr. Carver not been there, Rebecca would have answered with the anger she felt. As it was, she merely stared back, tight-lipped. "If you will excuse me," she said, "I shall continue on my way. I fear the rain is about

to start in earnest.'' She held out a hand and looked up to
the heavy clouds overhead.

"It is too far for you to walk in such weather," he said.
"Come, take my hand and step on my boot. I shall pull
you up and take you home."

"No, really," Rebecca said, pulling her shawl closer
around her and stepping back, "I shall be quite warm once
I start walking again."

But he would not let her pull her eyes away from his.
"Come," was all he said, his hand still outstretched.

If only Mr. Carver were not there! Rebecca could feel
her face burning, cold or no cold. She stepped forward
again and placed her hand timidly in his. She raised her
skirt with the other hand and placed a foot on his Hessian
boot. He was very strong, she thought through the confusion of her mind. Beyond those two actions, she seemed to
make no effort at all, yet a mere few seconds later she was
seated sideways on the horse in front of his saddle, one of
his arms firmly holding her in place.

He prodded the horse into motion. Rebecca was utterly
mortified. She tried to sit upright, away from him, but it
was impossible to do so. The only way she could keep
from losing her balance was to lean sideways, one shoulder and arm pressed firmly against his chest. His arm
stayed around her.

"Wish now that I had thought of playing Sir Galahad,"
Mr. Carver said. "Only trouble is, ma'am, that m'horse
would probably sag in the middle if it were forced to bear
one ounce more than my weight." He laughed as he rode
on slightly ahead of his companion on the narrow country
lane.

When they came to the point in the road at which it
branched in two, one fork leading to the Sinclair home and
the other to Limeglade, Christopher spoke again.

"You go on home, Luke," he said. "I shall take Miss
Shaw home and be back in no time at all. Tell Mama to
keep the tea hot for me."

Rebecca felt utterly dismayed. She had assumed that

both men would ride to Limeglade with her, though now she thought of it, of course, it made no sense at all for both of them to ride out of their way.

"Right," Mr. Carver said. He touched his hat with his whip. "Pleased to have met you, Miss Shaw. Glad one of us could be of service to you. Looks as if the rain is going to hold off awhile longer. But very cold." He hunched his shoulders and turned his horse into the lane that led to his destination.

"Mr. Carver is right," Rebecca said hesitantly. "It is not going to rain yet after all. I could walk from here, Christopher, really I could. You need not ride out of your way."

He looked down at her. "You are just about blue with the cold," he said. "I thought you had more sense, Becky. You were too proud to borrow a vehicle, I suppose."

Rebecca would have replied, but she was suddenly made speechless as he transferred his horse's reins to the hand that also held her and with the other hand began to unbutton his greatcoat. A few seconds later she found herself enveloped in its warm folds and pulled even closer against him. She dared not trust her voice to say anything. All her efforts had to be used to keep her head from contact with his body. Even that battle was lost after a few minutes, though. The strain on the muscles of her neck was too great; she was forced to rest her head against his shoulder.

They rode in silence for the mile that still lay ahead before they came to the gates that opened onto the drive leading to the house. For all her resolves of the previous few days, Rebecca found that she could not prevent herself from feeling an overwhelming sadness. It was so long since she had been close to him like this. And he was different. He had lost his boyish leanness. His body had hardened into well-muscled maturity. Yet it could be no one else but him. There was a certain feeling about being with Christopher that she had forgotten, a feeling of safeness, of rightness. And there was a certain smell about him, of soap, cologne, leather, perhaps—she was not quite sure what. That too she had forgotten until now.

She wanted to do nothing more than turn her face into his neckcloth, wrap her arms around his waist, and cry. Instead, she held herself rigidly still, trying to fight her treacherous body, trying to think of Philip.

"You can set me down here," she said at last when they were one bend away from the house. She did not wish him to take her right up to the door. She would be obliged then to invite him inside. And she did not wish the others to know that she had ridden with him for a few miles. Uncle Humphrey, or even Harriet, might remember something from the past and tease her about it.

She was relieved when Christopher drew his horse to a halt. For reasons of his own he must agree with her. He did not want Harriet, perhaps, to know that he had been with her.

"Very well," he said. "You should not get very cold between here and the house. Tomorrow, Becky, if you are to teach, will you please take one of your uncle's carriages? I imagine that this weather will persist for a few days yet."

He swung down from the saddle and reached up to lift her to the ground. It was really not his fault. Rebecca was honest enough to realize that afterward when she had run to her room and had had time to calm down enough to think rather than merely feel. It was her fault entirely. His own arms stayed quite firm. He did not intend that she touch him on the way down. It was her own arms that went suddenly weak at the elbows. She had put her hands on his shoulders to brace herself, but suddenly she lurched toward him so that she slid the whole agonizing length of his body between her high perch and the ground.

She sucked in a ragged breath of air and looked up into his face in dismay. "Christopher!" was all she could think of to say. Pretty stupid, as she admitted to herself later. Why say that?

"Becky!" He whispered her name.

It was those blue eyes that were really to blame, of course, but then, in all fairness, she had to admit that he was not really responsible for those. She could not look away from them even when they came closer. Finally, when she could focus no longer she had to close her eyes. But that did nothing to break the spell because by that time his mouth was on hers.

It was easy enough afterward to tell herself that she should immediately have pulled away and run for her life. The trouble was that one's mind did not work quite rationally when one was being kissed by the only man one had ever loved, and the man one had loved so totally that no one had ever been able to take his place.

She was inside his greatcoat again, the coat and his arms wrapped around her, her own hands splayed warmly over the silk shirt that covered his chest. (How had his jacket and waistcoat become unbuttoned?) And his mouth was opened over hers, his tongue pushing urgently beyond the barrier of her lips and teeth. She had forgotten—ah, yes, she had forgotten just how much he could stir her blood and make her ache with longing for him. She pressed against him, the coat and his arms quite unnecessary to hold her close. She wanted this to happen, had wanted it from that first moment of meeting him on the laneway home a couple of weeks before. She wanted him. She loved him. He was Christopher, and she did not care about anything else. She did not care.

He ended the kiss and looked down into her bewildered eyes. His own looked unnaturally bright. "Becky," he said very softly. "Becky, I am sorry. I am sorry about everything. But this especially. I have no right. I have caused enough havoc in your life, I believe. Please forgive me."

Rebecca looked back, wide-eyed now. He was the old Christopher, human and vulnerable. But, of course, he was not the old Christopher at all. And even that man had been a figment of her imagination.

And then, finally, too late, much too late, she turned and fled.

Rebecca was walking in Maude's formal garden the next afternoon, breathing in the heavy scent of the roses. It was a warm day and the sun shone from a clear sky, despite Christopher's prediction of the day before. For once she had stayed at home all day. It was not her regular day either for teaching or visiting the sick, and she had decided that she would not invent an extra errand.

She had been full of self-loathing since the afternoon before. How could she have allowed it to happen? Had she spent all those years working him out of her system and building up self-discipline only to find that his mere appearance in her life again could bring all the barriers crashing down? Was she prepared to give up the secure and satisfying life that she had rebuilt from the ruins of her old life?

The answer to both questions certainly seemed to be yes. While she had been in his arms, his mouth on hers, she had surrendered completely to a physical longing that should have died years before. She had wanted him and given in to that desire. She had loved him.

Her self-loathing of the moment came entirely from the fact that she still could not convince herself that she had not meant it. She did love him. She always had, even when she had hated him most. She loved Christopher Sinclair, a man who had used her for his own satisfaction during a few months when he had had nothing else with which to amuse himself and had callously abandoned her as soon as he found someone who could cater more satisfactorily to his tastes. He had had the money and all the exciting life of town with which to entertain himself in the six and a half intervening years. And he still had the money.

Now he was back again, bored again, looking for a female with whom to carry on a flirtation. It did not seem to matter who she was. Harriet had set her cap at him, and he had lost no time in taking up the challenge. And he had certainly not hesitated to accept the open invitation she herself had seemed to offer the day before by allowing her body to sway against his.

She could remember one occasion when she really had deliberately done just that. They had been in the woods beyond the bridge, both perched in the low branches of a tree while they talked and laughed over some nonsense that she could not recall. When he had lifted her down, she quite deliberately and provocatively rubbed against him, giggling as she did so. She could even remember his words.

"Becky!" he had scolded. "Are you playing temptress?"

"Yes, definitely," she had admitted, grinning up at him. "You have not kissed me all afternoon."

"Have I not?" he had said, putting his arms around her and pulling her hard against him. "What an oversight. I fully intend to do so now, though."

"Good," she had commented, putting her arms up around his neck and raising her chin. "It is about time."

She could even remember the kiss. It was the one that had got out of hand. His shirt had been unbuttoned to the waist, her hands on his chest, and her dress had been pushed from her shoulders, his hands on her naked breasts before they had come to their senses at the same moment. The incident had shaken them both. He had even suggested that they get married without further delay. She often wondered what would have happened with their lives if she had said yes.

Rebecca was agitated by the memory. Would he remember too? If he did, there would be no shadow of doubt in his mind that her actions of the previous afternoon had been deliberate.

Perhaps she should end her betrothal to Philip. It was not that she wished to be free to try to entice Christopher back again. There could be no question of that. Love him she might, but she was not foolish or degraded enough to want to resume a relationship in which she had been treated with such contempt. But could she in all fairness marry Philip when she had finally been forced to admit that she still loved Christopher? And after the afternoon before, she did not know if she would be able to bear being touched by Philip. She had often wondered; she had never had so much as a kiss from him by which she might judge.

Should she tell him? But how would she tell him? What would she do afterward? Could she go on forever living on the charity of Uncle Humphrey?

Her thoughts were mercifully interrupted by the sight of three figures approaching from the direction of the pasture. She smiled at Mr. Bartlett, who had Ellen on one arm and Primrose on the other.

"Ah, Miss Shaw," he called, "I see that my sister's roses only serve to make you look more lovely. I only wish the same might be said of me. But I fear that I merely look like a thorn among roses." He smiled at the two girls.

"We accused Mr. Bartlett of being a hothouse plant," Primrose called, "always in town and always riding everywhere. He had to prove us wrong by leaving his horse in our stable and walking all the way here with us."

"We have talked to him all the way," Ellen added, "to keep his mind from the terrible distance, you see."

"The countryside breeds cruel maidens," Mr. Bartlett said. "I would wager that these two will sleep dreamlessly tonight without sparing one thought to the blisters on my feet."

They all laughed. Rebecca felt her mood lift somewhat. She had been brooding on her own problems too long and forgetting that there were pleasant companions within easy reach.

It was almost as if Mr. Bartlett read her mind. "The Misses Sinclair have come all this way for the pleasure of taking tea with my sister," he said. "But I must confess that this hothouse plant has become accustomed to the fresh air and likes it. May I walk with you, Miss Shaw?"

She smiled and moved toward him. His company would be a welcome relief from her own broodings. Ellen and Primrose walked the rest of the way to the house while Rebecca and Mr. Bartlett began to stroll across the extensive lawns that stretched to the west of the house.

"This is an extremely pleasant place to be," he said, holding out an arm for her to take. "The countryside is delightful and the company most congenial. I am only afraid that I shall become so happy here that I shall outstay my welcome."

"I do not believe you need fear that, sir," Rebecca said. "It seems to me that everyone is the happier for your presence here."

"How kind of you to say so!" he said, patting the hand that lay on his arm. "You are a very kind lady, Miss Shaw. I have not been unaware of how much time you devote to those less fortunate than yourself. We all might learn something from your example. Of course, perhaps I am more sensitive to your good works because life has not always been kind to me."

"Oh?" she said.

"My family is not wealthy, as I am sure you are aware," he said. "Maude, alas, was not able to bring much of a dowry to her marriage. Lord Holmes is a generous man, and I do believe it mattered not at all to him that she could offer only her sweet self. But my father feels it, Miss Shaw, and I feel it. Staying here, for example, is pleasant; the hospitality of my brother-in-law is excellent. But it does pain me that I cannot return that hospitality."

Rebecca smiled. "I know how you feel," she said.

"I believe we are alike in many ways, Miss Shaw," he said, "except that you have been more useful in your life than I have been. Both of us grew up, I believe, knowing how to live frugally. I have never expected much by way of the goods of this life. And I never had the opportunity to go to university or to travel. Even so, I might have been happy." He sighed.

"Education and travel do not necessarily bring happiness," Rebecca said reassuringly. "One can learn a great deal just from reading, I firmly believe."

"Ah, you are right," he said. "And what would one do without books, Miss Shaw? My happiness, though, might have come from love."

She looked at him inquiringly.

"She was lovely," he said. "Not perhaps beautiful in the eyes of the world. But to me she was perfection. We wished to marry. The only stumbling block as far as I was concerned was that she was extremely wealthy and like to inherit a very large fortune from her papa. I hated to be able to bring no answering wealth to the marriage. But she assured me that the fact made no difference, and I insisted that before we marry a written agreement be drawn up whereby her wealth would remain wholly hers. Alas, all our planning came to nothing."

"She—died?" Rebecca asked softly.

"Not then," he said with a twisted smile. "She was forced to marry a man whom her father preferred, although he was my equal in both birth and fortune."

"Oh," Rebecca said, "you are talking of Mrs. Sinclair, are you not?"

He bowed his head. "I could have borne it had she been happy or even moderately contented afterward," he said, "or perhaps even if he had taken her away where I would not have seen her frequently and known how he abused her."

So, Rebecca thought, there was no escaping her thoughts. They were back on the topic of Christopher. And she hated him with a new vehemence. By what right had he come back here to torment her again when she had won a hard-fought battle with her own feelings? And by what right had he come to torment Mr. Bartlett, when that poor gentleman must be deeply grieving the loss of the woman he had loved?

"I am sorry, Miss Shaw," Mr. Bartlett said, his voice contrite. "I did not intend to talk about Sinclair or Angela. It is all past history and I have no wish to burden anyone else with my unhappiness. Come, let us talk of more cheerful things. Maude tells me that you are to attend the ball the day after tomorrow?"

"Yes," Rebecca said, "I have accepted the invitation."

"I am so pleased," he said. "May I hope that you will dance the opening set with me, Miss Shaw?"

Rebecca smiled warmly at him, thankful for the change in topic. "I should be delighted, sir," she said.

• 8 •

"You should be sitting on this side of the carriage, Rebecca, dear," Lord Holmes said. "This lap-robe is quite large enough to cover your knees too. I fear the draft in this conveyance, though I have given repeated instructions for the doors and windows to be refitted."

"I am really quite warm here, Uncle Humphrey," Rebecca replied. "We are fortunate that the weather has turned mild again. I believe even an open carriage would feel quite pleasant this evening."

"Never say so!" the baron said with a shudder. "But, of course, you are funning me, Rebecca. Night air is the very worst bringer of dangerous chills. Maude, my love, put your hands beneath the robe. Your knuckles will be unbecomingly red by the time we reach the Langbournes' house if you do not."

"Yes, my lord," Maude replied, obediently tucking her already warm hands beneath the fur-lined robe that her husband had insisted be laid across their laps during the six-mile journey to their destination.

All the occupants of the carriage except Lord Holmes were feeling the discomfort of the stuffy interior of the carriage long before they arrived. Somehow five of them had squeezed into a vehicle meant to hold no more than four. Lord and Lady Holmes sat facing the horses because having his back to them always made his stomach decidedly queasy, the baron said. Across from them sat Re-

becca, Harriet, and Mr. Bartlett. Harriet complained loudly
that her new turquoise-blue satin gown would be hopelessly crushed before they arrived in the ballroom, but Mr.
Bartlett soon restored her good humor by assuring her that
the great beauty of her face and the perfection of her
coiffure would render all beholders quite oblivious to a
few wrinkles in her gown.

Harriet had been in an exuberant mood all day, as
Rebecca had found to her cost. Again she was not teaching
school and had stayed at home all morning. Harriet had
visited her in her room, intent on talking about the previous day when she had journeyed to Wraxby, the closest
town of any size, in company with Mr. Sinclair, Mr.
Carver, and Ellen. The idea for the outing had been entirely Harriet's. She had mentioned in the hearing of Mr.
Sinclair that she really needed new blue slippers and a fan
for the ball, but the village could supply neither. Mr.
Sinclair had taken up his cue with flattering haste and
suggested that they must go into the town.

And he had been most attentive, Harriet told her cousin,
both during the journey and in the town. He had not
seemed to mind that they had had to visit three separate
establishments in search of just the right fan and that even
then she had not been able to make a choice between two.
He had suggested that she buy one and he the other as a
gift, but she had not been so dead to propriety as to accept
that offer when they were not even betrothed.

Of course, Harriet added, that situation was like to
change very soon. She fully expected that Mr. Sinclair was
about to declare himself—perhaps even at the ball. Certainly he would do so soon.

That Mr. Carver was a perfectly horrid man. She really
did not know how Mr. Sinclair tolerated him. And it must
be perfectly dreadful for the Sinclairs to be obliged to be
civil to him for so long. She could not understand why he
had not taken himself back to London or wherever he
came from long before now. She had been understandably
weary after her busy afternoon of shopping and had wanted

nothing more than to sit down and have an ice before starting for home. Ellen had been whining forever about a length of ribbon she wanted to take back for Primrose as a surprise, and Mr. Carver had insisted that they complete the errand.

That would not have been so dreadful, perhaps, if he had offered to accompany Ellen while she and Mr. Sinclair had gone for the ices. But he had insisted that all four of them go—merely to purchase one length of ribbon, and he had dared—dared!—to reprimand her when she had protested.

"He had the effrontery to look at me with that odious smile that he pretends is so amiable," Harriet said indignantly, "and tell me that I must not behave like a spoiled brat. Can you imagine, Rebecca? I was so angry I could not speak. I think Mr. Sinclair showed admirable restraint in not calling him out on the spot. It really would not have done in the middle of a street in Wraxby, you know."

Rebecca had the good sense to make no comment but to let Harriet's monologue flow over her head. She had really not enjoyed hearing about the attentions Christopher was showing her cousin. She could have wished that he had been the one to give Harriet the well-deserved setdown.

The Langbourne mansion was an imposing building, though Lord Holmes had never been induced to admit as much. The driveway led straight from the gates to the main doors and was lined with tall elm trees. On this occasion, as always during the annual ball, the trees were hung with lanterns, and the front of the house was ablaze with lights.

"What a magnificent sight!" Mr. Bartlett was unwise enough to remark.

"Well enough," Lord Holmes said, not even deigning to glance out of the window. "*Nouveau riche,* my dear Stanley. The style of the house is totally derivative. Nothing original whatsoever. Yes, it is well enough, I would grant you, but it lacks character."

"Oh, precisely," Mr. Bartlett agreed. "I was, of course,

comparing the house to most that have arisen during the last twenty years or so. I did not imply any comparison with established country homes like Limeglade, naturally. The idea is quite laughable.''

The baron inclined his head graciously.

The stairway leading from the tiled hall of the manor to the ballroom above was crowded with a surprising number of people. The Langbourne ball was considered to be one of the major social attractions of the year and drew guests from miles around. The five members of Lord Holmes's party joined the group on the stairs that was waiting to pass the receiving line. The Sinclairs were up ahead of them, Rebecca could see, and she lowered her eyes to avoid any accidental eye contact with Christopher. Even as she did so, though, she realized how foolish she was being. Could she avoid looking at him all evening?

She was relieved to be claimed for the first dance by Mr. Bartlett. She felt unaccountably nervous at the splendor of the occasion; it was several years since she had attended anything so lavish. The ballroom was decorated with what must have been hundreds of flowers. The room was heavy with their perfume. And the chandeliers, filled with candles and reflected in the floor-to-ceiling mirrors that stretched one length of the ballroom, were dazzling to the eyes. Philip was not yet there. He had told her that he would probably be late as this was the evening when he liked to compose his Sunday sermon.

Christopher was leading Harriet out for the first set, Rebecca saw even as she laid a hand on Mr. Bartlett's arm. And she looked at him for the first time. He was wearing black, the new fashion that Mr. Bartlett had described to an incredulous Uncle Humphrey a few weeks before—and he looked quite magnificent. The contrast between the black and the startling, almost luminous white of his linen and stockings was quite breathtaking. He succeeded in putting all the other men in their bright colors quite in the shade.

"I see that Sinclair is exercising his usual bad judgment,'' Mr. Bartlett said. ''Such a controversial fashion is totally inappropriate for a country ballroom, do you not agree? But then I understand that being noticed is of great importance to the man. He thrives on attention.''

''Then I would suggest that we pay him none,'' Rebecca suggested, smiling dazzlingly at Mr. Bartlett. Somehow she was going to enjoy this evening. And even if she could not enjoy it, she would appear to do so. She had not seen Christopher Sinclair since their disastrous encounter in the country lane, and she had no intention of showing him that she had been in any way affected by that experience.

It was not difficult for Rebecca to live up to that resolve for the first part of the evening. She was looking well, though she did not fully realize the fact. A new rose-pink gown flattered her coloring and added a glow to her cheeks. She had not been seen in any large company for a long time. She was, therefore, much in demand as a partner. She danced with men she had not seen perhaps for a few years. And she danced with Julian and with Philip when he finally arrived.

Philip was a good dancer. He despised the activity, but he always felt it important to socialize with all classes of his parishioners. And as always with Philip, if he was going to do something, he would make the effort to do it well.

''Did you finish your sermon, Philip?'' Rebecca asked him. She looked at his tall, slender figure, dressed in green, at his good-looking face and his shining blond hair and tried to feel an attraction to him.

''Yes, I did,'' he said. He smiled suddenly, a rare enough sight to capture Rebecca's attention. ''I have a surprise for you tomorrow, Rebecca. You will be pleased.''

''Oh?'' she said. ''Tell me, Philip. Suspense makes me ill.''

''You will find out at school tomorrow,'' he said, his manner almost teasing for a moment.

''Philip!'' she said, exasperated.

"I am pleased to see Lord Holmes still in the ballroom," he said, looking around the room. "I thought he would have disappeared to the card room long ago. He really does not have enough exercise, you know."

"It is surprising," Rebecca agreed. "He has even danced twice, once with Lady Langbourne and one—of course— with Maude."

Philip frowned, his eyes coming to rest on the last-named lady. "Lady Holmes looks like a girl at her come-out," he said, "and not at all like a matron."

"And very glad I am of it," Rebecca said warmly. "She is very young, Philip. Younger than I am, you know."

He looked at her. "Yes," he said, "I suppose you are right. I had not thought of it that way. However, Rebecca, she is a married lady, and I cannot approve the frivolity of her gown."

Rebecca too looked at Maude. She had thought the white silk underdress covered with delicate white chantilly lace a particularly glorious creation. And it suited its wearer, emphasizing the lovely auburn of her hair and the daintiness of her figure.

"And the neckline is quite indecently low," Philip continued. "If you were ever to wear something so immodest, Rebecca, I should tear it to shreds and throw it away."

Rebecca had to bite her lip and turn away. It was a small point and not worth arguing over. But for some reason, she felt more irritated with Philip than she had ever been before. Why must he always single out Maude for criticism? Lady Holmes's behaviour was always above reproach, as far as Rebecca could see, especially when one realized that she was not a happy person. And who could be happy married to someone like Uncle Humphrey? It was easy enough to tolerate him, even to be amused by him, as an uncle. But as a husband? Maude conducted herself with admirable dignity.

Fortunately for Rebecca, she was saved from further irritation by a new partner, who had signed her card earlier and had now come to claim his set. And she was kept busy until after the supper break. She was able to stay away from Philip and the decision about him that she knew she was going to have to make very soon. She still was not quite sure whether she should break off their betrothal or whether she should try to continue with her plans to marry him. But this was neither the time nor the place to worry over such a thorny problem.

And she was able to avoid Christopher. She had seen him frequently, had even danced past him on a number of occasions. But somehow she had contrived to avoid looking at him or meeting his eyes in all of that time. She was, of course, aware of him every moment of the evening. She knew exactly with whom he had danced. She knew that he danced both the opening set and the supper dance with Harriet. And she was aware of the fact that neither of them was at the supper for a full twenty minutes after everyone else was sitting down. The evening was warm; several couples had left the ballroom through the French doors in order to stroll in the garden.

Mr. Carver asked her to dance after supper, and Rebecca smiled mischievously at him. It was a waltz, the second of three that the Langbournes had planned for the more daring and fashionable of their guests.

"You are very trusting, sir," she said. "Are you willing to risk having your toes trodden on when I have had merely one lesson in the waltz?"

"Well, ma'am," he said, "if you tread on m'foot, I might tread on yours. And I can vouch for th'fact that you would get th'worst of it."

Rebecca could feel laughter bubbling up inside her as he rumbled with mirth. "Very well," she said. "I shall endeavor to keep my feet to myself, sir."

"You really are a naturally good dancer," he commented after a minute. "Sometimes waltzing can be suspiciously like lugging around a sack of meal."

"Oh," Rebecca said, "now you have made me really nervous, sir."

Mr. Carver was unable to keep up the repartee. The tempo of the waltz was very lively, and soon he was almost audibly counting steps. He stopped when they were opposite the French doors.

"Very sorry, Miss Shaw," he said. "Bit off a little more than I can chew this time. Dancing ain't quite my thing unless the tempo is slow and sedate. Would you care for a turn in the garden, ma'am?"

Rebecca smiled. "I should be delighted, sir," she said. "The smell of the flowers in here was quite lovely at first, but now, I must confess, it has become oppressive."

They strolled in silence at first across the lawn, Rebecca's hand resting on the massive and very solid arm of her companion. The night was lit softly by lanterns set in the trees that bordered the grass.

"Have you made any progress on expanding your school to include girls?" Mr. Carver asked.

"I have not broached the subject for a while," Rebecca said. "I shall wait until the results of the present school are quite obvious and then renew the campaign."

"Diplomatic," Mr. Carver said. "Should have come with Sinclair to see you teach, Miss Shaw. Can never drum up as much interest as he in such things. Should be ashamed of myself."

"Not at all," Rebecca said. "I should prefer you to stay away altogether than pretend to a charitable interest that you do not really feel. I cannot stand pretension like that." Her tone was more vehement than she had intended.

"Eh?" Mr. Carver said. "Y'ain't referring to Sinclair, are you?"

"Yes, actually I am," Rebecca said. "He came to the school merely to look good, I am convinced. What does he really care?"

"Eh?" Mr. Carver said again. "Y'don't know?" He looked away from her. "No," he said, "seem to remember he mentioned something of the sort. Sorry, Miss Shaw, excuse me. Talking to m'self. Often do it, y'know. Sign of advancing senility." His arm beneath hers shook with the mirth that she was becoming accustomed to.

"Are you trying to tell me that Mr. Sinclair really is interested in the school?" Rebecca asked incredulously.

"Oh, assuredly so," Mr. Carver said. "Never knew anyone like Sinclair for always having some charitable concern eating at him. Puts me to shame. Never think of it m'self unless someone reminds me. Unfortunately for me, m'mother or Sinclair are constantly reminding me."

Rebecca was silent. She was feeling somewhat stunned. Could Mr. Carver be exaggerating? Christopher concerned about the welfare of others? He had in the past, of course, but she had long ago discovered that the real Christopher Sinclair was a selfish, mercenary man, who rode rough-shod over the feelings of others. Yet Mr. Carver seemed to be an honest and a trustworthy man. Well, perhaps there was a grain of truth in what he said. She would be glad now to know that there was some trace of conscience or kindness in the man she had loved and still loved.

They reached the end of the lawn in silence and would have turned back toward the house again. However, both became aware suddenly that they were not alone. Someone wearing light-colored clothes was among the trees, and both realized with some embarrassment that there were actually two people there in very close embrace. Mr. Carver turned away with rather more haste than he would otherwise have employed and walked Rebecca quickly across the grass until they were out of earshot.

"Never could stand that sort of thing," he said indignantly. "Young fools should wait until they can be sure no one will come upon them and be mortified with embarrassment. No sense of restraint. M'apologies, Miss Shaw."

"It was in no way your fault, sir," Rebecca said lightly. "Let us forget about it. The incident is not worth remembering."

The music had ended by the time they returned to the ballroom. Rebecca excused herself and pushed through the crowd that surrounded the floor. She did not know where to go. If she went to the ladies' withdrawing room, she would encounter the maids who were there at all times to help unfortunates mend sagging hems or detached bows. She ran hastily down the staircase and found a shadowed alcove where she could find privacy for perhaps a few minutes. She had to have privacy. She had to have a few minutes in which to collect herself before having to face any more dancing partners.

She was very thankful that Mr. Carver had not seen. He could not have seen or he would surely have been even more embarrassed than he had been. He had thought the two people strangers. But she had seen. She had recognized them, both of them. It seemed incredible. She was almost inclined now to think that her eyes must have been deceiving her, but she knew they had not. The gleaming gown of the lady and the light hair of the man had belonged quite indisputably to Maude and Philip. And they had been in very deep embrace, their bodies touching at all points, completely lost to their surroundings in the kiss they had been sharing.

Ten whole minutes passed before Rebecca came out of her place of hiding and climbed the stairs to the ballroom again. She had blanked her mind. It was merely one more problem that she must consider when she had leisure in which to do so. Her face was composed, her walk unhurried.

The first person she saw when she reentered the ballroom was Maude, who was standing close to the door, apparently in the process of refusing to dance with an earnest young man, who was bowing elegantly before her. She was, Rebecca saw in one hasty glance, as white as the gown she wore and in very obvious distress. Her hands twisted the fan that she held as if she were intent on breaking it. There was no sign of Philip.

The trouble with coming to a social event with other people, Rebecca thought ruefully, was that one had to await their pleasure at the end of the evening. She would have liked nothing more than to return home so that she could crawl into bed and escape into merciful sleep. Her life and emotions were becoming hopelessly tangled. She very much feared that she was about to lose all her faith in humanity. Could no one be depended upon to act true to character? Philip! He had never so much as kissed her. And Maude? Rebecca could have sworn that she was the soul of dignity and honor and sweetness.

Rebecca looked around her. Harriet, she was relieved to see, was not with Christopher, though she could no longer be sure even of her own motives. Was she watching that relationship out of a concern for the welfare of Harriet, or out of a concern that Christopher might be ensnared by her and lead a life of misery with such a selfish partner? However it was, all seemed safe for the moment. Harriet was being led onto the floor by a smiling Mr. Bartlett. She too was smiling and blushing. He must have just paid her a compliment. She hoped that poor Mr. Bartlett would not develop a *tendre* for Harriet. He deserved better than that.

"Will you dance, Becky?"

She spun around to look into the blue eyes very close to her.

"It is a waltz," Christopher said, "and I observed earlier that you perform the dance with great competence."

Even as she placed her hand in his and allowed him to lead her onto the floor, Rebecca's mind began to come out of its stupor. Was she mad? This was the very last thing she wanted to be doing at the moment. And how could he have the effrontery to have asked her? A waltz, too—the third and last of the evening. She would have thought that he would be as anxious to avoid her as she was to avoid him. Or did he want the satisfaction of conquering her heart again? Rebecca turned to face him, her expression grim, and placed one hand on his shoulder and the other in his.

He said nothing for a while but held her loosely and guided her expertly and gracefully through the movements of the dance. Rebecca kept her eyes on the silver buttons of his waistcoat.

"I knew," he said finally, "that the longer I left it

without saying anything to you, the more embarrassed we would be to meet. I had to talk to you this evening, Becky.''

''I cannot think that there is anything for either of us to say.'' She spoke so quietly that he had to bend his head toward her to hear the words. ''Our acquaintance came to an end many years ago. We are strangers now.''

''Yes,'' he said after a short silence. His voice was strained. ''You are right. You have made a good life for yourself, Becky. You do a great deal of good; you matter to a large number of people. And you have chosen a good man for a husband. Philip Everett must be one of the few men worthy of your love. These facts make my behavior of a few afternoons ago the more reprehensible. I can say in my own defense only that I did not intend to do what I did. My behavior was unforgivable. I ask your forgiveness, Becky. You have a generous heart, I know.''

She darted him an astonished look. What game was he playing now? She could not understand and dared not try. Her faith in her own judgment had been severely shaken over the last few hours.

''I think we should forget the whole matter,'' she said to his silver buttons again. ''I would prefer to forget it, Christopher.''

''Yes,'' he said, ''if you wish.''

They danced silently for a few minutes, Rebecca almost dizzy with her confused thoughts and with his nearness. She was afraid that her hand was trembling in his, but she could neither know for sure nor do anything to prevent its happening.

''What do you know of Stanley Bartlett?'' he asked unexpectedly at last.

''Mr. Bartlett?'' she asked, looking directly into his eyes in her surprise. ''He is Maude's brother. He knew you in London, I believe.''

''Oh?'' he said. ''He admitted as much, did he?''

''Is there any reason that he should not?'' she asked. She could feel indignation rising in her. Was he anxious to

know how much of the truth about himself Mr. Bartlett
had told?''

He looked searchingly into her eyes. ''I wish you would
have a care for your cousin, Becky,'' he said hesitantly.

''What?'' she said. ''You mean Harriet? Are you trying
to tell me that she may be in some danger from Mr.
Bartlett?'' She almost laughed in her incredulity.

''I would not wish to be so melodramatic,'' he said. He
took a deep breath and continued with seeming hesitation.
''But your cousin is a wealthy heiress, Becky, even if
Lady Holmes should produce an heir, and Bartlett is not a
wealthy man.''

''You are accusing him of being a fortune hunter!''
Rebecca said, stopping in the middle of the dance floor
and staring at him with wide-eyed indignation. ''How
perfectly despicable you are! It is true that he has no
money—he is the first to admit the fact. But he has
qualities that are vastly superior to all the wealth in the
world. He has kindness and integrity and concern for the
welfare of others.''

''Becky,'' he said sharply, ''are you sure you wish to
create a public scene? Shall we dance? You may continue
your tirade into my ear.''

Rebecca felt as if she would explode with anger, but the
wisdom of his words was not to be denied. She forced
herself to smile as they began to dance again and composed her face.

''I will not allow you of all people to throw suspicion
upon Mr. Bartlett,'' she said with controlled fury. ''He has
told me about you, sir. I know that you have already
ruined his life and that of the woman he loved. Can you
not be content with what you have done and cease tor-
menting him now?''

''Do you refer to Angela?'' he asked quietly.

''You must know that I do,'' she said. ''And you must
know that I despise you, sir. You may believe that everyone whose pockets are to let is scheming to acquire someone else's money. But not every man is like you. I would

consider Harriet fortunate to receive an offer from Mr. Bartlett and I would applaud her good sense if she accepted him.''

"I see," Christopher said, his voice almost unnaturally calm. "There seems nothing more for me to say then, does there? Pardon me, Becky, for trying to offer advice where it is not wanted. The music is ending—to our mutual relief, I am sure.''

And the ball was ending too, Rebecca discovered. She had never been so glad of anything in her life. She could not have imagined an evening more full of emotional upheaval.

• 9 •

Rebecca saw very soon the next day what Philip's surprise was. The boys came into the schoolhouse more quietly than usual, but with stifled giggles. She did not look up from the book she was scanning until they were all inside and seated on the benches. Then she raised her head and looked straight into the bespectacled eyes of an uncomfortable-looking Cyril. The boys burst into open laughter at her expression, and Cyril squirmed in discomfort.

"What?" she said. "Cyril, how perfectly splendid! But how did this come about?"

Cyril merely grinned sheepishly.

"The reverend took him into Wraxby yestiddy, miss," one of the other boys volunteered.

"The Reverend Everett?" Rebecca asked in surprise. "He bought the spectacles for you, Cyril?"

"Yes, miss," the boy nodded.

But how could he have done it? What sacrifice had he had to make to be able to buy eyeglasses for one of his pupils? But was not that just like Philip? One day he was talking about dismissing the boy from the school; and the next, he was making quite sure that the boy had as much of a chance to learn as the others.

"And do they make a difference, Cyril?" she asked. "Can you see more clearly with them?"

"Oh, miss," he said, his eyes wide behind the glass lenses. "I didn't know there was so much to see. When I went home, me mum laughed because all I did was look at the blanket on me bed. I could see all the threads woven together, miss, all in and out in a perfect pattern.''

The boys all roared with laughter at the excitement in Cyril's voice. Rebecca had to clap her hands for silence.

"That is wonderful, Cyril," she asked. "And now we will be able to find out if you can also read."

No miracle had occurred, of course. Cyril had not suddenly become a fluent reader. Nevertheless, Rebecca was encouraged by the fact that he could puzzle over each word and sometimes work out in his mind what one was. It seemed obvious at least that now he could see clearly what letters were in each word. She felt confident that with a little time and practice he would soon catch up to the rest of the pupils.

Philip did not put in an appearance at all during the morning. Rebecca did not know whether she wanted to see him or not. She was eager to question him about Cyril and to find out how and why he had helped the boy. On the other hand, her mind was still in turmoil from the night before. They had been very late arriving home, and knowing that she had to teach the following day, she had forced her mind blank so that she might sleep. And this morning, knowing that she had a day of teaching ahead, she had kept her mind blank. She would think later, she had decided, when she had the time and the privacy.

She knew only that the evening before had been like some kind of nightmare in which everything that could have gone wrong had done so. And somewhere in the jumble of problems that she was going to have to face soon were those concerning Philip—not only her feelings for him, but also his for her. Had she really seen him kissing Maude? The idea seemed quite preposterous in the cold light of day. But she would not think of it now.

Philip came to the schoolroom during the afternoon, only a short while before the boys were to be dismissed. He was holding himself more than usually upright, Rebecca noticed at a glance. And his face was even sterner than it usually was and very definitely pale. He merely nodded to her, greeted the boys, who had all risen to their feet at his entry, and walked to the back of the room, where he stood, hands clasped behind his back, staring out of the window until the day's lessons were over.

Rebecca joined him there when the last of the pupils had left. "Philip," she said, "I very much liked your surprise."

He looked blankly at her for a moment. "Ah," he said, "Cyril. And have the eyeglasses made all the difference, Rebecca?"

She smiled. "Not in one day," she said. "But they will, Philip. His eyesight must be extremely poor. All day he kept us amused by his excitement at discovering some new detail that he has been unaware of until now."

"Yes, I know," Philip said. "I had that all the way home from Wraxby yesterday."

"Philip," she said timidly. "How could you do it? I do know that Cyril's father could not afford to buy him the eyeglasses if he saved for five years. Did you pay for them yourself?"

Philip looked uncomfortable. "There was some money left from the school that I had been saving for emergencies," he said. "I considered this emergency enough."

She smiled. "I am so glad," she said. "Sometimes one tends to think of the school in the abstract and forget that it is here to serve individual boys. I am glad you considered Cyril important enough to be called an emergency."

"I am not at all sure that it was the right thing to do," Philip said, "but it is worth a try, anyway."

"When you report this to your patron," she said, "will he disapprove, do you think, Philip? Will he think that you have spent his money on a triviality?"

"I am sure he will not," Philip said, and he moved abruptly away from the window and a short distance from Rebecca. He stood with his back to her.

"Rebecca," he said, "our betrothal has gone on too long, do you not agree?"

Oh dear, she had not had time to sort out her thoughts

and feelings. She was not ready to discuss this topic. She said nothing.

"Shall we marry soon?" he asked. "Let us say at the beginning of September?"

Less than a month away!

"I—" Rebecca laughed nervously. "This is so sudden, Philip. I do not know what to say."

"Sudden?" he said, turning to her. "We have been betrothed for almost a year."

"Yes," she said. "Yes."

He looked at her in the ensuing silence. His eyes were not the calm and confident ones she was used to. They were tormented. "I need you, Rebecca," he said.

She swallowed. Then she smiled a rather wobbly smile. For some reason she felt very close to tears. "Oh, Philip," she said, "I think I need very much to be needed right now."

They both moved forward. And for the first time they were in each other's arms. Rebecca rested her cheek against his chest and closed her eyes. She could hear his heart beating. After a while he put a hand beneath her chin and lifted her face to his. And he kissed her.

There was no passion in the kiss. It was a mere meeting of lips. But there was enormous comfort in it for Rebecca. It was like an unexpected anchor in a very turbulent sea. Whatever had happened in the last few weeks and especially the night before, the old life, the one she had fought so hard to build, was still there for the taking. And she wanted so desperately to recapture the tranquility and the security of that life.

Philip was looking down into her eyes. "September, then?" he asked

"Yes," she said. "Oh, yes, Philip, I should like that very much."

Maude was alone in the drawing room when Rebecca returned home that afternoon. Her head was bent over her embroidery. However, she looked up with a rather jerky movement of the head when the door opened. She blushed hotly and bent over her work again, folding it with meticulous care.

"Ah, Rebecca," she said, "I have been waiting for someone to arrive home so that I might have tea. I shall ring for it now." Her voice was unnaturally bright.

"Are you all alone, Maude?" Rebecca asked. "Where is everyone?"

"His lordship has been in bed all day," Maude said. "He rather fancies that he might have caught a chill last night and is taking the precaution of keeping himself warm. The Langbournes must like fresh air, I believe. Not only were the French windows in the ballroom kept open all night, but there was a window open in the card room too."

"Well, I do hope Uncle Humphrey does not take a chill," Rebecca said. "He is very susceptible to colds."

"Sometimes I think that he coddles himself too much," Maude said in a rush. "If he took more air and exercise, perhaps he would be more healthy. But of course I should not say so. I do not know what it is like to be of a delicate constitution. Forgive me, Rebecca."

Rebecca smiled and sank gratefully into a chair. "And where are your brother and Harriet?" she asked.

"They have gone riding together," Maude said, and she unfolded her embroidery and bent her head over it again. She seemed to have forgotten about ringing for tea. "They left shortly after luncheon. I thought they would have been back by now."

"I would not worry about them," Rebecca said. "Harriet is a perfectly competent horsewoman and I am sure Mr. Bartlett is an accomplished rider too. And you need not fear about the weather. It is warm and quite calm today."

"Oh, I am not really worried about any of those things," Maude said. "It is just that . . . I feel responsible for Harriet, Rebecca. She is my stepdaughter, you know, absurd as it seems. And for all her confidence and headstrong ways, I do believe that she knows very little of the world. I am afraid she is no match for Stanley. Had I known they planned to be gone so long, I would have insisted that they take a groom with them.''

"I am afraid Harriet would not have taken kindly to such a suggestion," Rebecca said. "Here in the country, we tend to behave in a far more relaxed manner than we would if we lived in town."

"Yes," Maude said, "but Stanley is from town."

Rebecca laughed. "But a more gentlemanly person it would be hard to find anywhere," she said. "I do not imagine Harriet's honor could be safer if she had taken a dozen grooms with her."

"You are right, of course," Maude said. "He knows that she is my stepdaughter. He would know better than to compromise her. You must think me very foolish, Rebecca."

"Yes, indeed I do," Rebecca said. "Shall I ring for tea, Maude? My throat is so dry I can hardly swallow."

Maude almost threw her embroidery onto the table beside her and leaped to her feet. "Oh," she said, "how very rag-mannered you must think me. I shall do it."

The tea tray was brought into the room only a few minutes before the arrival of Harriet, Mr. Bartlett—and Mr. Carver. Harriet was in a temper, Rebecca could see as soon as the girl walked into the room. Her movements were abrupt, her voice overloud and overbright.

"Well," she said, "every other day we have to await tea until Rebecca comes home from school. Yet no one seemed to consider it necessary to wait for me today."

"If I had known when you would arrive, I would have waited," Maude said. "But when you left, Harriet, you gave no indication of when you would return. Anyway, dear, the tray has just arrived. You may have fresh tea without even having to wait for it."

Rebecca had greeted the two men. She smiled warmly at them. She liked both, and was considerably relieved that Mr. Carver was without his friend on this occasion.

"Miss Shaw," Mr. Bartlett said, "I suppose you have been putting us all to shame by working hard all day while we have been sleeping off the exertions of last evening and generally idling. And how do you contrive to look so fresh and lovely, ma'am, after such a busy day?''

She smiled. Such compliments did not call for an answer.

''Did you meet Mr. Carver outside?'' Maude was asking Harriet.

''No,'' Harriet said rather shrilly. ''He was returning from the village as we were leaving here. It was such a lovely afternoon that he decided to join us. He had no other pressing business.''

Harriet said no more, but Rebecca could tell from her tone and expression that she was furious. And indeed it did seem strange that a man with Mr. Carver's good manners would have attached himself to a couple who could hardly have wanted his company. And he had stayed with them for the whole afternoon.

''It was a shame the party could not have been larger,'' Mr. Bartlett said, bowing with a polite smile in Mr. Carver's direction. ''It was a perfect afternoon for a ride.''

Mr. Carver did not stay long. After drinking one cup of tea, he rose and took his leave, explaining that the Sinclairs would be wondering what on earth had happened to him.

The drawing-room doors had hardly closed behind him when Harriet exploded. ''Well,'' she said, ''I have never in my life met such a thick-skulled, bad-mannered clod!''

''Harriet!'' Maude admonished, shocked.

''I am sure I have never given that man cause to believe that I so much as tolerate his company,'' Harriet said. ''And he has been downright rude to me on more than one occasion. Yet he forced his company on us this afternoon just as if he were conferring the greatest honor. And he hardly spoke a word the whole way.''

''My dear Miss Shaw,'' Mr. Bartlett said soothingly. ''I must say I agree that I found the situation somewhat awkward. Mr. Carver is not the sort of person with whom it is easy to converse. He is of a somewhat taciturn disposition. But one must have pity on the man. He does not have many friends, I believe. And he must feel all the awkwardness of his situation at the Sinclairs'. He is totally dependent upon their hospitality. Seeing us must have given him the idea of giving them an afternoon at least free of his presence.''

''He might have done that alone,'' Harriet said bitingly. ''He did not have to spoil our afternoon merely because he did not want to go to the Sinclairs'. Why does he not pack himself off where he belongs, anyway? No one wants him here.''

''Harriet!'' Maude protested again. ''That is not fair, you know. He is Mr. Sinclair's friend and guest. As such he has every right to be here and to visit at this house.''

''Well, if you ask me,'' Harriet said, ''Mr. Sinclair has invited him only because he feels sorry for him. And I do not see why we should be made to suffer. Do you know what he said when he first saw us? He asked who was riding with us, and when we said no one, he asked where we were going and how long we intended to be away. Can you imagine the effrontery of the man? And then he said that he thought he would ride along with us.''

''Have some tea,'' Maude said. ''You look hot, Harriet.''

Rebecca excused herself soon afterward. She was feeling extremely tired after a night with very little sleep and after a busy day. Most of all, though, she was aware that her tiredness was largely an emotional thing. So much had happened in the last twenty-four hours that her mind had not had a chance to assimilate half of it. Her brain, in fact, was shutting down, refusing to take in any more information before its present overload had been digested.

She went up to her room, took off her dress and stockings, washed herself off with the cold water that stood in the pitcher on the washstand in her dressing room, and lay on top of the covers on her bed. She wanted to sleep, to forget everything until she had more energy to cope with her thoughts. But it did not take her many minutes to know that she would not sleep, tired as she was.

There was the problem of her relationship with Philip to work out. Just a couple of hours ago she had agreed to

marry him within the next month. And she had been quite
convinced during those few minutes with him that her
decision was the right one. He was a good and a kind man,
despite the outer sternness of his manner. With him she
would be safe; she would be able to continue the kind of
life she had led for much of her life. She could return to
the house that she still considered her home. It would be
her own home; she would be mistress there. And Philip
needed her.

It was that final point that had swayed her there in the
schoolroom. It was the first time she had heard Philip
admit to a need. And it is as flattering, she found, to be
told that one is needed as that one is beautiful or desirable. At
Uncle Humphrey's she was not needed. She was treated
kindly there, never made to feel like a poor relation. She
was even held in some affection, she believed. But she
was not needed.

And she needed Philip. Once married to him, she convinced herself, she would be able to accept her place in
life and all the emotional upheavals of the previous few
weeks could be forgotten. She would be safe!

But all that had been a few hours ago. Now already she
was not so sure. Marriage was a very final step. It would
be too late to discover after the wedding that she had done
the wrong thing. Wrong for her, perhaps, and perhaps
wrong for Philip.

She really had seen him with Maude, had she not?
There could be no possibility of mistake? But no, she
knew there could not. Even if she had doubted the evidence of her own eyes the evening before, the behavior of
both that day had indicated that something abnormal had
happened. And what had happened? Were Philip and Maude
carrying on an illicit affair? Had it been going on for some
time?

The thought had only to be formed in her mind for
Rebecca to realize how preposterous it was. Her faith in
her own understanding of human nature had been severely
shaken recently, but she could not have been so mistaken

in either of those two persons. Philip definitely had his faults; she was quite aware of them. But they were faults all on the side of virtue. He was too demanding of other people, too intolerant of weakness. Philip could no more conduct a clandestine affair with a married parishioner than he could curse from the pulpit.

And Maude? She was very young and very unhappy with Uncle Humphrey, but all her behavior since Rebecca had known her had suggested a young woman of high moral principles, who would put duty before personal happiness. Even her quite unnecessary concern for Harriet's reputation that afternoon had demonstrated her moral values. She would never willingly be unfaithful to her aging husband.

What had happened then? Rebecca let her mind rove over the previous few months. Maude and Philip, she could see now, had been growing more aware of each other for some time. Maude was constantly praising Philip. She admired him greatly. Philip was quite the opposite; he was forever criticizing Maude for what he considered her frivolity. Was it a mutual attraction that had really been causing that awareness? If so, probably neither had been aware of the truth. Maude would not have talked so openly about him before her husband and his family if she had realized that she was attracted to him. Philip would have ruthlessly suppressed all feelings had he suspected the truth.

But it was the truth, was it not? Rebecca stared up at the canopy above her bed. The attraction had grown gradually and had finally taken them unawares so that they had been indiscreet enough to embrace the night before where they had been in great danger of detection. It had had time to take deep root in the feelings of both. Was it possible that their feelings were ones of more than attraction? Were they in love? It seemed highly probable.

It did not take much pondering to know why Philip had finally decided that he and Rebecca must marry. He might have been taken by surprise the night before. But Philip was not the sort of man who would indulge in feelings that he would consider sinful in the extreme. Like her, he must be seeking safety in a flight toward marriage. It was hurtful to admit this possibility, but Rebecca had also to admit that she was no different. And was there anything so very wrong in what they planned? They did need each other and they were fond of each other. They would live a good and worthy life together. It was unlikely that either of them would be actively unhappy. Time was a healer of bruised emotions, as she knew from experience.

Rebecca put her hands loosely over her face and rolled over on the bed so that she lay facedown. She had thought she would never feel that pain again. Seven years ago she had battled it for what had seemed an endless time. And later she had looked back with some satisfaction. At least, she had thought, she would never have to go through a period like that again. Why had he come back? Oh, how could he have been so thoughtless and so cruel!

She was disappointed in herself. She had thought she was a stronger person. Although she had dreaded meeting Christopher again when she heard that he was coming home, she had thought that she could remain indifferent once the embarrassment of the first meeting was over. But in the event her emotions had put up almost no fight at all. She loved Christopher Sinclair with just as much passion as she ever had. And she despised herself for doing so. She had never thought it possible to love someone who was so obviously unworthy of that love. But love him she did, and she was helpless to do anything about it.

She must marry Philip. There was no alternative. Yet she could not marry him. Being in flight from one man was no reason at all for marrying another.

Perhaps it would be easier to fight against her feelings for Christopher if he were clearly indifferent to her. But his behavior was a puzzle. On the one hand, he behaved as she had expected him to behave from the start, consorting with the younger set, paying court to Harriet, taking her about. Yet she had to admit that his manner toward Harriet was not unduly flirtatious, and she doubted that he was close to making her an offer, despite what Harriet herself had said the day before.

And his behavior toward herself was certainly not indifferent. He had been as embarrassed as she during their first meeting in the lane. The only reason she could think of for his visit to the school was that he wished somehow to impress her and redeem himself in her eyes to a certain degree. And then there had been that ride home with him and that kiss. Rebecca's hands unconsciously clenched her pillow as she remembered. He had not been unaware of her nearness when she rode with him. She had been too aware of her own terrible embarrassment at the time to really notice, but looking back now she could recall the tautness of his muscles, the unnatural silence in which they had ridden.

And he had kissed her with as much hunger as she had felt. For the minute or two that they were in each other's arms, she was sure, the years had been swept back for both of them.

Then there had been the evening before. She had really not expected him to ask her to dance. She had not expected even to be acknowledged. Yet he had asked her. And it had not been that he might flirt or gloat or sneer. He had wanted to apologize for some of the damage he had done to her life. He had been almost humble. He had made no attempt to defend himself against any of her charges. In fact, she remembered now, he had apologized to her after their kiss too.

Was it possible that he still retained some of the old regard for her? Was he regretting now that he had put fortune before love all those years ago? It really made no difference to anything if he did, of course. Even if he still loved her, and even though she still loved him, there could never be any question of resuming any relationship. She would never be able to forgive him, at least not to the extent of being close to him again. She could not have a relationship with a man she did not respect.

But it increased the pain tenfold to wonder if he did still

retain some of his love for her. It seemed so cruel that they now lived close to each other, meeting with fair frequency, and both free, yet that they could never mean anything to each other. She loved him so, and she had been horrid to him the night before. In fact, she had been quite unforgivably impertinent. She had no right at all to make any reference to his wife or his treatment of her. Her cheeks burned now to remember some of the things she had said. It was a miracle that he had retained some modicum of coolness, enough to prevent her from making a public scene.

Why had she lost her temper and become so personal in her insults, anyway? Why had she mentioned his wife? Of course, he had started insinuating preposterous things about Mr. Bartlett. He had actually tried to sully the poor man's reputation by hinting that he might be a fortune hunter. He must have known that his wife and Mr. Bartlett had loved each other, and consequently hated the man. Though why he should, Rebecca could not imagine. He himself had wanted nothing from his wife except her fortune.

Yes, she was not sorry after all that she had said those things. At least she had made it clear to him that she was not unaware of the kind of life he had lived since he abandoned her. And she had made it clear that she despised him and wanted no part of his attentions. She was glad too that she had remembered that episode of the night before. The memory of his treachery would harden her against her own heart.

Oh, Christopher, she thought, burying her face in her hands again, why? Why did you have to turn out this way? Or why did you not show yourself in your true colors before I was foolish enough to love you?

She started to cry, despising herself heartily as she fumbled in the side pocket of her dress for a handkerchief.

· 10 ·

Harriet's birthday was approaching. She did not want a dinner or a ball or a party of any sort. Sandwiched as such an event would be between the Langbourne ball and the village fair, it would lose a great deal of its luster. An outing was what she wanted, a picnic of some sort, to include everyone from her own household and everyone from the Sinclairs'.

"You must ride over there with me after luncheon, Rebecca," she said at breakfast the morning after her outing with Mr. Bartlett and Mr. Carver. "They will be sure to come. They will be only too glad of some entertainment. But we must ask them today. It would be too dreadful if they accepted some other dreary invitation for that day and were unable to come. What would be the point of a picnic with only us there?"

"I would rather not go," Rebecca said. "I have planned to use today to alter those two dresses you asked me about a few days ago."

"Pooh," said Harriet, "they can wait. I am in no hurry. They are just old rags, anyway. They might as well be thrown away as I told you at the time. I shall have some new ones made."

"I would be happy if you would accompany Harriet," Maude said. "Stanley and I have already promised to visit the Farleys. It is a long drive, and I do not believe we will be back until late afternoon."

"You must take a carriage instead of riding, Harriet, my love," the baron said, looking out of the window with a frown. "I see the branches of the trees are swaying. There must be a wind, and I would not want either you or Rebecca to take a chill."

"Oh, Papa," Harriet protested crossly, "the sun is shining and it is August. We would positively cook in the carriage. No, we shall ride."

"This younger generation is so incautious," the baron said, turning to Mr. Bartlett for support. "They will ruin their health and their complexions rather than endure a little discomfort away from drafts." He drew his snuffbox from a pocket and proceeded to comfort his agitated nerves with a pinch of his favorite blend.

"One can tell that you have always been sensible about such matters, sir," Mr. Bartlett said. "Indeed, I find it almost impossible to believe that Miss Shaw is your daughter. But"—he smiled and inclined his head in the direction of the ladies,—"I have observed that both your daughter and your niece protect themselves very wisely from the elements. In my eyes, their beauty has suffered no adverse effect whatsoever from their occasional walks or rides."

The outcome of the whole conversation, Rebecca realized philosophically, was that she was to accompany Harriet to the Sinclair house that afternoon and that they were to ride there. It seemed that she would also be obliged to go on Harriet's birthday outing. And there was the fair only a week after that. Three occasions at least on which she would be forced to be in company with Christopher. She wondered how long he planned to stay. She could not endure too much of such torture, she felt. She must marry Philip. Only by doing so could she protect herself.

Harriet did not talk much during the ride. She appeared to be in a thoughtful mood. They were more than halfway to their destination before she broke the silence that Rebecca had welcomed.

"Do you not agree," she said, "that Mr. Christopher

Sinclair's somewhat inferior upbringing still shows on occasion?''

"Gracious, Harriet," Rebecca said, "whatever do you mean?"

"He is very handsome and fashionable and wealthy and all that," Harriet said, "and I still think I might have him. I am not quite sure. But he seems to lack something of the breeding of a true gentleman."

"Oh?" Rebecca prompted.

"Well," Harriet said, "I told you that he did not really defend me from the rudeness of that dreadful Mr. Carver when we were in Wraxby. And at the ball the other evening he danced the last set with Miss Susan Langbourne when everyone knows that he is my suitor."

"But, Harriet," Rebecca said, "he had already danced two sets with you. It would have been considered improper for him to solicit your hand for another."

"Nonsense!" Harriet said. "Country manners are not so strict, Rebecca." She seemed to see no contradiction with her earlier charge that Christopher was not a perfect gentleman. "Besides," she added, "Mr. Bartlett told me some things about him that I did not very much like."

"Oh," Rebecca said, and frowned. What had he said? She did hope that he would not talk too freely about Christopher's behavior in London. She could see why he had done so to her and even to Harriet. He was trying to protect the girl by opening her eyes to the truth. Yet Rebecca was not very confident of Harriet's discretion. She hoped that no word would reach Mr. and Mrs. Sinclair. They were so obviously proud of their son that it would hurt if they discovered the true nature of his relationship with his wife.

"Of course," Harriet said, "one likes a man to be interesting, and one expects one's husband to have outside interests. It would be mortally dull to have him hanging about one's skirts for the rest of one's life. I shall have to ponder the matter."

Rebecca, thinking back over what her cousin had said,

drew the conclusion that Harriet was more disgusted by Christopher's slowness in coming to the point than by what she had found out about him. Her pride was piqued. She had been fully expecting some sort of declaration during the evening of the Langbourne ball, and none had been forthcoming. Perhaps she was beginning to fear that she would after all be unable to snare him. Hence she was beginning to withdraw gradually herself so that her pride would be salvaged if she failed to bring him up to scratch. It would be she who had rejected him, not the other way around.

Rebecca's hopes that perhaps some of the Sinclair family would be from home were quickly dashed. When the butler showed them into the sitting room, a buzz of conversation stopped, and she could see that they were all there. The buzz resumed, and the two visitors were welcomed into the group.

"Young ladies," Mr. Sinclair said, "you have arrived just in time to save the young people from tearing one another to pieces. The question is what to do for the duration of the afternoon, and the argument has gone on for a half hour or more."

"Julian and I want to walk down to the bridge," Ellen said. "It is a perfect day for a walk. It is too hot and dusty to ride, as Prim wants to do."

"Mr. Carver is willing to ride too," Primrose said, "but he wishes to go into the village to make some purchases, and I would prefer to ride in the opposite direction."

"And I am quite neutral," Christopher said with a grin. "And perhaps it is as well that we did not make up our minds before now, or we would have been from home when the Misses Shaw arrived."

"Oh, you must all ride home with us for tea," Harriet announced. "Maude and Mr. Bartlett have gone to the Farleys and will not be back forever. Rebecca and Papa and I would merely get on one another's nerves if we had no other company."

"Oh, good," Primrose said, "I shall get to exercise Peter after all today, then."

"And you must all keep the afternoon of Wednesday next free," Harriet said. "You too, if you please, Mr. and Mrs. Sinclair. It is my birthday and we are to go on an outing. Even Papa has said he will come provided that the weather is not too uncertain."

"How very delightful, my dear Miss Shaw," Mrs. Sinclair said. "Are we to go to the river again? I always did think that the perfect site for a picnic. Though you really must not be so naughty this time and worry your poor papa almost to his grave by walking along the wall of the bridge."

"No," Harriet said, "I have decided that we will drive farther afield than that. We are going to go to Cenross Castle."

Both Rebecca and Christopher turned their heads to look sharply at Harriet. Their eyes met over the top of her head.

"Harriet," Rebecca said, "Cenross Castle is ten miles away. It would take us almost the whole afternoon just getting there and back. There are many pretty and suitable places a great deal closer."

"Oh," Primrose said, clasping her hands to her breasts, "I love Cenross Castle. Mama and Papa took us there two years ago. It is an old ruin, Mr. Carver, but a person can still climb to the top of some of the old battlements and see for miles in all directions."

"And one can still go down to the dungeons," Julian added. "Ellen got stuck on the stairs last time."

"Well," Ellen said, "it is hardly surprising. They wind round and round in a tight spiral, Mr. Carver, and are very narrow even on the outside edge. And many of them are broken. And they are very dark. I was terrified. There must have been thousands of them."

"One hundred and sixty-four," Julian said. "Prim and I counted them."

"Uncle Humphrey would never travel such a distance, Harriet," Rebecca said.

"He will," her cousin said airily. "When he complains, I shall threaten never to talk to him again if he does not come."

"I would be delighted to see this old structure," Mr. Carver said amiably. "But don't expect me to climb battlements or descend to dungeons, Miss Shaw."

"Oh, I will not, sir," Harriet said, such ice dripping from her voice that Rebecca felt ashamed.

"Perhaps it would be wise, Miss Shaw," Christopher said, his voice expressionless, "to start early since the distance is quite great."

"What a good idea!" Harriet said, flashing him her most charming smile. "We shall leave in the morning, of course, and take a picnic luncheon with us. Oh, it is going to be a splendid birthday, I know."

He smiled back at her and for a mere second his eyes met Rebecca's again.

On the ride home, Harriet immediately singled out Julian for attention. It seemed very obvious to Rebecca that she was deliberately ignoring Christopher, trying to prompt him into jealousy, perhaps? The rest of the party rode in a close group. Rebecca stayed as close as she could to Ellen, terrified that she might become paired off in an undesirable way. However, it was Mr. Carver who finally drew her attention.

"I was disappointed not to see you this morning, Miss Shaw," he said. "Went to the school with Sinclair only t'find the vicar there. Meant t'impress you, and you weren't there." He laughed.

"I am so sorry, sir," Rebecca said, smiling, "but I notice that you have managed to tell me about it, at any rate, so that I might still be impressed."

He shook with laughter. "Saw through my ruse, did you, ma'am?" he said at last. "Must say I didn't feel comfortable at all. Disliked school enough when I had to go as a pupil. Had a deuced time getting Sinclair away, though."

"Really?" Rebecca said, making a poor job of keeping the sarcasm from her voice.

"Sat down next to that young fellow with the eyeglasses to help him read," Mr. Carver said, "and seemed t'forget all about me and the vicar and our luncheon."

"He might have saved himself the trouble," Rebecca said. "Cyril is an extremely shy boy. He probably blinked and stammered and fidgeted until he had convinced Mr. Sinclair that he was an idiot."

"On the contrary," Mr. Carver said. "The lad was smiling and talking in no time, and then had his head into the book until I thought it would never come out. He was making progress too, by all accounts. Even that poker-faced vicar admitted it. Oh, pardon me, ma'am—most indelicate." Mr. Carver started to cough and turned away his head.

"Did I hear my name?" Christopher asked, easing back on his horse's reins to allow the two stragglers to catch up to him and his two sisters.

"Was telling Miss Shaw about that lad with eyeglasses that you helped this morning, Sinclair," Mr. Carver explained.

Christopher smiled. "I merely sat and listened to him," he said. "It is Miss Shaw who has done all the hard work."

Rebecca did not reply. She was trying to maneuver her horse forward so that she would be riding with Ellen and Primrose, but Mr. Carver had the same idea and executed it before she could do so. To her dismay, she found herself riding alongside Christopher, a little way behind the others.

"Did you know that you have a willing slave in that boy?" Christopher asked.

"Cyril?" she said. "I am fond of him. But really one must not exaggerate what I have done for either him or the other boys."

"I think he would not even be at the school if it were not for you, Becky," he said.

"Oh, nonsense," she said. "I believe I helped Philip to see what Cyril's problem was, but it was Philip himself who decided to buy the eyeglasses and who took the boy to Wraxby in order to purchase them."

Christopher smiled. "You have not changed at all, Becky, have you?" he said. "You still hate to be praised."

"Will you go to Harriet's birthday outing?" Rebecca blurted suddenly.

"Yes," he said after a pause. "It would be bad-mannered not to."

She did not look at him. "I thought you would perhaps find some excuse to avoid it," she said.

He did not answer for a while. "Becky," he said at last, quietly, "I shall be leaving soon. I would have been gone already, but my mother has been very happy with my visit and has set her heart on my being here for the village fair. But soon after that I shall return to town. I will not come again, and you need not fear that I shall break the promise this time. I did not know that my presence here would upset you after all this time, but I can see that it has. I am sorry. But you can be at peace again soon."

"Why did you come?" she asked passionately, and then looked across at him aghast, wishing beyond everything that she could recapture those words.

He looked back at her, his face stiff with some sort of inner tension. "I don't know, Becky," he said. He drew breath to say more, but closed his mouth again and stared ahead. "I don't know," he repeated lamely.

They rode in silence for the rest of the way to Limeglade.

So he was leaving soon, Rebecca was thinking. The fair was eight days away. He would stay perhaps two or three days after that. In two weeks' time at the most, he would be gone. And this time, he had said, he would keep his promise not to come back. After perhaps ten or eleven days she would never see him again. Never. It was a long time. An unbearably long time. Better, surely, the torture of seeing him occasionally, of having her whole life upset by his presence.

She could raise her eyes and see him now if she wished. She was sitting in Mr. Sinclair's open barouche, one arm resting across the top of a door, staring at her gloved hand. But she knew that he rode just a little ahead of them on her side of the vehicle. Julian was with him. She did not look up.

"Now, Miss Shaw," Mrs. Sinclair said from the opposite seat of the barouche, "do tell us how your cousin succeeded in persuading his lordship to come this afternoon. I said to Mr. Sinclair that he would never consent if she pleaded and threatened for a week and Mr. Sinclair agreed with me. You might have knocked me down with a feather when we arrived at Limeglade earlier to find his lordship all ready for the outing."

"It was not easy, ma'am," Rebecca said with a smile. "But you underestimate Harriet's powers of persuasion. She succeeded finally when she convinced Uncle Humphrey that his health would not be in jeopardy. She even agreed to ride with him in the closed carriage, and that has turned out to be a greater sacrifice than she bargained for. It is an extremely hot day. The inside of the carriage must be sweltering. And we have agreed to picnic in the old courtyard of the castle. It is surrounded by the ruins of the walls, you see, so that it is perfectly sheltered from the wind no matter what direction it blows from."

It really had been a stormy argument, Rebecca thought privately. Harriet had won her point with a great deal of pouting and head tossing and threatening. The baron had resorted to three separate pinches of snuff before giving in and graciously agreeing to favor the picnic with his presence. Maude had been distressed, Mr. Bartlett conciliatory. Only Rebecca had stayed completely out of the discussion.

Fortunately for Rebecca, the baron's carriage was crowded when it contained more than four persons. Although Mr. Bartlett graciously offered to ride, Harriet had been most

insistent that he accompany her in the carriage. In fact, she
had been unusually friendly with him in the last few days,
another ruse to force Christopher's hand, Rebecca guessed.
She herself hastened to offer to ride in the Sinclair barouche. Mrs. Sinclair had already offered it to anyone who
needed a ride, though it would already be almost filled
with Mr. and Mrs. Sinclair, Ellen, and Primrose. Mr.
Carver and Philip rode up ahead of the carriage. Christopher and Julian stayed closer to their own family.

Philip had been hesitant about coming. It would mean
closing the school for the day. And there had been altogether too many social activities in the last few weeks to
take him from his parish duties, he said. However, he had
talked with the vicar of Wraxby the day before and arranged for him to come to the village in two and a half
weeks' time to marry Rebecca and him. He felt it was time
that Rebecca's family and closest neighbors be told of the
plans. The birthday outing seemed a suitable occasion to
announce the coming event.

Cenross Castle could be seen for several miles before
they reached it, built as it was on the top of a wooded hill.
From a distance it looked impressive, its gray stone walls
massive, its slit windows, from which archers would have
defended its keep against attackers, sinister. Only as one
drew closer was it possible to see that the castle now was a
mere shell, its outer walls sheltering only crumbled ruins
and a grassy courtyard.

Yet one part of the battlements remained almost intact
and the stone steps leading to it passable, though crumbling. And one of the dungeons, which had been con-
structed deep inside the hill, was still there and could be
reached by a dangerously disintegrating spiral stone staircase. It was a very pleasant site for a picnic. The old walls
sheltered visitors from the winds, yet the battlements and
the window slits afforded a quite breathtaking view across
the countryside for miles in all directions. And at the foot
of the hill to the west ran a river, wide and fast flowing, a
natural moat on one side of the castle at least.

The carriages and the horses had to be left at the eastern foot of the hill. Christopher, Julian, and Philip carried the picnic baskets and blankets to the top while Rebecca took one of Lord Holmes's arms and Maude the other and led him slowly up the incline.

"Really," he complained when they paused halfway up for breath, "I would have positively forbidden Harriet to bring us here had I known the site to be so primitive. Such exercise is extremely bad for the legs. It causes gout, you know. Mark my word, Maude, I shall be laid up with it all winter."

"There is but a short way to go, my lord," Maude said encouragingly, "and then you will be able to sit and rest. The journey down will not be nearly so strenuous."

The tone of her voice was entirely flat and colorless, Rebecca noticed, glancing across at her uncle's wife. In fact, Maude had been pale and listless for several days— since the Langbourne ball. If Rebecca had not known what had occurred there, she might have worried that Maude was sickening for something, or that she was increasing, perhaps. But she did not think either was the case. Maude was either suffering terrible pangs of guilt for what she had done with Philip, or else she was suffering with the knowledge that her love for him would never be able to find expression. Perhaps both.

By the time the three of them reached the courtyard within the walls, the blankets were spread on the most sheltered and shady part of the lawn and Primrose was impatiently eyeing the food baskets.

"Wine for Papa!" Harriet cried. "Do let us all have a drink before we eat." She was flushed and looking extremely pleased with herself.

"Indeed, I must agree," Mr. Bartlett said, bowing and smiling in Harriet's direction. "We must toast Miss Shaw on her birthday. I am sure everyone will agree with me that one more year to her age has merely added more beauty and more glow. Allow me, ma'am?" He stooped to open the wine basket and proceeded to do the honors of pouring everyone a glassful.

Harriet laughed. "I am sure I am no more beautiful than any of the other ladies," she said, smoothing the front of her new sprigged muslin dress and checking the large bow that tied her bonnet beneath her chin. "But I am surely the happiest. Thank you, sir." She took the glass of wine that Mr. Bartlett offered and smiled dazzlingly at him.

When everyone had toasted Harriet and flattered her to her heart's content, they sat down on the blankets, which had been set closely enough together that everyone could sit in a large group.

"I have an announcement of a happy nature to make as well," Philip said.

Everyone's attention turned his way.

"Rebecca and I have set the date of our nuptials," he said. "The Reverend Paul Warner of Wraxby has agreed to perform the marriage ceremony two weeks from next Saturday. We wanted our friends to be the first to know that soon I am to be the happiest of men."

Rebecca kept her eyes on the glass of wine that she held in her hands.

"Oh, a wedding!" Primrose squealed. "How marvelous. And Ellen and I were saying just yesterday that there will be absolutely nothing of any interest to do after the fair."

"Splendid, Reverend," Mrs. Sinclair said. "You could not have chosen a more deserving bride."

"Maude, my love," the baron said, "you must immediately start to organize a wedding breakfast. Let it not be said that I treated my niece with less than her proper due on her wedding day."

"You really need not bother, Maude," Harriet said. "I shall see to everything. I really thought you were never going to marry, Rebecca. You have been betrothed forever."

"I would wager that Miss Shaw will be the most beautiful bride these parts have seen for many a year," Mr.

Bartlett said, wasting one of his most charming smiles on Rebecca's bowed head.

"I think the occasion calls for another toast," Christopher said. "Let us drink to a couple whose goodness sets them apart from the general run of mankind, and wish them the happiness they deserve."

Rebecca finally looked up, a smile of embarrassment on her face as everyone took up the toast. She found herself looking at an ashen-faced Maude, whose hand shook so when she raised her glass that she had to put it down again untasted.

• 11 •

Mr. and Mrs. Sinclair were prevailed upon to play a hand of cards with Lord Holmes and Maude after everyone had eaten his fill from the luncheon baskets. All the others, led by a high-spirited Harriet, made a careful ascent of the worn stone steps to the part of the battlements that still stood. Rebecca would have remained behind on the pretext that someone needed to repack the baskets, but Philip stopped beside her.

"Come, Rebecca," he said, "let us go up with everyone else. I have been told that the view is magnificent from the top."

"Yes, it is," she agreed. "But one must be most awfully careful. The wall is gradually crumbling away. One must not lean too heavily on it."

"Take my arm," he said gravely. "I shall see that you come to no harm."

The others were in high spirits. Harriet, Rebecca noticed, as soon as they finished the ascent, was clinging to Christopher's arm and standing close against him in pretended fright. Julian had an arm around the shoulders of each of his sisters and was pretending to push them over the low parapet. They were both squealing loudly. Mr. Bartlett was offering his assistance to Ellen. Mr. Carver was suggesting to Primrose that perhaps she should detach some of the ribbon from her bonnet so that he might tie his own hat more firmly to his head.

"Might blow away in the wind," he said, "and I might topple over if I lunge to catch it."

Primrose shrieked anew. "Pray do not even talk of such a thing, Mr. Carver," she said. "My legs go weak at the knees at the very thought."

Then she giggled as Mr. Carver shook with silent laughter, holding on to the brim of his hat the whole while.

"Perhaps we should go down again," Philip suggested. "It does not seem to be windy at ground level, but it is quite gusty up here."

"I find it most invigorating," Harriet announced, turning to face the wind and allowing it to blow against the flimsy muslin of her dress. She showed to great advantage with the fabric thus molded to her figure. She still clung to Christopher.

Rebecca looked down to the river and one corner of the grassy bank that was enclosed by a horseshoe of trees. It would be peaceful down there, quiet, sheltered. If she walked there, circling the wall of the castle until she came to the narrow, overgrown path that led down, she would be able to sit and think for a while, the only sounds the rushing of the water and the singing of birds.

"We really could not come all this way without going down there," Harriet was saying.

"Oh, no," Ellen said. "Not me. You would not be able to drag me down to the dungeons. Please let us forget about it, Harriet."

"No one is compelled to come, of course," Harriet said, smiling gaily around at the group. "But I shall certainly have a poor opinion of anyone who fails to do so."

"Those steps were dangerous when I was a boy," Christopher said. "They can only have got worse since then. I think we had better find some other diversion, Miss Shaw. A walk around the base of the hill, perhaps?"

"I could have stayed at home to walk," Harriet said rather petulantly. "What a poor-spirited lot you all are. Will no one dare go to the dungeons with me?"

"I would, Harriet," Julian said, rather shame-faced, "but Papa would have my head if I took the girls into danger like that. I am for the walk."

Harriet released Christopher's arm and swept across to the steps leading down to the grassy courtyard. "I thought people's wishes were catered to on their birthdays," she said. "I see I was mistaken." She began to descend the stairs without assistance.

Mr. Bartlett leapt to her aid and the others, more subdued than they had been a few minutes before, followed. Philip laid a hand on Rebecca's arm as she turned toward the steps.

"Let them go," he said. "I see no need for us to become involved in that argument. I shall be so glad, Rebecca, to take you away from that little hussy. It may be her birthday, but she behaves like a perfectly odious child."

Rebecca waited for the blame to be laid at Maude's door, but Philip said no more. He turned and placed his arms along a fairly solid part of the parapet.

"Would you be very upset if we were to move away from here?" he asked.

"You mean permanently?" Rebecca asked.

"Yes," he said, "I think it might be good for you, Rebecca, to be taken away from your family's shadow. And I think I might like to start again, perhaps in a somewhat larger place, though size does not really matter."

Rebecca was stunned. Somehow she had never thought of moving away. She belonged here. Her roots and her memories were here. If she moved away, she would be cut off forever from Christopher. She would never see him again, never hear of him again. It was when she caught herself in these thoughts that she looked at Philip and answered.

"I am going to be your wife, Philip," she said steadily. "I shall go with you wherever you wish to go."

He flashed her a look of gratitude and held out an arm to her. When she came closer, he put the arm around her shoulders and drew her close to his side. "You are a good woman, Rebecca," he said. "I shall try to be worthy of you. I shall try to make you happy."

She laid her head on his shoulder and closed her eyes. They burned behind her eyelids.

When they came down to the courtyard several minutes later, all was deserted except for the four card players, who were still engrossed in their game. Rebecca could tell by the condescension in her uncle's manner that he was winning. Mr. Sinclair looked weary.

"Ah, Reverend," he called in obvious relief, "how would you like to take my hand? I am so accustomed to taking a rest after luncheon that I am finding it deuced hard to keep awake. If I were more alert, his lordship here would have to work harder for his points."

"Hmm!" was the baron's opinion.

Philip obligingly crossed to the group, though he looked like a man going to his own execution, Rebecca noticed in a quick glance. Maude's head was bent over her cards, which she was inspecting with minute care.

"Where did the others go?" Rebecca asked.

"Oh, walking somewhere," Mr. Sinclair replied, finding himself a place in the sun to recline and close his eyes. "Can't think how the young find so much energy all the time."

Poor Harriet, Rebecca thought. So she had lost on this occasion. She would not like that. It was likely to make her cross for the rest of the day. It looked as if she would have her own wish, though. The walkers had gone off in some unknown direction, though she supposed it would not be at all difficult to find them if she wished to do so. The card players needed to concentrate on their game. Mr. Sinclair certainly did not need any company. She would slip down to the river, see if it was the way she remembered it.

She should not, of course. Some parts of the past were best not relived, and she had trained herself years ago not to relive that particular episode. She was to marry Philip very soon and it seemed likely that he would take her away to an entirely new place. She would be able to begin life anew, the slate of the past wiped completely clean. She should practice for that future now. She had to let go of the past. Yet even as she told herself this, she walked out through the archway and around the base of the castle until she was at the top of the steep path that led downward.

The pathway was almost totally obliterated now. It was seven years since she had walked it, and obviously not many people had used it since. Of course then it had been late autumn; the grass had not been as thick as it was now in August. She stood looking down to the cluster of trees below and eventually sighed and began to descend. She knew she had to go. Why delay the inevitable? She could not stay long, anyway. The others would worry about her if they returned and she was missing.

The trees opened out quite suddenly to reveal a grassy bank beside the fast-flowing waters of the river. It was an enchanted place, enclosed on three sides by the trees and on the fourth by the wide expanse of water. Sounds seemed to be cut off; the world receded. One could imagine one-self totally alone, completely private.

Rebecca stood with her back against a tree, staring at the carpet of grass and wild flowers at her feet. She put her head back against the tree trunk. Almost seven years! Time had seemed to pass quickly, yet it was like a scene from another lifetime, the one she was seeing in her mind. She was seeing herself and Christopher here, both wrapped warmly against the crisp chill of a glorious autumn afternoon, both flushed and happy at a stolen day together.

They should not have been there, of course. Her father had always been very careless about chaperoning her. He had loved her, trusted her utterly, treated her always as if she were fully adult. She had had a great deal of freedom in which to see Christopher. And she had not abused that freedom, beyond the few hours when they deliberately wandered off by themselves so that they could talk, dream, and kiss. But this had been a particularly glorious day, two days before his intended visit to London. Neither of them had any obligations for the day. They had decided on the spur of the moment, and quite recklessly, to go to Cenross Castle. Christopher drove them there in his curricle.

And they had found their way to this very spot. They had been enchanted. And they had sat on the grass, their arms around each other, and talked for a long while. Rebecca had felt so cozy, huddled inside her warm cloak and drawn against the warmth of his greatcoat, that she had fallen asleep. She did not think she had slept long, but he had laughed and teased her when she woke up. And she had lifted a warm and sleepy face to his, her whole body relaxed against him.

He had kissed her, and it had taken far less time than usual for them both to become enflamed with passion. His hands beneath her cloak had pushed urgently at her dress until her shoulders and breasts were bare to the touch of his hands and mouth. Somehow she had unbuttoned his greatcoat and all the layers that were between her and his warm chest.

And then he had been on top of her, his weight creating unbearably erotic sensations in her womb, his mouth ravaging hers with an urgency that they had not approached before.

"Becky," he had said into her opened mouth. "Becky, my love, my life."

And then his face had been above hers and they had stared into each other's eyes for timeless moments. She could remember now with what heightened senses she had looked up at him. She had been very aware of the grass beneath her head, of the crispness of the air, the sound of flowing water, the song of a lone bird.

"Yes," she had said, her palms moving over his bare shoulders. "Yes, Christopher."

He had continued to look into her eyes as her breathing quickened, her surrender made. And then he had buried his face against her neck for a few moments and rolled away from her.

When she had turned onto her side to look at him,

bewildered and hurt, he reached out and took her hand in his. He smiled shakily.

"No, Becky," he had said. "I love you too much. Not like this. When I first enter your body, my love, I want to do so with all the rights of a husband. I don't want you to have to feel shame afterward."

She had shaken her head slowly, tears in her eyes. "I could never feel shame at loving you, Christopher," she said.

And he had hugged her to him again, the passion gone, only a deep and warm affection holding them together for many minutes.

"When we are married," he had said against her hair, "I shall bring you back here, Becky, and make long and slow love to you." He had drawn his head back and she saw that he was grinning.

She had smiled back, brushing away her tears with the back of her hand.

"Promise?" she had asked.

"The very next time," he had said before placing a smacking kiss on her lips and hauling them both to their feet. . . .

Rebecca stared at the grass before her, her face expressionless. Strange to imagine that that had happened here. Almost seven years ago. She should not have come down here. The pain was becoming unbearable. She was going to have to go back within the next few minutes and be sociable again, cheerful.

"It is even lovelier in the summertime, is it not?" Christopher said quietly.

Rebecca turned her head sharply. He was also leaning against a tree, not far from her, his arms crossed over his chest.

"How long have you been there?" she asked.

"A little longer than you," he said. "If I could have moved away without disturbing you, I would have gone. But it was not possible."

Rebecca turned her head away and stared out over the

water. He pushed away from the tree and walked over to stand in front of her. He put one hand on the trunk beside her head and leaned his head to one side so that he was looking directly into her eyes.

"Becky," he said, "there is one thing I want you to know. Perhaps it is unnecessary, but it has haunted me for years. I have always feared, you see, that in addition to hurting you I might have given the impression that you were somehow at fault, that perhaps you were in some way unlovable. I want you to know—and I swear by all that I once held honorable that I tell the truth—that I loved you when we came here together." He indicated the grassy area behind him with his free hand. "I loved you, Becky, with the whole of my being."

Her head was pressed against the tree, her palms flat against the bark on either side of her. She looked back into his eyes. "Did you, Christopher?" she said. "Did you? I loved you too, you know. I understood that a pledge had been made here. I thought we were committed to each other for a lifetime. I did not know that one could love one day and marry someone else almost the next. I think we have different definitions of the word *love*."

She continued to look into his eyes. She would not flinch. Let him be the first to move.

"My life came to an end the day I left you," he whispered fiercely. "I have lived in hell since then. I do not need to die, Becky. Nothing could be worse than what I have lived. If you wished to see me punished, know that your wish has been granted a thousandfold."

He turned abruptly and went crashing off through the trees, climbing quickly back up to the castle. Rebecca closed her eyes and stayed where she was. She clamped her teeth together, willing herself not to call his name until he was out of earshot.

Something was wrong when Rebecca entered the courtyard again fifteen minutes later. Uncle Humphrey was standing, leaning heavily on Maude's shoulder and waving a lace handkerchief in front of his nose. His face was more than usually pale. Maude had one arm around his waist and was clearly supporting much of his weight. Mrs. Sinclair was standing close by, openly weeping. Mr. Sinclair was patting her on the back rather ineffectually and absentmindedly. He was staring across the courtyard.

Christopher, Julian, Philip, Ellen, and Primrose were clustered together close to the entrance to the dungeons, all talking at once. Harriet, Mr. Bartlett, and Mr. Carver were nowhere in sight. Rebecca took in the scene at a glance and had a horrid presentiment of what was wrong. She hurried across the grass toward the larger group.

"What has happened?" she asked.

"Probably nothing at all," Philip said calmly. "But your cousin seems to be missing, and it seems likely that she has gone down to the dungeons."

"Surely she would not be so foolish," Rebecca said. "Did she not go walking with the others?"

"Yes," Julian said, "she started to. She was walking with me. But she don't seem to enjoy my company these days," he added humbly. "She took Bartlett's arm and they were walking more slowly than the rest of us. They never did catch up."

"But you must have noticed if they turned back," Christopher said impatiently.

"We just assumed that they were lagging," Julian said, "but when we turned back, we did not meet them at all."

"Would you not have seen them, Philip, if they had come to the dungeon steps?" Rebecca asked.

"Not necessarily," he replied. "We were sitting out of the wind over there, and the entryway here would be hidden from view."

"I am sure they must have gone down," Ellen said. "Harriet would not have given in so meekly when she had her heart set so on going, and Mr. Bartlett is so obliging that he would find it hard to say no to her."

"They should be up by now," Christopher said uneasily. "I had better go down and see what is happening."

"Oh, please do not," Primrose pleaded. "Mr. Carver has already gone down. You will all be tripping over one another if you go too."

They stood around uneasily for a few minutes, peering ineffectually into the darkness that quickly swallowed the narrow winding stone steps at the top of the spiral. Finally Julian made an impatient gesture and announced his intention of going down.

"No, Jule, I'll go," Christopher said. "No offense, old man, but I am stronger than you to help if anyone is hurt. If we just had a light it would help. The dungeons themselves, of course, are lit faintly by a small opening onto the hill, but the staircase is infernally dark, if memory serves me right."

He disappeared from sight after pressing himself against the stone wall on the outer edge of the steps. Rebecca found herself clinging to Philip's arm and leaning quite heavily on him. There was a ringing in her ears. She thought she might faint.

Fortunately for the anxious group in the courtyard, the wait was not a long one. Christopher was the first one to come into view again. Behind him came Mr. Carver, his face glistening with perspiration, carrying Harriet in his arms. Behind them came Mr. Bartlett.

Everyone spoke at once.

"Harriet, are you all right?"

"What happened?"

"Where did you find her?"

"Did she fall?"

"Did she faint?"

"Someone fetch her some water."

"Bring a blanket. She must be cold."

"I knew something like this would happen if you insisted on going down there, Harriet."

Everyone talked; no one listened.

Harriet said nothing. She was looking rather pale and disheveled. As soon as they were safely clear of the steps, Mr. Carver stooped down and placed her on the grass.

"One of the steps crumbled under her," Mr. Bartlett explained. "Fortunately it was almost at the bottom. She has sprained an ankle, I believe. But I was having a deuced hard time getting her back up again."

"Nothing for it but to pick her up and carry her," Mr. Carver said. He was wiping his face with a large linen handkerchief.

"I was unwilling to take the risk," Mr. Bartlett said. "If I had slipped with Miss Shaw in my arms, I might have killed her."

"Not t'mention yourself," Mr. Carver mumbled into his shirtfront.

"It seemed safer to walk beside her and encourage her to climb slowly," Mr. Bartlett said. His eyes were steely, his lips thin. "Though it was very dangerous to have to climb the narrow part of the steps myself. Of course, it was very heroic to climb to the top with the lady in your arms, Carver."

Maude had hurried over with one of the blankets, which she wrapped around Harriet's shoulders. Rebecca meanwhile had kneeled down beside her cousin and was gently exploring her ankle to try to estimate the damage. It was already badly swollen; it was impossible to tell if it was merely sprained or if perhaps there was a broken bone.

"What I would like to know, Bartlett," Christopher said, "is what you were doing down there in the first place."

"It is Miss Shaw's birthday," Mr. Bartlett said, "and she wished to see the dungeon. Where I was brought up, Sinclair, men were taught to respect the wishes of ladies. No one else had the courage to accompany her; I did so."

"You're a damned fool, Bartlett!" Christopher said. "Did the lady's safety mean nothing to you? Must you be forever trying to impress the ladies?"

Mr. Bartlett did not respond to the anger in Christopher's voice and manner. He remained cool. "You and I both know that there is no love lost between us, Sinclair," he said. "I suggest we show enough good breeding not to air our differences in public. If you wish to pursue our quarrel, perhaps we could make a private appointment?''

Harriet was beginning to recover from her fright, though she grimaced in pain when Rebecca tried to move her foot. She looked around her with interest.

"Why is everyone talking about me as if I were not here?" she asked. "I am not at all sorry that I went down the steps. It was by far the most exciting part of the day. And I would not have twisted my ankle had not someone been inconsiderate enough to leave a loose stone on the step. Do please stop fussing, everyone." But she looked as if she was thoroughly enjoying the attention she was receiving.

"You are not sorry!" Mr. Carver exclaimed. Rebecca looked up in surprise. She had not imagined that his voice could sound so formal or so cold. "It don't matter, I suppose, that everyone up here was worried half to death? Look at your papa! And it don't matter that Sinclair and I might have been in danger coming to rescue you."

"Well," Harriet said, tossing her head, "I might have known you were poor-spirited, sir! I don't know why you came down to find us. No one asked you to, I am sure."

"Harriet, love," Maude said, "Mr. Carver carried you up most of those steps. You should be grateful. And he is right about your papa. He is very upset. And really Stanley was greatly at fault in agreeing to accompany you down there. He should have known better."

"Oh," Harriet said, "you are all horrid. No one here has an ounce of spirit except Mr. Bartlett. This has not been a pleasant birthday after all. I wish to go home at once."

"Come on, Sinclair," Mr. Carver said, "let's carry Miss Shaw between us to her carriage. If you ask me, ma'am, you are fortunate not to be given a sound beating for this and a ration of bread and water for the next few days."

"Well!" Harriet said. "Well! I have never been so insulted. How dare you! Get away from me, sir. I would

rather crawl every inch of the way to the carriage than
have to be beholden to you for the smallest favor. Get
away from me!''

The last words were almost shrieked as Mr. Carver
advanced menacingly on her, scooped her up into his
arms, and marched off with her in the direction of the
stone archway that led to the hill and the conveyances.
Rebecca, gathering up the discarded blanket, glanced uneasily after them. Mr. Carver, especially in his present
mood, looked quite large enough to squash the life out of
Harriet. Both Christopher and Philip, she noticed at another glance, were grinning.

· 12 ·

Harriet was almost subdued for the next few days. Her ankle really was severely sprained, as the doctor confirmed on the evening of the outing. Consequently, she was confined to the house until she could get about again. She sat on a sofa in the morning room for most of each day, her injured foot propped on a cushioned stool in front of her.

She need not have been unduly bored. Her own family and the Sinclair family did their best to ensure that she constantly had company, and news of her mishap brought many other visitors, too. But Harriet had decided to be bored and generally out of sorts. The only person with whom she was in charity was Mr. Bartlett, who had not only been the only one with the courage to accompany her to the dungeons, but who also was the only one who had in no way blamed her for what had happened. In addition, he had been ill-used himself, notably by Mr. Carver and Mr. Christopher Sinclair, and it was up to her to console him.

The two spent hours together, talking, playing cards, reading—Mr. Bartlett read aloud to Harriet. On two occasions, he carried her out onto the terrace so that she might sit in the fresh air for a while.

Maude seemed not to like her brother and her stepdaughter being alone together. Whenever possible, she brought her work into the room and sat silently, her head bent to the embroidery until someone else arrived. But

Maude could not always be there. Lord Holmes—claiming
that the long journey to Cenross Castle, the wind and fresh
air in the courtyard, and the shock of his daughter's accident had quite undermined his delicate health—had taken
to his bed. The doctor was sent for daily to examine some
new symptom. And Maude was the only nurse allowed
near the somewhat petulant patient. She was constantly in
attendance on him when he was awake. Fortunately for
her, he slept quite frequently.

Harriet was quite out of charity with both Christopher
and Julian. She did not quarrel openly with them, but she
behaved with cold hauteur during their daily visits, to the
frustration of Julian and the apparent amusement of
Christopher.

"I say, Harriet," Julian said unwisely one afternoon,
"you ain't going to go around with your nose in the air for
the rest of the summer, are you? It's deuced uncomfortable
trying to converse with a female who is on her high
ropes."

"I do not recall asking you to converse with me, Julian," Harriet said with such a bored drawl that Christopher got to his feet and strolled to the morning-room
window so that he might have his back to the company for
a few minutes.

Harriet was civil to Ellen and Primrose, though she
behaved as if she were twenty years older than they and
condescended so shockingly that both became quite indig-
nant and confined their conversation to the ever-charming
Mr. Bartlett for all subsequent visits.

Almost undoubtedly Harriet would have treated Mr.
Carver with a special disdain. However, she was not given
a chance to do so in the days of her confinement to home.
He did not visit even once or send any messages that she
might have answered in a suitably contemptuous fashion.
It was left to her, in fact, to show an awareness of his
existence.

"Never tell me that Mr. Carver has finally gone home,"
she said to Christopher one afternoon. "I thought perhaps

he was planning to take up permanent residence with your mama and papa.''

"Luke?" Christopher said in some surprise. "Oh, he is still here. And when he came, he accepted a very firm invitation to stay until my own return to town in September. He is in the village this afternoon, visiting Miss Shaw at the school, I believe. He seems to have developed a social conscience since coming into the country. His mother will be delighted.''

"Well," Harriet said acidly, "it is as well that he has some feelings for the poor. He seems to have none for the sufferings of his own class.''

Mr. Carver was indeed at the school. Rebecca had been surprised to find him standing on the doorstep soon after luncheon when she answered his tap on the door. She looked nervously around, fully expecting to see that Christopher had accompanied him, but he was apparently alone.

He smiled, removed his hat, and bowed. "Came to see how you were doing, ma'am," he said. "Can I be of any assistance?''

Rebecca raised her eyebrows in surprise. "I am sure the boys will be delighted by your presence, sir," she replied. "Pray come inside."

She had discovered from experience that, though somewhat nervous at the presence of visitors, the boys were also exhilarated by it. It was novel for them to be the focus of attention to persons of quality.

Mr. Carver strode to the back of the room and stood with his hands behind his back for several minutes while Rebecca continued with her lesson on Greek mythology.

"Coo, miss," one of the bolder boys said when she had described the Parthenon to them, "do any of them buildings still exist?''

"I would not think so, Teddy," she said, "though there are many buildings in England now, you know, that imitate ancient Greek architecture.''

"Pardon me," Mr. Carver said in his deep voice, "but

you are quite mistaken, Miss Shaw. There are still many signs of ancient Greek civilization in Greece. Been there," he ended lamely.

"Oh, have you?" Rebecca said. "How I envy you! Do share your memories with us, sir."

The boys turned around to him with eager faces.

And so Mr. Carver found himself in the unlikely role of guest speaker at the village school, telling an enthralled audience about his travels in Greece and answering innumerable questions. When the time came for school to close for the day and Rebecca announced the fact, there was a collective moan of disappointment from the boys.

She turned to Mr. Carver, laughter in her eyes as the last of her pupils dragged himself almost unwillingly from the building. "You have missed your calling, sir," she said. "If you could just see these boys as they usually are when the end of the day comes. If they were just a little stronger, I believe they would leave the school without even opening the door first, such is their haste to be outside."

"Glad to be of assistance," Mr. Carver said. "Ain't much of a speaker, though."

"How can you say that," Rebecca said, "when you saw how delighted the boys were with what you had to say? And I too," she added. "I have never before had the chance to speak to someone who has actually been to Greece. It is the ambition of my life to travel there and to Italy."

"Could come in next time you are here," Mr. Carver said, "and tell the boys about Italy."

"Oh, would you?" Rebecca said, her tone dispelling any fear he might have had that she was being merely polite.

"Walk you home," Mr. Carver offered. "I can lead m'horse by the reins. Unless you would like to ride, that is. Won't suggest that we ride together. Poor animal would collapse in the middle." He gave a short bark of a laugh.

"I would far prefer to walk," Rebecca said, "and I should be delighted with your company, sir."

They talked about the school for part of the journey until Mr. Carver changed the subject. "I hear Miss Shaw's ankle is bad enough to confine her to home," he said gruffly.

"Yes, indeed," Rebecca said. "But poor Harriet hates to be immobile. I predict that she will be up and about within the next day or so."

"Serves her right," Mr. Carver said. "Hope the injury will teach her some sense. Glad she didn't break any bones, though. Wouldn't wish the little chit any real harm."

"Well, I would have to agree with you that she deserved the accident," Rebecca said candidly. "She has been dreadfully spoiled all her life, you see, and still feels that all her whims should be gratified instantly. I think a really strong person might still force her to grow up. Despite all evidence to the contrary, I have always believed that there is some good in Harriet. However, I do believe that any man with the necessary strength of character would cry off as soon as he saw how selfish and willful she is."

"Hm," Mr. Carver said, "all she needs is one good thrashing when she does something like that escapade at the castle. I would have given it to her in a moment had I been her papa or her brother."

"Yes," Rebecca agreed, "or her husband."

It had been a totally innocent remark. Yet glancing up at the big man who walked beside her, Rebecca was completely taken aback at the flood of color that rushed to his face. He withdrew a large handkerchief from his pocket and affected a coughing spell that lasted for all of one minute.

"Pardon me, ma'am," he said when he had recovered himself, "not used to so much walking."

Rebecca said nothing but resumed the walk, which had halted while he coughed. She was feeling somewhat stunned. Had she been mistaken? Did Mr. Carver have a *tendre* for

Harriet? It was not possible, surely. Since his arrival a few weeks before, he had shown nothing but contempt for her cousin. And well he might. Harriet had made no effort to hide the disdain she felt for his giant figure. Poor Mr. Carver. If he really were nursing tender feelings for Harriet, he was doomed to nothing but disappointment.

Mr. Carver was obviously concerned with changing the subject. "Sinclair was at the school yesterday," he said. "Seems to have become attached to that protégé of his."

"Protégé?" Rebecca said.

"Young lad with the eyeglasses," Mr. Carver said. "Says that he saw promise in that lad from the first day he saw him—time when you pointed out that he could scarcely see, I believe."

"Protégé," Rebecca repeated. "He has the nerve to use that word. Well, that is the outside of enough. Philip went out of his way to finance a school; both he and I have worked hard to teach Cyril; I discovered his disability; Philip used money he can ill afford to buy the boy eyeglasses—and he is Mr. Sinclair's protégé! Merely because Mr. Sinclair has spent a few hours with the boy, helping him to read. He is nothing but a town dandy."

"I say," Mr. Carver exclaimed, "not quite fair, Miss Shaw. Sinclair don't like it to be known that he helps the poor, but he has already spent a large part of his fortune on projects like this school of yours, y'know."

"No, I do not know," Rebecca said. She was so irritated by the presumption of the man in calling Cyril his protégé that she was not prepared to listen to reason. "If he has so much money to give to charity, where was he when we needed a school here, and where was he when we were puzzling over the problem of purchasing eyeglasses for Cyril? It is said that charity begins at home, Mr. Carver."

"Oh, lord," that gentleman said, mopping his brow with the handkerchief that he still clutched in one hand, "I should not have started this, ma'am. Sinclair wouldn't like it. But I hate to see m'friend maligned. I think you should ask your betrothed, ma'am, about Sinclair's connection with your school.''

"I would not think Philip would have much knowledge of Mr. Sinclair and his charitable endeavors,'' Rebecca said. "Anyway, sir, it is easy enough, I suppose, to be charitable with someone else's money.'' She was feeling thoroughly out of sorts and beginning to say things that were really none of her concern. She did not stop even when a remote corner of her mind reminded her that she would regret having spoken later when she had had time to cool down and consider.

"Mr. Sinclair had no money of his own,'' she said, "until he married. Is one supposed to admire him now for spending a small portion of his wife's money on the poor?''

"Eh?'' said Mr. Carver. "Many men marry rich wives, Miss Shaw. And many of them never give a penny to the poor.''

"Many of them do not treat their wives abominably, either,'' Rebecca said incautiously.

"Are you referring to Sinclair?'' Mr. Carver asked, stopping and turning to look full at her.

Rebecca had the grace to blush. "Forgive me, sir,'' she said. "I really have spoken quite out of turn. It is none of my concern how Mr. Sinclair treated his wife. I never even knew the lady.''

Mr. Carver's eyes narrowed as he continued to look closely at her. Rebecca almost squirmed with mortification. How could she have given in to such childish spite?

"Is this Bartlett's doing?'' he asked. "Has he been talking to you, Miss Shaw?''

Rebecca blushed again. "I would much prefer to say no more,'' she said. "Please forgive my impertinence, sir.''

Mr. Carver ignored her plea. "You would do well to ignore Bartlett, Miss Shaw,'' he said. "He is a viper in the guise of a man.''

"Oh, come now,'' Rebecca said, recovering herself. "I can see that you would dislike him if you are Mr. Sin-

clair's friend, but even you must admit that he was a much
wronged man. At least, it must have been painful for him
to see the woman he loved so mistreated by her husband.''

Mr. Carver frowned. ''I don't know what you are talking about,'' he said, ''but it sounds as if he has been
telling you some Banbury tale. My only criticism of Sinclair was that he treated that baggage of a wife of his with
unfailing courtesy even when she was so obviously . . . I'm
sorry, ma'am. Am being indiscreet too, talking about matters that are none of my concern. But I will say this. If you
want to know the truth of Sinclair's marriage, Bartlett ain't
precisely the one to talk to.''

They walked on in silence after one attempt to talk on a
different topic. The new subject sounded so artificial that
they both seemed to prefer not to talk at all. When they
came to the stile that led into the pasture and Rebecca
suggested proceeding alone, Mr. Carver made no objection
but helped her over the stile and then swung himself into
the saddle and rode away in the direction of the Sinclair
home.

Rebecca had plenty of time to think. She slowed her
pace and resolved to take as long as possible to reach
home. She knew that she would in all probability miss tea,
but tea meant visitors more than likely. Yesterday she had
invented some errands to keep her away during the afternoon, but when she returned the Sinclair party had still
been there and she had been forced to tiptoe to her room
and hope that no one realized that she was at home.

She had not seen Christopher since the disastrous afternoon at Cenross Castle, and she was willing time to pass
quickly so that the fair would come and go and he would
leave her life forever. The week after that she would be
married, and soon, probably, she and Philip would move
away to begin life anew somewhere else, he to kill his
memories of Maude, she hers of Christopher. It was not a
satisfactory way to begin a marriage, she supposed, but it
seemed to be the only way out of problems for both of

them. She had no doubt that Philip and Maude really did harbor a deep and hopeless love for each other.

Rebecca was more disturbed than she would admit over what had happened at Cenross. The memories themselves had been bad enough. It was almost unbearably painful to remember how close they had come to giving themselves to each other, how deep and lasting their love had seemed to be. It was impossible to understand how he could have changed so utterly and in such a short time. She shuddered at the memory of his coldness and callousness when he broke the news of his impending marriage.

And then there was the other thing that had happened at Cenross—that very disturbing encounter with Christopher himself. Why had he been there? Why would he want to resurrect the memories of what had happened in that place almost seven years before? It was hard to remember what he had said to her. She had been in such an emotional state herself that her brain had not been functioning with great clarity. And he had stood so close to her, his hand beside her head against the trunk of the tree, his blue eyes on a level with her own and gazing into them. She had been too disturbed by his physical nearness to understand his words.

She had heard them, of course. They were waiting somewhere in the jumble of her mind to be brought forward, fitted together, and comprehended. He had wanted to tell her something, had taken great pains to say it slowly and clearly. He had loved her when they visited that place before. That was what he said. He had loved her with his whole being. How could that be? How could he have loved her and married someone else just a few months later? It was not possible. Love could not be very strong if it could be displaced so easily by greed for money. She could not believe him.

Rebecca's footsteps lagged. She gazed down at her feet as she walked slowly across the pasture. What had made him leave so hastily at the end? She could remember now how he had gone crashing through the trees, leaving her still standing against the tree. She could recall her own pain, the almost overpowering urge to call him back. It had been the universal maternal need to comfort. Comfort for what? What had he said? Whispered, rather. He had whispered, as if his voice was not steady enough for the words to be spoken. She could not remember.

What had Mr. Carver meant by suggesting that she talk to Philip about Christopher? The two men had become surprisingly friendly, and Christopher had apparently been spending some time at the school when it was Philip's day to teach. But what would Philip know about Christopher's life beyond these few weeks? Probably nothing. He was doubtless impressed by the visitor's behavior and interest in his work. But he could not know the man as she knew him.

It seemed, though, if one were to believe Mr. Carver, that Christopher was a charitable man. He always had been, of course, until greed had changed the course of his life. If he had turned back now to his old ways, there was perhaps a chance that he felt remorse for what he had done and that he was determined to make up in small part for the wasted years. She hoped so. She was finding it increasingly painful to hate him. She hoped he would be able to rise above his past.

My life came to an end the day I left you. I have lived in hell since then.

Rebecca stopped walking completely. She could almost hear him saying those words. Whispering them. Oh God, that was what he had said to her before rushing away up the hill. He had lived in hell, he had said. He did not need to die. She closed her eyes and put her hands over her face. Dear God, he had suffered too. He had never been happy with his wife despite all the money.

Then why had he done it? Why had he married Angela? Why had he abandoned her?

Why, Christopher, why?

Rebecca removed her hands from her face after a while and gazed wearily ahead. She started to walk again. Mr. Carver had been puzzled when she had alluded to the shabby way Christopher had treated his wife. He had always treated her with unfailing courtesy, Mr. Carver had said, even when . . . He had not completed the thought. Even when she was with child? Had Christopher not wanted a child? She supposed it was possible to be unfailingly courteous to someone and still neglect her shamefully. Perhaps both Mr. Bartlett and Mr. Carver were right. A viper, Mr. Carver had called the other, though, a viper in the guise of a man.

Whom was one to believe? Life had become so complicated in the last few weeks that there seemed to be no certainties any longer. And she did not feel that her mind could cope with what was happening. She clung as to a lifeline to the knowledge that in two weeks' time she would be married to Philip and could devote herself wholeheartedly to making him a good wife and helpmeet. She would be able to stop worrying. Life would become simple and tranquil again.

Rebecca looked ahead to the house, which was quite close now. A group of people was gathered outside the front door, four on horseback, one on foot. Three of the riders raised their hands and waved in her direction as they rode off. Christopher affected not to see her, or perhaps he really did not. He was bent forward talking to Maude for several seconds after his brother and sisters had moved off in the direction of home.

Maude saw Rebecca approaching and waited for her to come up before returning to the house. "Oh, Rebecca," she said, "you have been working too hard, dear. We have already finished tea and sent the tray back to the kitchen. You really must be careful for your health. You have been gone since early this morning."

"I walked home in disgracefully leisurely fashion," Rebecca said cheerfully, "with Mr. Carver as far as the stile and then alone. The weather seems too lovely to be cooped up indoors. Do you think Cook will be dreadfully cross, Maude, if I ring for a cup of tea?"

"Of course not," Maude said, "and what does it signify if she is? But do please take it in the morning room, Rebecca. Harriet and Stanley are in there, and I must return to his lordship's room. He is sure to be waking up soon, and he frets if I am not there.''

"You must be careful not to overwork too, Maude," Rebecca said, taking in the pallor of her uncle's wife. Surely Maude had lost weight too in the last little while.

Maude smiled rather wanly. "I shall be fine, Rebecca," she said. "But I am afraid that the excursion to Cenross Castle really did tax his lordship's strength too much. I believe he is feeling definitely unwell this time. Oh dear, and I was uncharitable enough to say to you only recently that I thought that sometimes he imagined his maladies."

She hurried up the staircase ahead of Rebecca and continued on up to the third floor and her husband's bedchamber. Rebecca reluctantly turned in the direction of the morning room. The very last thing she felt like at the moment was a dose of Harriet's peevishness and even—surprisingly—of Mr. Bartlett's charm. Sometimes, she reflected, one could have too much even of a good thing.

• 13 •

Two days before the fair, Philip came into the school-room while Rebecca was teaching and announced that school would finish early. It was the last day before a month-long holiday. The harvest would begin soon; the fair had always been set at the end of August to give the laborers a last fling, so to speak, before the hard work of gathering in the grain began. And when the work did start, as many hands as possible would be needed. There would be no excusing the boys then for matters of such peripheral importance as education.

The boys cheered and rose to leave. Rebecca had not quite finished the history lesson she was giving, but she smiled and closed her book.

"One good thing about history," she said, "is that it will always wait for another occasion. Well, boys, I have been proud of your progress in the last few months. Did you believe then that by the end of summer you would all be able to read?"

Some of the boys grinned; others looked sheepish.

"Me dad said that if the good Lord had meant for me to read, he would have made sure I was born to the quality," one lad said.

"I thought I was nothing but a blockhead, but it was just me eyes, wasn't it, miss?" Cyril said.

"Cyril," Rebecca said, "with your eyeglasses you look

so learned that you might easily be mistaken for a young professor.''

All the boys roared with laughter and pushed and shoved one another against the benches.

''Mr. Sinclair said that if I work hard he might hire me in a year or two's time to help his bailiff,'' Cyril said eagerly. ''I'm good at figures, and it's getting so as I can read. 'Course, it would mean leaving me mum and dad and going away.''

Philip stepped forward, hands clasped behind his back. ''Well, young men,'' he said, ''school is dismissed. I just hope that when you come back at the beginning of October, you will not have forgotten all you have learned.''

The boys needed no more encouragement to crowd out through the open door into the air and freedom.

Philip turned to Rebecca. ''Have we accomplished anything?'' he asked ruefully. ''They always seem so eager to get away from the learning and back to the very life from which we are trying to free them.''

Rebecca laughed. ''Philip,'' she said, ''were you such a model pupil during your boyhood that you welcomed all your lessons? Would you not much have preferred to be out riding or climbing trees?''

''No,'' he said with a puzzled frown.

''Then I assure you,'' she said, ''that you were quite atypical. It seems that one has to be adult before one appreciates the benefits of learning. Unfortunately it is necessary to force youngsters to achieve what they will value only later in life.''

She proceeded to pack away her own books in a valise that she had brought with her for the purpose. There was no point in leaving them in the schoolroom for upward of a month. Philip moved to the back of the room and stacked the few books there neatly.

''Philip,'' Rebecca asked, ''has Mr. Christopher Sinclair ever done anything for the school or the boys other than visit a few times?'' She did not look at him; she kept busy with her task.

"Why do you ask?" Philip said after a short pause.

"For no particular reason," she said. "Just something Mr. Carver said a few days ago and what Cyril said just now. I have been left wondering."

Philip was silent for a while, his hands still on the books beneath them. "I do not know what to say," he said. "I have promised secrecy, though I have never seen that anything can be served by keeping you uninformed."

"You mean that Mr. Sinclair paid for Cyril's eyeglasses?" Rebecca asked, unconsciously holding her breath.

"Oh, yes," Philip said. "That too."

"That too?" Rebecca's attention was focused full on him now. "There has been more?"

Philip raised his eyebrows and half smiled. "I did not know that you suspected only about the eyeglasses," he said. "But since I have hinted at more, I had better tell you all, I suppose. I really feel you should know, anyway, since you have as close a link with the school as I have myself. Mr. Sinclair is the man who has financed the school from the beginning."

Rebecca really thought she might faint. Everything around her had become unreal. There was only Philip standing there across the room, looking at her almost apologetically, and the appalling words that still seemed to hang in the air between them.

"Mr. Sinclair?" she said stupidly. "We owe all this to him?"

"Yes, indeed," he said. "He arranged an introduction when I was in London for a few days before I took up my appointment here. He explained then that he was interested in my career as I was to succeed a friend of his as vicar in this parish. And he told me that if I ever needed money to aid the poor of the area I was to apply to him. I remembered what he had said when you and I had our dream of the school a year or so ago and I wrote to him. I did not really expect that he would be interested in such an ambitious and expensive scheme, but he was. He knew you too, he said, and seemed convinced that you would be an excellent teacher. He agreed to give as much help as we needed provided no one but I knew of his involvement. I am sure he did not really mean you too, Rebecca. Now, especially, I have wanted you to know so that you might show him your gratitude.''

Rebecca finally broke eye contact with him and looked down at the valise that she clutched in her hands. "Yes," she said, "I am glad that you told me, Philip. It is right that I should know. I shall have to find an opportunity before he leaves to speak with him."

Philip excused himself soon after. He still had several visits and errands to accomplish before the afternoon was over. Rebecca was left alone with her bewilderment. Christopher the unknown benefactor of the school! It made no sense at all. She had seen during the past few weeks that he was not the selfish, greedy man that she had expected him to be. But she had assumed that the change back to the way he had used to be was of a very recent date. Yet he had sought Philip out several years ago for the express purpose of offering his help to the needy in his own birthplace.

Several years ago! And it had been no empty gesture. He had given more than generously on the first occasion he had been applied to. And it had been no minor charity that would have made almost no dent at all in his pocketbook. He had provided them with a building as well as all the furnishings and equipment for their school.

She could not even explain his behavior by imagining that it had all been a showy gesture to impress the neighborhood. He had wanted no one to know. Unlike Philip, she was convinced that he had not wanted even her to know. If he had, he had had ample opportunity to tell her in the past few weeks. Yet he had not breathed a word. And he had made it seem as if Cyril's eyeglasses had been all Philip's idea and doing.

The mystery of the last seven years was becoming more and more puzzling. Indeed, until recently she had not even realized that there was a mystery. He had merely seemed a weak man who had given in to the temptations of greed.

The explanation could still hold, she realized. A man who gave in to temptation did not necessarily change his whole character as a result. She supposed it had been rather naive of her to imagine that suddenly, almost overnight, as it were, Christopher had turned from a loving, caring human being into a selfish, avaricious monster.

She would just have to face the truth of the fact that his love for her had not been strong. It had been a pleasant flirtation. He had probably even intended to marry her. It might have been a reasonably successful marriage. But his visit to London had opened his eyes to the kind of life that he could live if he only had money. And suddenly it had all been within his grasp. Giving up the woman he had loved to a moderate degree must have seemed a small sacrifice to make for all the rewards of life with another woman who had the attraction of being rich. That must be it.

I loved you, Becky, with the whole of my being.

He had said that to her at the castle. Were those the words of a man who had loved only moderately?

My life came to an end the day I left you. I have lived in hell since then.

Were those the feelings of a man who did not know what deep emotion was?

Rebecca jerked the valise off the table as if by mistreating this inanimate object she might satisfy all her frustrated feelings, and made for the door. This was surely the worst summer of her life. She was very thankful that it was almost at an end. She made her way to the stables at the back of the parsonage, where her uncle's horse and gig had spent the day. She had been forced to bring the conveyance today because she had known that she would have a heavy load to carry home.

Harriet was almost back to normal again. Dr. Gamble had instructed that she was to keep her foot off the floor for another week, but there was no keeping her down once she could get to her feet without screaming in agony. At first she took short walks around the garden, leaning heavily on Mr. Bartlett's always available arm. But the day before she had crossed to the stables, had her mare saddled, and gone riding triumphantly off with her usual faithful companion.

Rebecca was surprised, in fact, to find her at home after the school had closed. She came marching into Rebecca's room almost on her heels. Rebecca could see immediately that she was in high dudgeon about something.

"Papa is just going to have to choose between me and that woman," she blurted without any preamble. "There is not room in this house for both of us."

These words were not a mystery to one who had lived in the house for several years. "What has poor Maude done now?" Rebecca asked mildly, untying the ribbons of her straw bonnet and tossing it onto the bed.

"Poor Maude!" said Harriet. "She is an upstart and a fortune hunter, that is what she is. And she thinks she can pose as my mama. The absurdity of it, Rebecca! She is only three years older than I am. It is even more ludicrous than your trying to tell me what to do. Thank goodness you never try, at least."

"If I do not, Harriet," Rebecca said, "it is because I know I should be only wasting my breath. Do sit down if you plan to stay. And not on that stool, please. I wish to sit before the mirror to brush my hair. What has Maude done?"

"She has asked Stanley to leave, that is what," Harriet said. "Her own brother! And when I expressly invited him to stay and told her so, she told me that she is mistress in this house and my wishes on the topic were not to be consulted. Imagine! This is my house, Rebecca, not hers. The nerve of the woman! And when I was going to go to Papa to tell him that Stanley was to stay because it is my wish, she forbade me to go to his room. My own papa! She said he is too sick to be pestered—pestered! Everyone knows that Papa is never sick. He merely pretends because he likes attention and does not like to exert himself to get up."

Harriet finally stopped for breath. Stanley, Rebecca thought. Was he Stanley now?"

"I am sorry if Maude has asked her brother to leave," she said. "But, you know, Harriet, she has every right to do so. He has been here for several weeks, and she is very busy now with your father. I am sure she is feeling weary and finding the burden of entertaining just too much to cope with."

"Stuff!" Harriet said. "How could Stanley be any trouble to Maude or anyone else? You speak as if she has to do all the cooking for him and the extra washing and everything else. She is afraid that I will marry him, that's what, Rebecca, and that I will have children. Then Papa will again love me more than he loves her—though I think he already does, anyway. I don't think Maude can have children. At least she has shown no sign of increasing since she has been married to Papa. Now she is jealous. She does not wish to see me married."

"Harriet," Rebecca said, removing several hairpins from her mouth in order to speak, "slow down. Surely there is no question of your marrying Mr. Bartlett anyway, is there?"

"And why not, pray?" Harriet asked tartly. "I am sure he is more of a gentleman than Mr. Christopher Sinclair or Julian or any of the other suitors I have had."

"Indeed," Rebecca said. "I agree that Mr. Bartlett has very superior manners and is excessively amiable. I have just been taken by surprise. I had not thought of him in terms of a suitor for you."

"You think him too poor, no doubt," Harriet said. "It is true he has little money and no prospects. And he does not try to hide the fact. And it is not his idea that we should be wed. He says it would not be the thing at all. But I do not care a fig about money, Rebecca. I have enough for both of us."

Rebecca removed the pins from her mouth again. She had not touched her hair with the brush since she had put them back there. "Harriet," she said faintly, "if Mr. Bartlett has not had the idea of marrying you, how did the subject come up between you?"

"Oh," Harriet said, "He said that it would be the dearest wish of his heart to offer for me, but he cannot. He is really a tragic figure, you know, Rebecca. He once loved another. But she died. And now I have helped him recover from his loss. He really is quite handsome, is he not, despite his red hair and his rather short stature?"

Rebecca was beginning to understand why Maude was trying to remove her brother from the house. It was true that he was an amiable man and that he would probably make Harriet a tolerable husband. He would be indulgent, anyway. But Uncle Humphrey would not see it as a good match. He expected greater things for his only daughter. Maude must be living in terror of his finding out about the budding romance and blaming her. It really was a pity, but Rebecca could sympathize.

"And is Mr. Bartlett going to leave?" she asked.

Harriet scowled. "He may stay until the day after the fair, according to her high and mighty ladyship," she said. "But I shall see Papa before then, never fear. I do not intend to be bossed around by that intruder."

Rebecca secretly thought that Lord Holmes would, for once, stand up to his daughter if he knew the truth of what was developing beneath his roof, but she held her counsel.

Harriet giggled unexpectedly. "We were out riding this afternoon," she said, "when we saw Mr. Carver again. He was riding to the village. He raised his hat and looked very stern. Stanley bowed, very civil, and I nodded my head, but neither one of us smiled. It was really very comical, Rebecca. He asked about my ankle and I said— very haughty—'Pray, sir, have you not been told by the Sinclairs, who have visited me every day since my accident' —I emphasized the *every*—'that I am now going along tolerably well? I am surprised at their silence, sir.' Then I turned and said, 'Come along, Stanley, the horses are getting skittish at the delay.' You should just have seen his face, Rebecca."

"Yes," her cousin replied, "I can just imagine, Harriet. I suppose you did not consider thanking Mr. Carver for the assistance he gave you at the castle?"

"Thanking him!" Harriet said. "That odious, pompous tyrant? Did you hear what he said? He said I deserved a thrashing! Any gentleman would have been all attention and solicitous concern. I might have been dead!"

"Precisely," Rebecca said. "And it would all have been your fault, Harriet."

Harriet fixed her cousin with a severe eye. "Sometimes, Rebecca," she said, "I think you are positively stuffy. You are actually taking the part of a man who can behave with such a want of conduct? I can just picture him thrashing a female, too. It would doubtless make him feel manly. He would find himself with a few bruises of his own if he ever tried to lay a hand on me, I can tell you."

"Well," Rebecca said soothingly, "I think you can rest assured, Harriet, that he never will. Mr. Carver is enough of a gentleman not to try to lay hands on any female who was not either his sister, his daughter, or his wife." She thought again of the reaction she had evoked quite unwittingly from Mr. Carver when she had said something quite similar to him a few days before and looked curiously at Harriet in the mirror.

Harriet, though, was not blushing and coughing at the thought. "His wife—ugh!" she said, and clutched her throat and stuck out her tongue.

Maude was quiet at the dinner table that evening. She was looking pale and weary, Rebecca thought. She was quite surprised, in fact, that her uncle's wife had put in an appearance at all downstairs.

"How is Uncle Humphrey?" she asked when she was alone with Maude before the meal. "Is he sleeping?"

"Yes, at present he is," Maude answered. "He really is not well, and the doctor told me today that he suspects a weak heart. Oh, Rebecca, and I have been so impatient with his ailments."

"Nonsense," Rebecca said, going to her and putting an arm around her shoulders. "You have been nothing but patience, Maude. You will have to be careful that you do not become sick too. You are looking very tired. Had you not better have some fresh air? Perhaps a walk afterwards? The evening air will be cool and very refreshing.''

"How I would love that!" Maude said wistfully. "If his lordship is still asleep when dinner is over, perhaps I will walk, Rebecca, if you will join me. If he is awake, he will doubtless want me in attendance. Besides, he does not like me to walk in the evening air. He is afraid that I will take a chill.''

She lapsed into silence again. It was altogether a strained meal. Harriet was showing silent displeasure to her stepmother, pointedly ignoring her and addressing the few remarks she did make to Mr. Bartlett or Rebecca. Mr. Bartlett himself did his best to charm everyone back into a good humor, but it was completely beyond his power to do so.

Lord Holmes was still asleep when Maude went up to his bedchamber to check on him. She left his valet in attendance and came back downstairs, a shawl around her shoulders, to claim her walk with Rebecca. They strolled south across the lawn and into the pasture.

Maude breathed deeply and lifted her face to the late evening sky. "Oh, Rebecca," she said, "you cannot know how good it feels to escape into the outdoors once in a while. How I envy you your life of activity and usefulness.''

Rebecca bit her lip. "I certainly would not say your life is useless at the moment," she said. "I am sure you are bringing great comfort to Uncle Humphrey.''

Maude sighed. "He will not let me out of his sight when he is awake," she said, "yet I cannot do anything right for him. If I plump up his pillows, I leave them lumpy; if I read to him, I read too quietly or too loudly. And now it seems that he really is ill. Poor Humphrey! Sometimes I wonder if I am of any use to him or anyone else in the world.''

"Oh, please do not talk like that!" Rebecca said, distressed. ''Indeed, at times it does seem that life is tedious and pointless, but those times always pass. You are of great value to me, Maude. I believe I would find life at my uncle's house less easy to support if it were not for your calm and sweet presence.''

"How kind of you to say so," Maude said, flashing the other a grateful smile. "But I do know what you mean. I hate to criticize Harriet; she has many good qualities that I do not possess—vitality, strong will, determination. But she is very undisciplined. I am only three years older than she, Rebecca, and I have lived a sheltered existence. Yet even so, I know a great deal more about life than she, though she would never believe so. I think having Stanley as a brother has taught me many of the harsher truths of life.''

"Harriet is selfish and she does not always display the greatest good sense," Rebecca agreed, "but I still hope that one day she will grow up and turn out not so badly after all.''

"I have always believed so, too," Maude said, "and indeed I still hope so. But I do fear, Rebecca, that she will do something foolish that will blight the whole future course of her life.''

"She told me this afternoon about your trying to separate her from your brother," Rebecca said gently. "Do you really believe it would be such an imprudent match, Maude?''

Maude shot her one penetrating glance and looked ahead again. "I find it hard to speak ill of my brother," she said, "but really he is not the man for Harriet.''

"Just because he has no fortune and no prospects?" Rebecca asked. "Do those facts matter so much when he has qualities enough to compensate for the lack? Harriet does not need to marry for money. Indeed, I am convinced that she would be fortunate indeed to attract such an amiable husband. He seems to feel an affection for her.''

"Stanley feels affection for no one but himself!" Maude said bitterly. "Nothing has ever mattered to him but the gratification of his own desires and the everlasting search for wealth and comfort.''

"You surely cannot be serious," Rebecca said. "You are tired, Maude. You are perhaps afraid that Uncle Humphrey will be displeased with you if he learns of this attachment between Harriet and Mr. Bartlett. But you cannot really mean what you just said."

"Oh, can I not?" Maude said, her voice breathless. "I did not mean to say so much, Rebecca, but since I have begun, I might as well continue. Sometimes I feel so lonely having no one in whom to confide. Stanley is coldhearted and totally lacking in morals. He is a consummate actor, as you have seen, but I have known him all my life. And he has never been any different. We were not always poor. Papa was never wealthy, it is true, but there was always enough. There was money for Stanley to live in modest comfort all his life and money for a respectable dowry for me. Stanley gambled it all away within a year of leaving home, and Papa was foolish enough to pay all his debts rather than see him go to debtors' prison."

Rebecca stared incredulously at the hard profile of her companion, who was striding across the meadow with probably no idea of where she was going.

"He was always clever at seeming sincere," Maude continued. "He was always a great favorite with the ladies even when he was quite a young boy. He used that charm to try to attract a rich wife when there was no money left. He almost succeeded once, I believe, until he was cut out by someone else. Now he is after Harriet. He has been very clever. He has waited until it has become unlikely that I will ever bear an heir. Harriet would not be such an heiress, you see, if I had a son. But now he thinks it reasonably safe to put his plan into effect. I thought even Harriet would have had enough sense to discourage his suit, but she has begun to favor him, I think because she has been disappointed by Mr. Sinclair's lack of ardor."

Rebecca was silent. She did not know what to say. She could not doubt the truth of what Maude said. Mr. Bartlett was her brother, and Maude was not one to indulge in spite for no reason. Yet she found it almost impossible to adjust her mind to the new image of the charming and amiable gentleman she had known for several weeks. Mr. Carver, too, had called him a viper. Could it be possible that he had done so with good reason, and not merely in defense of his friend whose enemy Mr. Bartlett was?

"Fortunately," Maude said, slowing her pace and seeming to recollect herself somewhat, "his lordship has given me his support, though he does not know the truth about Stanley. Harriet went to see him before dinner while I was downstairs fetching his medicine. I was very vexed; I had forbidden her to worry her papa when he is so obviously unwell. But she gained nothing. When I came back into the room, he was telling her quite roundly that Stanley has been here long enough and that if I saw fit to tell him to pack his bags, then that is the way it must be. She was very chagrined, knowing that I was there to hear what he said. But I am relieved, Rebecca. In three days' time Stanley will be gone and Harriet will be safe from that peril, at least. Not much harm can come to her in the meantime, I believe."

"I am sure Harriet does not feel any deep attachment to Mr. Bartlett," Rebecca said. "Once he has gone, she will turn her attention to someone else, I am sure. She has always been the same, Maude. I am afraid constancy is not one of her chief virtues. Please do not worry about the matter. Everything will turn out well. Uncle Humphrey will probably feel more himself in a day or two—indeed, I have never known him to miss the fair. He loves to present the prizes at the end of the day. And Harriet will soon have her head full of some new attraction. You will be free to concentrate on gaining back your health and spirits."

"Bless you," Maude said. "I do love you, Rebecca, and I shall miss you dreadfully when you are married and removed to the parsonage."

And quite inexplicably she stopped in the middle of the pasture, put her hands over her face, and burst into tears.

· 14 ·

The annual village fair really had far more to offer the people of the lower classes than the gentry. The games of skill, the races, the exhibitions of needlecraft and baking, the food stalls and tearoom, the stall that sold ribbons and cheap and garish baubles, the jugglers, the fortune-teller, and the dances around the maypole seemingly had nothing to attract the superior minds of the rich and educated. Yet for as far back as she could remember, Rebecca has always looked forward all spring and summer to this particular day.

And she was not alone. Uncle Humphrey and Aunt Sybil had always spent the better part of the day and the evening in the village, graciously bestowing nods and bows on lesser mortals and presenting the prizes at the end of the day. That description was unfair to Aunt Sybil, she admitted. Her aunt had never condescended. She had mingled with her husband's tenants and laborers with the greatest delight, as had Mama and Papa. And the Sinclairs were always there and all the other landowners for miles around. It was one of those occasions that was popular for no explainable reason.

Only twice could she remember the day being spoiled by rain. The first time she had been ten years old and had cried and cried, her nose pressed miserably against the window of her room in the parsonage, because she had new white gloves and would not be able to show them off to Christopher Sinclair—even then there had been Christopher. The other time was the summer after her unofficial betrothal came to an end, a summer when she had been so out of spirits that she really had not cared.

This was not to be the third occasion, Rebecca saw as soon as she woke up and glanced to the window of her bedchamber. Even through the velvet curtains she could see that the day was bright. She was glad. For the first time in several weeks she felt positively cheerful and full of energy. For several days now she had looked forward to the day of the fair as a kind of boundary marker in her life. It was a day that was somehow to mark an end and a beginning. It was probably the last day that Christopher and Mr. Carver would be there. Tomorrow or the next day they would leave for London.

She would be sorry to see Mr. Carver go. She liked him and saw him as a gentleman of good humor and good sense. And she dared not consider her true feelings on Christopher's departure. When her mind came close to realizing that she would probably never see him again, she had to focus it quickly on other topics in order to avoid panic. But even so, she was glad the day had come. Once they were gone she would be able to concentrate on the future as it must be. And it was not by any means a bleak future that she faced.

She was glad too that this was the last day of Mr. Bartlett's stay. She had liked him and still found it difficult to believe all that Maude had said about him. Yet it must be true. And indeed, the day before, when he had been alone with her on the terrace for a short while and had tried to enlist her sympathies for his predicament—in love as he was with a wealthy girl and innocently open to suspicion as a fortune hunter—she had found herself looking at him with new eyes. And she had been able to see that perhaps it was all an elaborate act: the charm, the humility, the sincerity.

Once this day was over, perhaps she would be able to believe in the reality of her own wedding plans. It was

hard to believe that in little more than a week's time she
would be Philip's bride. There was to be nothing elaborate
about the day, but Maude and Harriet had already planned
a wedding breakfast at which they hoped more than twenty
of their neighbors would sit down.

Most of all she welcomed the day because she had
decided that something must be done and she wanted it
over and forgotten. She would have to talk to Christopher.
She had to thank him for what he had done for the school
and for Cyril in particular. She did not know why she felt
this was necessary. It seemed clear to her that he had not
wanted her to know about his involvement. But she did
know, and she felt embarrassed about the contempt she
had shown for his interest in the school since his return
home. She had to let him know that she knew and that she
appreciated his efforts despite her personal feelings about
him.

The thought of seeking him out and deliberately initiat-
ing a conversation with him terrified her and excited her
all at the same time. It would be the last time, the last
chance to establish something of goodwill between them.
And it was important to her to do so. She could no longer
even pretend to hate him. She could still, of course,
despise his weakness, and she could still believe that he
had treated her about as badly as it was possible for a man
to treat a woman. But she could not hate him. Putting
aside all personal matters, she could even begin to respect
him again. And she clung to this possibility. Christopher
had been first and foremost a friend, someone she had
looked up to despite all his mischief for as far back as she
could remember. Had she not fallen in love with him,
perhaps she would never have stopped liking him.

Lord Holmes finally convinced even the most cynical of
his household that he was not in good health by refusing to
rise from his bed even for the fair. Maude had told no one
except Rebecca about the doctor's disturbing suspicion. He
did, however, insist that Maude run along and enjoy herself. She was to deputize for him and present the prizes on

his behalf. She agreed to drive into the village in the gig with Rebecca.

Harriet was in an almost dangerously gay mood. She chattered to everyone at breakfast, even Maude, whom she had pointedly ignored for two whole days. And she was wearing a new dress of figured pink muslin, which looked very fresh and youthful with her dark hair and eyes. Rebecca had expected her to be sulky, knowing that this was Mr. Bartlett's last day. Perhaps she was merely determined to make the most of it, Rebecca thought, and felt renewed relief that Maude's brother was soon to be safely out of the way.

Harriet expressed her determination to drive into the village in Mr. Bartlett's curricle and tossed her head as if expecting to have to do battle. But Maude wisely offered no comment. They were all to leave the house at the same time and the journey was to be made in broad daylight. It was perhaps best to allow Harriet one small victory when soon the war would be won.

Rebecca saw Ellen and Primrose as soon as they entered the village. The sisters were standing at the market stall, an array of brightly colored ribbons dangling from the hands of each. Her heart began to thump uncomfortably. The Sinclairs were here already, then, and in a small place like this there would be no avoiding any of them for long. Now that the moment was upon her, she found that she was not prepared at all for her planned meeting with Christopher. She took the coward's way out and ducked into the schoolroom, which they had been able to offer this year as a tearoom, where the weary could come and sit for a while out of the sun and refresh themselves with tea or lemonade and cakes.

She was not surprised to find Philip there, standing in his usual straight-backed way with his hands clasped behind his back. He was talking to a cluster of women who were setting out cakes and scones on plates.

"I was just saying, Miss Shaw," one of the women sang out across the room, "that we are right proud of our

Dan'l. Him able to read and all! Soon he won't even be talking to his mum and dad, I said to him last night. But he hugged me that tight, ma'am, and said he wouldn't never forget who brought him into this world and fed and clothed him.''

Rebecca smiled broadly. "Daniel has been one of our star pupils," she said. "I am so glad you are pleased with his progress."

"My Lucy says why can't she learn as well, Miss Shaw," another of the women said. "Her father said to her what nonsense it was for a girl to want to read. Such notions they do get!"

Rebecca was not sure if the head-shaking contempt for the notions was directed at Lucy or Lucy's father. "I believe it is just as important for your girls to learn as it is for the boys," she said. "It is the dearest wish of my heart that soon we will be able to educate them too."

A lively debate ensued in which, rather surprisingly, there were heated opinions on both sides. Rebecca would have thought that an all-female audience, with the exception of Philip, would have strongly favored her opinion.

Philip finally took her by the elbow and steered her from the building and into the garden bordering the parsonage. She relaxed beside him. It was quiet here, away from the bustle that was already developing in the street. She smiled up at him.

"Is it not lovely to have the school closed for just a while and to be able to relax?" she said. "We seem to have so little time just to be together, Philip."

He did not return her smile and he did not take up her topic. "I would rather you did not talk in such a way before the villagers," he said curtly.

Rebecca frowned in puzzlement. "What do you mean?" she asked.

"Putting ridiculous notions in their heads about educating their daughters," he said. "Have you no sense, Rebecca? Soon we will be having all these mothers demanding that we take in their girls."

"Perhaps it would be a good thing if we did," Rebecca said. "We would be forced to move a little faster than we originally planned, it is true, but we could rise to the challenge. We have been very successful during our first year."

"Rebecca," he said, turning to face her, "I must tell you now once and for all that the school will never include girls. The idea is ridiculous. Why should we waste our time on educating females? What possible use could there be in our doing so?"

She flushed. "I am a female, Philip," she said, "and I happen to feel that my life is a little more complete for my ability to read and write and compute and for my knowledge of history and of French and music."

He made an impatient gesture. "You are not a member of the lower classes," he said. "Of course it is necessary for ladies to have some smattering of knowledge so that they can participate to some small degree in social conversation. For these girls, Rebecca, an education would serve no purpose at all."

"Are we really such inferior creatures?" Rebecca asked very quietly. "And tell me, Philip, do I successfully participate to some small degree in social conversation? Do I save the gentlemen from the boredom of having to listen to an utter ninnyhammer all the time?"

"You are becoming angry, Rebecca," Philip said calmly, "and speaking unreasonably. You know that you are twisting my words. I am not saying that these girls are useless. They have infinite value. They are God's creatures, fashioned to be a help and a comfort to their menfolk. We would spoil them by educating them, spoil their God-given beauty."

"Woman achieves worth and beauty only through the service she renders her menfolk," Rebecca said.

Philip almost smiled. "I could not have said it better," he said. "I must try to remember those exact words."

"I will reach final fulfillment as a woman and as a person when I become your helpmeet," she said.

This time he did smile. "What a beautiful idea," he said. "You will be a good wife, Rebecca. I am a fortunate man."

"Poppycock!" was all Rebecca said.

"I beg your pardon?"

"I said, 'Poppycock!' " she repeated very distinctly.

Philip frowned. "Yes, I heard you the first time," he said, "but thought I must have mistaken. I have never heard such an inelegant word on your lips."

"It comes from having an education," she said. "I have read the word somewhere. I am already one of the spoiled, Philip. You know, there has always been something about you that has made me somewhat uneasy. I have never been able to identify what it is. I think I know now. You are pompous in the extreme. Yes, you really are."

Philip turned very white. He looked down at her, his face expressionless. "I think you are not quite well today, Rebecca," he said. "Perhaps you should go and take some tea and sit down for a while before you say something that you will really regret."

Rebecca stared at him. "It has ever been thus, has it not, Philip?" she said. "Several times in the past we have approached the point at which we might really communicate and discuss differences in our ideas. And always you close the door to me. Are you afraid of a healthy argument? Or is it that you are so convinced that you are right that my opinion is of no interest to you?"

"Enough, Rebecca," he said. "I have no wish or intention to stand here brawling with you. And when you are my wife, I shall certainly expect you to bow quietly to my will, even if you do not always like it. You will promise in the marriage service to obey me."

"No," she said slowly, "I do not believe I will, Philip."

"I am sorry if you do not like it," he said, "but I can tell you with all confidence that the Reverend Warner will not proceed with the ceremony until you have done so."

"I do not believe there will be any ceremony," Rebecca said quietly, looking steadily into his eyes.

He looked back. "What are you telling me?" he asked.

"I don't think I am going to marry you, Philip," she said.

There was silence between them for a while. He laughed briefly and passed a hand across the back of his neck. "And all because I object to having girls in the school?" he said. "Do you not think this quarrel has got a little out of hand, Rebecca? Let us not do anything hasty. Run along and enjoy yourself for a while. We will meet again later when our tempers have cooled. Perhaps we will be able to laugh at what has just happened."

Rebecca looked away from him and down at her hands. "I do not think so, Philip," she said sadly. "I believe we have just discovered what perhaps we have always been aware of, that there is a fundamental difference in our outlook on life. But I shall do as you say. I wish to find Mr. Sinclair and talk to him for a while. I shall see you later?"

He nodded and turned toward the parsonage. Rebecca watched him go until he was inside the house and the door closed behind him.

Now what had she done!

Harriet was holding court to a circle of young men at the edge of the village green. Christopher, Julian, Mr. Carver, and Mr. Bartlett were all there, as well as a few other acquaintances. She was twirling her pink parasol behind her head.

"She said there was to be a big upheaval in my life soon," she was saying as Rebecca came within earshot. "And I shall soon be happily married to a man who is within the boundaries of the village at this moment." She looked coquettishly around at the interested faces surveying her.

"You don't really set any store by what fortune-tellers say, do you, though, Harriet?" Julian asked.

Harriet looked archly back at him and gave her parasol

an extra twirl. "Oh," she said, "when they tell me things
I wish to hear, I invariably believe them."

"Did she describe this fortunate man?" Mr. Bartlett
asked, bestowing a half bow and a smile of great charm on
Harriet.

"No," Harriet said, "not his appearance, that is. But
she did say that he would be a masterful man who would
sweep me off my feet, so to speak."

She and Mr. Bartlett exchanged what Rebecca could
only describe to herself as a meaningful smile. Her own
heart was knocking against her ribs again. There was
Christopher only a few feet away. A mere word on her
part would bring his attention. It would be a matter of a
moment to draw him away from the group so that she might
say her piece. She drew a breath and opened her mouth.

"Mr. Sinclair," Harriet said, closing the distance that
lay between them, "I have heard that you are to return to
town tomorrow, and I have the greatest curiosity to discover what lies in your future. Something incurably romantic I am sure, sir. Come, I shall accompany you to the
fortune-teller's tent."

"Hm," Christopher said, but he smiled down at Harriet. "I always consider that life is made more exciting by
our ignorance of what the future holds. However, to please
you, Miss Shaw, I shall go and discover the worst. Lead
on!"

"Miss Shaw," Julian said, turning to Rebecca eagerly,
"have you seen the juggler? He's a different fellow from
the one who usually comes here. And one must admit that
that one used to be a trifle pathetic. This one can keep six
balls in motion all at once while dancing the most strenuous jig."

"Indeed," Rebecca said, "that must be quite a sight."

"Come and see," he said. "Wish I knew how the
fellow did it. I have a notion to astound everyone by
learning, but I never could keep more than two balls at a
time off the ground."

Rebecca laughed and placed her arm through his. "I

think you might expend your energies on worthier accomplishments," she said. "What are your plans for the winter? Are you really considering a Grand Tour?"

"Oh, I don't know," he said vaguely. "Christopher is awfully keen to send me, but I hate to add one more burden to his load."

"I am sure he would not offer to send you if he did not really wish you to go," Rebecca said. "It would seem such a shame to miss an opportunity like that. It would probably please your brother to do something quite handsome for his family for once, too."

He laughed. "For once?" he said. "Christopher has been doing things for our family for years now. I hope the time is coming when we will be able to pay him back a little for all he has done, or at least stop being quite so dependent on him, Ah, here he is. It is hard to see through such a crowd. Here, Miss Shaw, let me go ahead of you. I shall get you a place in the front where you can see just how clever the fellow is."

And indeed Julian was quite right. Rebecca had never seen such an impressive display of skill as that shown by the new juggler. Soon she was applauding and exclaiming as loudly as the smallest child in the crowd.

Somehow after that Rebecca found that she had lost all her courage where Christopher was concerned. She spent the rest of the day avoiding him, telling herself each time she might have had an opportunity to approach him that the time was not just right. She wandered from attraction to attraction in something of a daze. What a mess she was making of this day, the day that was supposed to be the beginning of a newer and more tranquil life. Had she really almost ended her betrothal? She was to be married the following week. The wedding ceremony and breakfast had already been arranged. Yet she had told Philip that she did not think there would be any ceremony.

What had caused her to speak so rashly? He had said himself that it was ridiculous to allow a quarrel over a minor school matter to blight their whole relationship. But

was it a small matter? Could she marry a man who had
such a feudal notion of a woman's place in life? He had
made it quite clear that he would expect unquestioning
obedience from her after their marriage, not only because
that was the way things were, but because he really believed women's minds to be inferior to men's. No, she
could not. She really could not marry him under the
circumstances.

The realization terrified her. If she could not marry
Philip, what was to become of her? What else was there?
She would have to seek employment as a teacher or governess. When Papa died, she had quite cheerfully expected
to have to do so, but time had passed since then. She was
too old to begin such a new life. Yet she must. She could
not marry Philip, even if he still wished to continue with
their plans. And she had known all along, had she not, that
she was not really doing the right thing to betroth herself
to him? At least, she had known recently. It was the safe
thing to do, but that did not make it right.

Rebecca mingled and talked and laughed in an almost
desperate attempt to postpone the panic that she felt was
awaiting her when she finally realized the full implications
of what she was doing. She joined the ring of spectators
around the maypole late in the afternoon, watching the
young girls and lads dancing around it, each holding to a
brightly colored ribbon, each dancing in such a skilled
manner that the ribbons never became entangled.

The afternoon ended late with the presentation of prizes
for the various competitions. Maude took her husband's
place. She had seemed to enjoy the day, Rebecca thought.
Certainly she had been busy and sociable all the time.
They were all to dine at the parsonage that evening, the
members of Uncle Humphrey's household and the Sinclairs. Later in the evening there was to be general dancing
on and around the village green. She would talk to Christopher during the evening, Rebecca decided. It would be
easier then to speak with some privacy. In the meantime
she guessed that she and Philip would have to come to

some definite understanding about their betrothal and wedding plans. When would life become less complicated?

The dining room in the parsonage was quite overcrowded with all the guests seated around the table. However, no one seemed to mind. Only Rebecca, Philip, and Maude were relatively quiet during dinner. Everyone else was determinedly merry, and all agreed that the fair had surpassed itself this year. The gentlemen did not remain at the table after the ladies but accompanied them to the small sitting room, where Ellen and Primrose agreed to entertain the gathering on the spinet until it was time to go outside for the dancing.

Philip, having seen that all his guests had been served tea, raised his eyebrows in Rebecca's direction and suggested that she take a turn in the garden with him. Mrs. Sinclair smiled conspiratorially at Rebecca and nodded her head.

"Yes, yes, Miss Shaw," she said, "do not let our presence disturb you young people. You run along and have a little time to yourselves before the street is so crowded with people that you will hardly be able to move."

"I have been thinking and thinking all day about what you said earlier," Philip said as soon as they were alone together outside the house, "and I cannot help concluding that perhaps you are right to question the wisdom of our marrying. You have many excellent qualities, Rebecca, and I have always concentrated my attention on those. I have chosen to ignore your very independent streak, thinking that perhaps it would not matter. But now I am afraid that it might. What have your thoughts been?"

Rebecca sighed. "I am afraid I have not changed my thinking since this morning," she said. "I have been doing the same as you, Philip, concentrating on those qualities I admire in you and ignoring those I would find it harder to live with."

"I fear we both merely wanted to marry," Philip said, "as a convenience, perhaps. We seem to be suited, do we not? But we are not."

"I am sorry, Philip," Rebecca said, stopping and turning to look into his face. "Will this cause you dreadful embarrassment? Canceling our wedding plans, that is, just one week before the appointed day?"

He smiled bleakly. "It is better to discover now that we are not suited than one week after the wedding, do you not agree? I am sorry too, Rebecca. I like you and respect you a great deal, and even now part of my mind is telling me how foolish I am not to be begging you to reconsider."

"Yes," she said, laughing ruefully. "My mind is doing the same thing."

He held out his right hand. "Let us remain friends, shall we, Rebecca?" he said. "I should hate for there to be bitterness and enmity between us just because we have decided that we would not suit as husband and wife."

She put her own hand in his. "Oh, yes," she said, greatly relieved, "I shall need you as a friend, Philip. We will be doing a great deal of arguing over the school in the coming months, I predict, and really it is no fun at all to argue with enemies."

He looked down at her unsmilingly, but there was a gleam of appreciation in his eyes. "You will not win, I can tell you now," he said, "but it seems that I have just given up my right to insist that you accept my decision." He bent forward quite unexpectedly and kissed her on the forehead.

They turned back toward the house to rejoin his guests.

• 15 •

Rebecca had danced with Mr. Carver and Mr. Bartlett. The street and the green were crowded with people. She guessed that almost everyone for miles around had come into the village for the evening festivities. Harriet had danced constantly but had been nowhere near Mr. Bartlett. Maude must be feeling great relief. It looked as if her stepdaughter was going to accept the inevitable with the minimum of fuss. Maude herself had danced with Christopher, and she was standing now a little removed from the dancers talking to Philip. Both of them looked grave. It was the first time Rebecca has seen them together since the night of the Langbourne ball.

She looked at Philip quite dispassionately. He was extremely handsome in his dark clothes and with his gleaming blond hair. And she felt nothing. There should surely be some panic at the realization of what she had just given up. There should be some regret over the loss of a good man as a prospective husband. But she felt nothing, except perhaps relief that she no longer had to pretend even to herself that her life was taking a course that was pleasing to her.

It was becoming more and more difficult to seek out Christopher. It seemed clear that he had been making as great an effort as she during the day to avoid a meeting. Several times she had been close enough to him to speak or at least to smile, but he had chosen to pretend she was not there. Even at the dinner table he had not looked at her once as far as she knew. Tonight he had danced every dance and had always been intent on talking to his partner when she was dancing near.

How was she to approach him? Ask him to dance with her? The very idea was enough to make her feel quite faint. Tap him on the shoulder and ask if she could have a word with him? She would never pluck up enough courage. Perhaps it would be better after all to say nothing. If he had wanted her to know about his involvement in the school, he would have told her himself. He would not thank her now for broaching the topic. And the occasion was hardly suitable for such a conversation.

Rebecca leaned against a tree outside the tavern in an unconscious effort to avoid notice by would-be dancing partners. She should seek out Maude or Mrs. Sinclair. It was unseemly to be alone thus. But her eyes were resting almost absently on Christopher as he returned a flushed young lady to her mama's side. And finally, quite accidentally, their eyes met. They both looked away hastily and then back at each other again. And this time the look held for several moments until Rebecca looked down in confusion.

Julian was at her side, grinning with the joy of the evening's activities, asking her to join him for the next country dance. She pushed her back away from the tree.

"Sorry, youngster," Christopher's voice said, "this dance has been promised to me, I believe?"

He was smiling when Rebecca turned to him, and holding out a hand for hers.

"Thank you, Julian," she said, turning back to the younger brother. "Perhaps later?" And she placed her hand in Christopher's.

Even then she said nothing, but allowed him to lead her to join a set. It was a particularly vigorous and intricate country dance. They were separated frequently, and even when they danced together there were so many figures to execute and so many steps to remember that there was no chance to speak even a word. When it was over, he laid her hand on his arm in a courtly gesture that seemed strange in such a setting, and looked around him.

"Would you care to join my mother and sisters?" he asked. "I am sure they would be delighted with your company."

Rebecca tightened her grip on his sleeve and drew a nervous breath. "Christopher," she said, "I have been wishing to talk to you. All day."

He looked down into her face, a gleam of something in his eyes for a moment. "What is it?" he said. "Shall we walk?"

They walked in silence until they had passed the dense crowd around the dancing area and were strolling along the less crowded street outside the church. He had taken her hand and tucked it more comfortably beneath his arm. Rebecca could feel the blood pounding through her temples. Had she done the right thing? How was she to begin to speak to him?

"Is something troubling you, Becky?" he asked at last. "Can I be of any service to you?"

"No, there is nothing wrong," she said, "But I had to talk to you before you return to town. I have done you an injustice and I feel conscience-bound to apologize."

He laughed briefly. "You apologize to me?" he said. "What can you have possibly done to wrong me?"

"I have thought of you as being shallow and uncaring, and have treated you accordingly," she said. "I really believed that you visited the school only because you wished to impress others. I did not know that it is only through your generosity that the school exists at all. I might have known, of course. You were ever concerned about the plight of the poor. And I did not know about Cyril's eyeglasses. I thought that Philip had paid for them, you see, and I felt anger that you would still visit the school and show special interest in the boy when you had done nothing to really help him."

She was talking very fast.

Christopher lightly covered her hand with his. "Hush," he said. "You do not need to say more, Becky. I am vexed with Everett for telling you as much as you know. I thought I could have trusted him."

"I had guessed part of the truth," Rebecca said. "He merely confirmed my suspicions."

"Well," he said, "perhaps no real harm has been done. I am conceited enough to be pleased that there is perhaps at least something in me about which you will be able to think kindly. But I am not sure my motives have been as pure as you might think. I believe I was thinking less of the welfare of your boys than I was of enabling you to achieve one of your dreams. I like to think that I would have helped Everett even if I had not known of your interest in the scheme, but I cannot be sure that I would."

Rebecca looked up at him, a slight frown on her face. "You did it for me?" she asked. "Why? Was it a salve to your conscience?"

He winced. "You might call it that," he said. His hand was still over hers. They had walked, without realizing it, past the church and the schoolhouse and onto the country lane that led to both their homes. The crowds were all behind them.

"I thank you anyway," she said. "The school has meant a great deal to me."

"Then I am happy," he said. "And would you like another room added, Becky, so that you can have your girls' school too? I shall give it to you as a wedding gift, shall I?" His hand tightened momentarily around hers.

Rebecca did not answer immediately. "I think I have a long battle ahead before I can persuade Philip that there is a need for a girls' school," she said, "but I do mean to fight it. And I shall not say no to the gift if you still wish to give it when the time comes. But it will not be a wedding gift, Christopher."

"You do not wish me to give you a wedding gift?" he asked gently.

"There is to be no wedding," she said.

He stopped walking and turned to her. "What are you saying?" he asked. "The scoundrel has not let you down, has he? My God, I will not allow anyone else to do that to you. I'll kill him!"

"No," she said earnestly, laying a hand on his arm. "It was a mutual agreement, Christopher, made just today. We would not suit. I think we have both known it for quite a while, but it is hard to admit one has made a mistake when something as formal as a betrothal has taken place."

He was searching her face in the moonlight. "It seemed to me that you were eminently suited," he said. "I thought you loved him, Becky."

"No," she said, and for some reason, standing there and looking up at him, in surely almost the exact spot where they had stood seven years before, all the confusions and uncertainties of the previous weeks washed over her and she was powerless either to look away or to stop the tears from trickling down her cheeks.

He bent closer and put his hands on her shoulders. "Are you crying, Becky?" he said. "Oh, God, it has upset you after all. Don't cry, my love. Somehow everything is going to turn out well for you. It must. I don't know anyone who deserves happiness more than you do."

And he put his arms right around her and pulled her against him, cradling her head against his shoulder, rocking her comfortingly, murmuring unintelligible words into her hair.

Rebecca would not let herself break down completely. She leaned against him, relaxed into the strength of his body, closed her eyes to feel the comfort of his hand and cheek on her head, and brought herself slowly under control. But she did not want to break away. This moment was the whole of life. Tomorrow he would be gone. Perhaps in five minutes' time she would be thinking about his desertion again. For the rest of her life she would miss him and love him. But for this moment she was here in his arms and nothing else mattered. If he were a murderer and a traitor, it would not matter at the moment. Now was all that was important.

"You can let me go now, Christopher," she forced herself to say eventually. "I must be tired. I did not mean to cry." But she made no effort to pull away from him.

He too did not let go of her, but actually tightened his hold and rubbed his cheek across the top of her head. "I should not say this," he said. "I have no right. No right at all. But I have to say it just once as a self-indulgence. I love you, Becky Shaw. I have loved you for seven years and probably even before that, and I shall go to my grave loving you. It will not be very gratifying to you to know that you are loved by someone like me, but maybe sometimes when you are depressed as you have been this evening and perhaps feel very much alone, you may gain some fleeting comfort from knowing that there is one man to whom you are the whole world."

When she had finished taking some deep breaths in a conscious effort to keep control over herself, Rebecca found that her arms had somehow found their way around his neck. Her face was still buried against the lapels of his coat. "I don't love you," she said incoherently. "I can't love you, Christopher. I can't forgive you. I can't love you. I can't, Christopher, I can't."

She lifted her face to him and tightened her arms around his neck. "Tell me I am wrong," she cried. "Tell me that it is possible for me to love you. I can't. I can't forgive you."

"I know," he said, and his mouth was on hers, both arms bent beneath hers so that he held her head with both hands.

Rebecca did not fight his kiss or the hot passion that soon had her arching her body against the heat of his, tilting her head, and opening her mouth beneath his. She could not love him as she had in the past. She could not forgive him. But for this moment she did not care what her rational feelings might be. Her body knew that it was with the only man who would ever stir her, and she did not care what he was or what he had done. He was Christopher.

He released her mouth finally and gazed down into her eyes. He was not smiling and he was quite untriumphant.

"I can't ever forgive you, Christopher," she whispered.

"I know," he said. "I knew it more than six years ago. I knew it when I made the hardest decision of my life. I knew not only that I would lose you forever, but also that I would be hated and despised forever by the one person I love more than life itself. I made the choice. I have to live with the consequences."

He bent down and kissed her softly on the lips again. "Some kind angel must have granted me these few encounters with you in the past weeks," he said. "I will live on the memories. But I fear I have done you a great disservice, Becky, churning up old hurts when I had promised never to come near you again. Come, love, let me walk you back to the village. We have wandered too far already. Tomorrow I shall be leaving. I shall not trouble your peace again."

He took her hand and drew it under his arm again and they turned back in the direction of the village from which the sounds of music and merriment could still be heard. Rebecca felt totally powerless either to slow their progress or to say another word.

They had almost reached the church on their way to the area of the village where the dance was still noisily in progress. There was no one else at this end of the street. No one visible, that is. But there was the sound of voices raised in fierce argument coming from somewhere behind the parsonage. Christopher gripped Rebecca's arm a little tighter and would have hurried her past. But she stopped suddenly.

"Hush!" she said. "Listen."

He looked down inquiringly at her, but her face was intent.

"That is Harriet," she said. "One of those voices belongs to Harriet. She must be in trouble."

Christopher released her arm without another word and raced up the pathway leading to the parsonage and around the side of the house. Rebecca followed close on his heels.

They both came to a stop when they rounded the back corner of the house and saw the scene before them. Mr. Bartlett's curricle and grays stood ready for travel in the laneway that ran the length of the village behind most of the buildings. Harriet stood beside it, wearing a pelisse that she had not worn all day. Mr. Bartlett stood at the horses' heads and in front of him, almost nose to nose with him, in fact, stood Mr. Carver.

"I shall say it only once more, Mr. Carver," Harriet was saying shrilly. "You cannot stop us. What we do is absolutely none of your concern. Stand aside immediately."

"And I shall tell you only once more, ma'am," Mr. Carver said, an unaccustomed menace in his voice, "that I shall deal with you after I have dealt with this scoundrel."

Mr. Bartlett was looking quite relaxed, almost amused. "I have been very patient, Carver," he said, "but now I am afraid it really is time for Miss Shaw and me to leave. We have a sizable distance to travel tonight. I really will have to consider removing you with my whip if you will not stand aside of your own volition. Of course, I suppose I should render you senseless and bind and gag you, because doubtless you will run squawking your story as fast as your legs will carry you as soon as we have left, but pursuit may be difficult. There are those crossroads a mere three miles away, and it would be tricky for our pursuers to decide which one we will have taken." He smiled.

Mr. Carver did not shift his ground by so much as an inch. "You may leave anytime you please, Bartlett," he said, "and good riddance to you. But you ain't taking Miss Shaw with you. If she wasn't such an addle-pated female, she would know better than to have considered it. Eloping with a penniless good-for-nothing! Chit needs to be soundly thrashed."

"Oh!" Harriet said, her hands clenched into fists at her side, "You are always saying that. You are beginning to sound like a parrot who has learned only one phrase. Get away from here, Mr. Carver. I do not need you or anyone else telling me what I should do."

Rebecca finally regained the use of both her feet and her voice. She rushed forward. "Harriet," she hissed, "what is going on here?"

"Oh, not you too, Rebecca," Harriet said crossly. "The whole militia will be here soon."

"You were not really planning to elope, were you?" Rebecca asked incredulously, but she glanced at Harriet's pelisse and at the two bandboxes that had been half hidden beneath the seat of the curricle, and looked back accusingly at her cousin. "Oh, Harriet," she said, "how could you? I did not think that even you could be so lacking in conduct. You must come back with me at once to Maude. We must be very thankful that you have been discovered before it is too late."

"Ah, and here comes Sinclair too," Mr. Bartlett said. "The whole righteous crew. Are you forever to dog my footsteps, Sinclair? I quite fail to see what concern Harriet is of yours. However, it does seem that there is to be no elopement tonight. One can hardly wave good-by to a farewell party when one is eloping. The effect would be quite ruined."

Rebecca, glancing briefly at Christopher, was amazed to see just how furious he was. She was suddenly afraid and caught at Harriet's arm in an attempt to remove her from the scene. But Harriet shook off her hand impatiently.

"Leave me alone, Rebecca," she said. "And all of you can go to the devil for all I care."

To her chagrin no one appeared to pay her the least attention except Rebecca, who caught at her arm again.

"Come away, Harriet," she said urgently. "There is going to be violence here."

Christopher had moved across to stand in front of Mr. Bartlett, beside his friend. "Stand back, Luke," he said. "This is mine. Your behavior here is very much my concern, Bartlett," he said, his voice shaking with such anger that Rebecca pulled anew at Harriet's unresponsive arm. "I should have killed you several years ago, or at least punished you to such a degree that you would never have attempted anything like this ever again. I let you go then, thinking you were beneath my contempt. This time you will not escape so lightly. This time you have committed the mistake of making an innocent though headstrong young girl of good family your victim. You had better prepare to defend yourself.''

He began methodically to remove his coat and roll back his shirt sleeves. Without turning around or removing his eyes from his adversary, from whose face the unruffled calm had vanished, he said, ''Becky, will you take your cousin away from here, please? What is about to happen is not for the eyes of ladies.''

Suddenly Harriet's arm was no longer resistant. She looked at Rebecca, bewildered, the beginnings of fear in her eyes.

''Stop them!'' she said. ''Stop them, Rebecca.''

''Come,'' Rebecca said calmly, ''we will go and find Maude. I don't believe there is any way to stop this fight, and I am not sure I would try even if I thought there were.''

Harriet allowed herself to be led around to the front of the parsonage and out into the street. It seemed something of a shock to both that the crowds and the noise and the dancing were proceeding just as they had been all evening.

Yet they were not the only ones who were not involved in the festivities. As they drew closer to the crowd, they became aware of Mrs. Sinclair and Ellen hurrying toward them.

''Ah, thank goodness,'' Mrs. Sinclair sang out when they were still several yards distant. ''We have searched all over the place for you two young ladies. Mr. Sinclair and Julian have gone looking in the other direction. And Christopher is nowhere to be seen either.''

''What has happened?'' Rebecca asked.

''My dear,'' said Mrs. Sinclair, ''a servant came riding in from Limeglade to say that his lordship has taken a turn for the worse and that Dr. Gamble was to come and Lady Holmes. Poor lady! She was almost distracted what with blaming herself for leaving him and looking in vain for Harriet. 'You take our carriage, your ladyship,' I said, 'and leave everything else to us. We will see that Harriet comes home as soon as may be.' Julian was going to drive her, but the Reverend Everett was kind enough to take her himself. He will be a comfort to her and to Lord Holmes if he really is poorly.''

"Papa?" Harriet said rather shakily. "He is really sick? I must go to him at once. Rebecca, come with me, will you?"

"Yes, of course," Rebecca replied. "We shall take the gig at once. It is such a bright moonlit night that there will be no trouble seeing our way."

"Not alone," Mrs. Sinclair said firmly. "I will not hear of it, my dears. Julian will take you when he comes back from searching for you in the other direction. Ah, thank goodness. Here comes Christopher."

They all turned to watch him walk along the street beside Mr. Carver. To Rebecca's searching eyes, he looked quite as calm and immaculate as he had looked earlier in the evening. There was no sign of Mr. Bartlett.

"Christopher," Mrs. Sinclair called, "here are the Misses Shaw with an urgent need to return home. Poor Lord Holmes has taken a bad turn and the doctor and the ladies have been sent for. The vicar has taken Lady Holmes already and left the gig for the young ladies. And I have just been saying that I will not hear of them going off alone."

"Indeed not," he said, looking with quiet sympathy at Harriet and Rebecca. "I shall accompany them, Mama. You need not worry. We had best leave immediately. Will you take my arm, Miss Shaw?" These last words were directed quite gently to Harriet, who indeed was looking as if she was not capable of getting anywhere under her own power.

It was an almost silent journey. Rebecca could not guess what Christopher's thoughts might be. He appeared perfectly calm, and there was no sign that he had just been involved in a fight—no black eyes or bloody nose or split lips. She longed to ask him what had happened, where Mr. Bartlett was now, how Mr. Carver had discovered the elopement plan, why he had been quite so angry with Mr. Bartlett, what exactly he had meant by his references to the past, if he was nursing some broken ribs or some other ghastly but invisible injury.

She wanted to question Harriet, to find out why the girl had been about to elope with Mr. Bartlett, where they had planned to go, what they had planned to do afterward. Her head teemed with enough questions to keep them all talking nonstop during five journeys from the village to Limeglade. But she said nothing. And what of Uncle Humphrey? Had the doctor been right and was he now really ill?

"It is all my fault that Papa is ill at all," Harriet said from her seat between Rebecca and Christopher. Her voice was unusually subdued. "That journey to Cenross Castle was just too much for him. Do you think he is really ill, Rebecca?"

Rebecca murmured something soothing.

"I know what you are both thinking," Harriet blurted a little later. "You both despise me."

"I believe your cousin loves you simply because you are her cousin," Christopher said. "And my feelings are merely ones of relief that you have been rescued from the clutches of an out-and-out bounder. You need not fear recriminations from either of us, I think, Miss Shaw."

"But I deserve to be despised!" Harriet said vehemently and quite unexpectedly. "It was a stupid thing to do. I only did it because Maude tried to separate us. I had not even thought seriously of marrying Mr. Bartlett before that. But I could not let her think that I would give in meekly to her bidding. I really am too stubborn for my own good."

Neither of her companions said anything to contradict this opinion of herself that Harriet had given. She looked down at her hands for the remainder of the journey home and said no more until Christopher drew the horses to a halt outside the main doors of the house.

"I do hope Papa felt better once he saw Maude," she said.

But when they went inside, a poker-faced butler directed them to the drawing room, where they found Maude and Philip standing at opposite sides of the empty fireplace. Maude, her face deathly pale, came hurrying across the room when they entered, her hands outstretched to Harriet.

"My dear," she said, "it was much worse than we could have imagined. He is gone, Harriet." Her eyes, fixed on her stepdaughter's, were dazed.

"What?" Harriet said on a gasp. "Papa is—dead? No, he cannot be. I won't believe it. I must go to him now."

"No," Maude said, catching Harriet by the shoulders as she turned. "We shall both see him afterward, Harriet. But not just yet. He is gone, dear. Your papa is dead. He had a heart seizure."

And Maude pulled the stunned girl into her arms.

Rebecca had not moved. She still stood just inside the door. She looked across the room to Philip, whose eyes were fixed on Maude and Harriet, and back to the doorway to Christopher, whose hand was still on the handle of the door.

It was Christopher who strode across to her, put a firm arm around her shoulders, and led her to a chair before crossing the room and pouring them all a drink of brandy from the decanter that was always kept on a sideboard there.

• 16 •

Maude, Harriet, and Rebecca were sitting in the garden. Each was wearing deep mourning, black shawls in place over black dresses. Early autumn was already in the air.

"It is all my fault," Harriet said, staring listlessly ahead of her. "Papa would never have died had I not insisted on going to Cenross Castle for my birthday. No one else wanted to go, but I would insist. And he had to climb all that way up the hill and sit in a windy courtyard for a full afternoon. And then I scared him by going down to those infernal dungeons and hurting my ankle. I had no idea that his heart could not stand the strain. Oh, I am so selfish! I killed Papa."

"Nonsense, Harriet," Rebecca said. "Of course you did not kill him. Your papa was an adult. He could choose for himself where he wanted to go and where not. And what was more natural than that a young girl whose birthday falls in August should want to go on an outing for the occasion? You must stop blaming yourself. Grief is hard enough to cope with without that."

"Yes, dear," Maude said, "Rebecca is quite right. You are in no way to blame. Your papa was afraid of fresh air and exercise. If he had taken his normal share of both through the years, I am sure his heart would not have weakened as it did."

"I would not even have been here on the night he died

if it had not been for Mr. Carver," Harriet said drearily. "I am the most selfish, thoughtless creature in the world."

"I think perhaps we should take a short walk, Harriet," Rebecca said, getting decisively to her feet. "There is nothing like exercise to calm the mind." She turned to Maude. "Mr. Carver was the one who brought Mr. Sinclair along in time to drive us home from the village that night," she explained,.

No one had told Maude of the failed elopement plan. She had had enough to cope with in the week that had elapsed since the death of her husband, receiving calls and preparing for the funeral two days before. Everyone who knew avoided the subject of her brother and left her to assume that Mr. Bartlett had decided to return to London the night of the fair instead of waiting until the next day. Indeed, Rebecca guessed that she was secretly relieved that her brother had not delayed. Had he done so, he might have used Lord Holmes's death as an excuse to stay awhile longer.

Harriet rose listlessly and obediently to her feet. She had been unusually docile in the past week. She and Rebecca strolled together along the winding driveway toward the gate.

"Harriet," Rebecca said when they were out of earshot of the garden, "please do not let Maude know what happened on the night of the fair. It would be very upsetting to her to know that about her brother."

"I think she already knows what he is like," Harriet said, "or she would not have gone to such lengths to warn me off. I have been such a fool, Rebecca. I did not even particularly like the man. I certainly did not wish to marry him. But I always have to assert my independence. I feel greatly mortified to think that several people had to become involved in order to rescue me. But I must admit that I am glad I was stopped. I would be married to him by now. And Mr. Carver has told me terrible things about him since that night."

"Well, it is all over," Rebecca said, "and I think it is

best forgotten. You have learned a lesson from it, Harriet, and that is the important thing.''

"He wants to marry me," Harriet said suddenly, a hint of the old spirit showing through the indignation in her voice.

"Who wants to marry you?" Rebecca asked, her stomach lurching uncomfortably.

"Mr. Carver," Harriet said. "Can you imagine, Rebecca? He wants to marry me. The nerve of the man!"

"He has asked you?" Rebecca asked incredulously.

"Yesterday, when he walked over here with Ellen and Primrose," Harriet said. "He did not exactly ask me, but he did say that with Papa gone I should need someone to look after me, someone who would not be afraid to tell me a few home truths. And someone to give me a good thrashing once in a while. Horrid man!" Her voice quivered with indignation.

Rebecca had a hard time keeping her face straight and her voice steady. "How do you know he was talking about himself?" she asked.

"Because I asked him!" Harriet said. "And he said that he would be committing himself to a life sentence if he took on the task, but he might be persuaded to do it. I really could have thrown something at him, Rebecca, and I would too, but the only thing to hand was that Wedgwood vase that Maude sets such store by. And I really did not think he was worth a Wedgwood vase and Maude's tears.''

"What will you do if he really does offer for you?" Rebecca asked curiously.

"I shall give him such a length of my tongue that he will never forget it!" Harriet said vehemently. "Horrid, presumptuous man. Though the challenge would be almost irresistible. It would be great sport to marry him and to bring him so under my thumb that he would cringe if I so much as looked at him. That would teach him a lesson.''

"Yes," Rebecca said dryly. "But somehow, Harriet, I do not think it could be accomplished. And what would happen then?"

Harriet considered. "Then I should probably have a sore posterior a few times," she said. "And I should probably fall in love with him because I have always longed to meet a man who would not put up with my whims and tantrums. Horrid man! He could never do it." She smiled.

Rebecca lapsed into silence, content with some very interesting thoughts for the moment. Harriet and Mr. Carver. It was almost too preposterous for belief. But it just might work. Her attention was caught after a while by the sound of horses' hooves and the almost immediate appearance of Christopher and Mr. Carver riding towards them along the driveway.

"Horrid man," Harriet muttered. "Here he comes again. I thought he and Mr. Sinclair were supposed to leave the day after the fair. Why did he have to stay and plague me with a visit every day since?"

"I believe they stayed to lend us some support," Rebecca said hastily, and composed her face to greet the two men, who were soon close to them and dismounting from their horses.

They turned back toward the house, Harriet walking ahead with Mr. Carver, and Rebecca and Christopher behind.

"How are you, Becky?" Christopher asked. "I was unable to come over here yesterday. It must be something of a relief to you and to Lady Holmes and Miss Shaw to have the funeral over."

They talked about inconsequential matters as they walked. Rebecca had at least part of her attention on the couple ahead of them. Harriet had chin and nose in the air in a theatrical effort to be disdainful. Mr. Carver walked along at her side, his face solemn, his shirt points digging sharply into his cheeks. They did not talk much.

Maude was still sitting in the garden when they reached the front of the house. With her was Philip. He hastily dropped her hand when the others came into sight.

"Lady Holmes," Christopher said, walking forward, his hand outstretched. "How are you?"

Maude smiled. "Better," she said. "Now that Lord

Holmes has been laid to rest and the will read, we can begin to recover again. Poor man. None of us realized just how ill he really was, even though Dr. Gamble had warned me that he might have a weak heart. I am very grateful to all your family and to Mr. Carver, Mr. Sinclair, for all the support you have given us in the last week. I really do not know how we would have gone along without you. I understand that you and Mr. Carver have even postponed your departure in order to be with us.''

"We leave tomorrow," Christopher said. "We have ridden over here this afternoon to say good-by. What are your plans, Lady Holmes? Will you remain here?''

"Oh, yes," she said, glancing hastily at Philip, "I shall stay here with Harriet for our year of mourning, anyway. Neither of us can really make plans for the future until then.''

Rebecca did not think it would be obvious to any of the others. She hoped it was not so; it would have been somewhat unseemly with Uncle Humphrey dead for only one week. But to her the rosy glow in Maude's cheeks and the almost chiseled set to Philip's face said worlds. Only time would tell, of course. But she would be very surprised if there were not a wedding to celebrate in little more than a year's time. And she would be very happy for them. They would suit.

"Miss Shaw," Mr. Carver was saying, "will you walk a little way?''

"If I do," Harriet said tartly, "I want Rebecca to come too. I am too young, sir, to be alone with a gentleman.''

Rebecca and Christopher exchanged a straight-faced grin. Now how could she know that he was grinning when not a muscle in his face had moved? she wondered. Probably in the same way that he would know she was smiling! They had often been able to communicate without words or even facial expressions.

Mr. Carver made a slight bow in Rebecca's direction. "Miss Shaw," he said, "can't I interest you in a walk? Your cousin has suddenly turned respectable.''

"Suddenly!" Harriet muttered, taking his proffered arm disdainfully. "Stay close, Rebecca."

They did not walk far, just a short way into the pasture. There Mr. Carver stopped, ascertained that they were out of sight of the group in the garden, and turned to Harriet.

"Don't know if you really want to embarrass Miss Shaw by having her here," he said. He paused for her reaction.

Harriet had turned rather pink in the face, but she looked severely back at him. "Rebecca," she said, without turning her head, "don't you dare move away."

"Think I had better marry you," Mr. Carver said without further preamble. "No telling what will come of you if I don't."

"Thank you," Harriet said. "I am about to swoon at the honor you have done me, sir. When do you get to the part about giving me thrashings?"

"Hope it won't ever be necessary," Mr. Carver said, "but I'll do it if I have to, Harriet."

"Oh!" she said, clenching her fists and pounding them on the air at her sides. "You are a horrid man. Is he not a horrid man, Rebecca?"

Rebecca wisely said nothing. She was somewhat embarrassed, as Mr. Carver had predicted. But she would not have missed the scene for worlds.

"Can't marry you for at least a year," Mr. Carver said. "Wouldn't be respectful to your papa. But want us to be betrothed so that I can come here occasionally to keep an eye on you."

"An eye is about all you will ever have on me, sir," Harriet said.

"Sinclair and I have to leave early in the morning," Mr. Carver continued. "Must have your final answer now. No time for games and nonsense, Harriet. Yes or no?"

"Is that all the proposal I get?" Harriet asked, very red in the face. "Do you call this the way to offer for a lady, sir?"

"Think yourself fortunate not to be slung over m'shoulder

and hauled off to the nearest parson," he said severely. "Yes or no, Harriet?"

"Ohhhh!" she wailed. "Yes, then. I see you will give me no peace until I consent. But you had better not ever try laying a violent hand on me, Lucas, or I'll, I'll—"

"May Miss Shaw leave now?" Mr. Carver asked. "She will be very mortified to have to stand there and watch me kiss you."

"You are not going to kiss me," Harriet said vehemently. "You stay there, Rebecca, if you please."

"Yes, I am," Mr. Carver said. "Man has a right to kiss his betrothed. You may leave, Miss Shaw."

Rebecca left.

A full ten minutes passed between the time when Rebecca returned to the group on the lawn and the arrival of Harriet and Mr. Carver. Harriet was looking very pink in the face as they approached.

"I know what you are all thinking," she sang out as soon as she could be heard, and she blushed a deeper shade of red, "and you are quite right. I have just consented to wed Lucas as soon as my year of mourning is over and I can leave off my blacks. I consider myself betrothed, though Lucas will have to call on Papa's cousin, of course, as he is now my guardian. Though why I should have to consult a man I have never even seen but once when Mama passed away, I do not know." Her face crumpled suddenly. "I wish Papa were here."

Christopher hastily rose to his feet. "I am more than delighted," he said. "I am sure you two will suit, though I cannot predict a tranquil relationship." He grinned. "One thing I can predict, though. Luke will be accepting the invitation that my mother has pressed on him to come back soon. Now I think it is time to leave."

He shook hands with Philip, Harriet, and Maude, and turned last to Rebecca. He had his back to the company as he held out his hand to her. He spoke for her ears only.

"Good-bye, Becky," he said, his eyes roaming her face. "I can leave with an easier mind knowing that your uncle has left you an annuity that will keep you in moderate comfort. You will continue with the school?''

"Yes," she said. There was a raw ache in her throat.

He retained his hold on her hand. "Be happy," he said. His eyes were holding hers almost desperately.

"Yes," she said.

He removed his hand and turned abruptly away from her. "Are you ready, Luke?" he asked.

Mr. Carver patted Harriet's hand, which was still linked through his arm. "Yes," he said. He turned to Maude. "Thank you, ma'am, for the hospitality you have shown me during m'stay," he said. "And accept again my deepest sympathies."

He raised Harriet's hand to his lips and turned to leave. He and Christopher walked away toward the stables, to which a groom had taken their horses when they arrived. Harriet and Rebecca stood looking after them while Maude got to her feet and invited Philip to take tea with them in the drawing room.

"Horrid man," Harriet said. "Why would he choose to offer for me only on the day he must leave and when I need him so with Papa gone?"

Rebecca did not answer. It was doubtful that she even heard. She was engulfed by mingled panic and indecision, and by a terrible depression. She would never see him again. He would come riding out of the stable in a moment and disappear down the driveway, and she would never see him again. Ever.

When the two men appeared on horseback, Harriet sighed and waved her hand. Rebecca swayed on the spot for perhaps half a minute, and then she lifted her black skirts and flew across the lawn as fast as her feet would carry her. There was no conscious thought in her mind, no idea of what she would do if she could reach him in time.

Christopher saw her coming and pulled his horse to a stop. He bent from the saddle as she got closer and reached out a hand for her. Even his movements seemed to be involuntary. "What is it, Becky?" he asked, searching her wild expression with concerned eyes. "What is it, love?"

She put her hand in his, but when she stood staring up at him, words would not come.

He let go of her hand, dismounted from his horse, and handed the reins to an interested Mr. Carver. "Take him back to the stable, will you, Luke?" he asked. "You might wish to take tea unless you would prefer to go home ahead of me."

Mr. Carver did as he was bidden, and Rebecca was aware with one part of her mind that Harriet was hurrying across the lawn toward the stable. She stared numbly at Christopher.

He tucked her hand through his arm and began to walk with her toward the driveway. "What is it, love?" he asked. "What can I do for you?"

"I have to tell you," she said. "I cannot let you go without telling you that I lied. I do love you. I do, Christopher, and at this moment I do not care what you did to me in the past. I can't let you go. Don't leave me. If you truly love me, as you said you did a week ago, don't leave me. I have no pride left. I love you."

She did not know what she expected. She had not planned this scene and had had no chance to form any expectations. But she began to turn cold when his only reaction was to walk steadily on without a word. They were well along the driveway, out of sight of the house, when he finally spoke.

"I cannot see any solution, Becky," he said. His voice was quite toneless. "We love each other. I would give my life for you. But we cannot marry, love. At the moment, perhaps, you do not care. But you would some time in the future, probably quite soon. You would remember that I once put my family before my love for you, and you would be bitter again. And I would not be able to defend myself, because I know you have every right to despise me. You were my betrothed. I had offered myself to you. And then I married someone else."

"What do you mean when you say you put your family before me?" Rebecca asked. "What did your family have to do with what you did?"

He looked down at her. "Is it possible that you never heard the real story?" he asked. "I would have thought the truth would have come out long ago, though at the time I chose to give you no reason for my actions. I preferred to have you think me a fortune hunter than to know the truth."

"I know nothing," Rebecca said, looking up at him wide-eyed, "beyond what you told me in the churchyard when you came home."

He took a deep breath. "I had to do it, Becky," he said. "There was no alternative except the ruin of my family. I had known for many years that my parents found it difficult to keep going, but I had not realized how desperate things really were until shortly before I went away to London. Papa was in so much debt that there seemed no way out at all, except to sell everything. Even then, he would barely have been able to pay his debts. I thought of everything, Becky. I thought of all the employment I could get and of taking my family to live with me. And at the same time I wanted to marry you and to start raising my own family. Nothing would answer. It could just not be done. I could not possibly have supported everyone on the salary of a schoolmaster or physician or clerk."

Rebecca stared at him. "You said nothing," she said.

"I could not worry you with my problems," he said. "It would not have been fair. And I wanted so much to be able to set the world at your feet."

"I never wanted anything but you," she almost whispered.

He covered her hand with his briefly. "I know that, love," he said. "But I did not even seem to have the freedom to offer you that much. I should have been hanged for all the promises I made you, especially at Cenross. I think I must have been trying to force my own hand, making it almost impossible for myself to give you up."

He laughed harshly. "So I ended up doing everything wrong. I promised you the world and I left you."

"You could have told me," Rebecca cried. "I could have helped you, Christopher. I could have worked too as a teacher or a governess. Why did you not tell me?"

He gave her a grimace of a smile. "I chose not to," he said. "I went to London to find what prospects there were of employment. And I discovered a gold mine!" His voice had become harsh. "I met Angela and her father, and for some reason her father made it very obvious to me that she was available. He was a man with one ambition in life: to reach the top of the social ladder by any means possible. He did not need a wealthy man—he had enough money for an army. He wanted a man of genteel birth. So I married her."

He looked down at Rebecca, but she kept her head lowered.

"I would not have done it for myself, Becky," he said. "Surely you will believe that. I do not think that I would even have done it for my parents. After all, it was Papa's compulsive gambling habits that had got them into the fix. But I looked at Julian and the girls, so young still, so oblivious to the ruin that was facing them, and I could not deny them the future when it was in my power to do something about it.

"Things have improved now. My actions jolted Papa back to a sense of his responsibilities, I believe. He has recovered well enough that he no longer needs my constant support. But at the time that marriage seemed absolutely necessary. I had to choose, Becky, between you and my family. And I chose my family, leaving you an abandoned woman. You see now why I cannot marry you? I would never be able to rid myself of the shame of my past. And you would not be able to forget, either."

"I would not want to forget," Rebecca said quietly but very firmly. "I want to remember always what you did, Christopher Sinclair. But why did you not tell me at the time? How could you have imagined that it would be worse for me to know the truth? Had I known, I would have urged you to do exactly what you did. You must know that. You do not imagine, do you, that I would have been selfish enough to keep you for myself when a whole family would have suffered as a result? I thought you knew me better.''

Christopher jerked to a halt and pulled her roughly into his arms. ''God, Becky,'' he said against her hair, ''you cannot know how filled with self-loathing I was for those five years of my marriage. I had to forget you, force you from my thoughts and my heart. I could not have stayed sane else. And besides, it seemed only fair that I marry Angela with the intention of making a proper marriage of it. I wanted to be able to give her all of myself. I tried. And I was never unfaithful to her, even when I realized that I had married a fiend and a slut.''

Rebecca shuddered within his arms.

''I was justly served,'' he said. ''She had married me too merely for convenience. She wanted respectability and easy access to the most exclusive of bedrooms. I discovered so many of her affairs that I eventually lost count. After the first few months ours was a marriage only in name. She had no attachment to anyone except perhaps to that scoundrel Bartlett, who I think had had hopes of marrying her himself, but who hung around even afterward because she lavished money on him. She seemed to believe it was his child she died bearing.''

''Oh, Christopher,'' Rebecca said, looking urgently up into his face, her arms clasped around his neck. ''And I thought I had suffered! Oh, my love, I wish I had known. No, I do not mean that, of course. I would have died, I think, if I had known the whole truth. But if I had just known why you left me. The worst part of these years has been thinking that all my life I had been deceived in your character. But you are far more wonderful than I ever dreamed.''

''Oh, no, Becky,'' he said with a shaky laugh, burying his face against her neck, ''no, do not put me on a pedestal, love. I will never be able to forgive myself for encouraging you to trust my love in the full knowledge that I might have to give you up.''

"Christopher, I love you," she whispered into his ear. "You will not leave me, will you? Please say you will not leave me. We can still have a life together. We are not so very old. I can still have a child or two."

He laughed and lifted his head to look down into her earnest face. "Becky," he said, "are you offering for me, love? Are you going to visit Papa and ask for my hand?"

She laughed uncertainly back at him. "If that is the only way to have you," she said, "then I shall do so. I shall even go down on my knees to you and ask formally, if you wish.''

He chuckled and caught her to him in such a tight hug that she felt as if all the air had been squeezed from her lungs. "Becky," he said, his cheek against the top of her head, "is it really possible that you can love me enough to forgive me? Will you have regrets later, love? I do not think I could bear that. Are you willing to marry me?"

"You have to marry me," she said into his neckcloth. "You have been alone with me, without a chaperon, for all of fifteen minutes. My virtue is hopelessly compromised."

He turned her face up to him with one finger beneath her chin. His face was very serious. "I love you, Becky," he said, "and I could think of no more fitting sentence for my wrongs than to be allowed to spend the rest of my days trying to make you happy. Will you marry me, my love?"

"Yes Christopher," she said, "Oh, yes."

His mouth on hers prevented any further talk for several minutes. And Rebecca's heart sang. This was not a sad or desperate kiss like the others they had shared since his homecoming. This was a kiss of love and affection, of promise, and—of passion. They broke away from each other, breathless.

"Ah," he said, "that brings back memories. I suppose I shall have to wait for you a deuced long time?"

"Not a full year," she said quickly. "Not that long,

Christopher. Uncle Humphrey was not my father or my husband. I won't have to wait a year for an uncle, will I?''

"I shall take you to London at Christmas time," he said, "and we will wed quietly. I don't believe that will be unseemly, Becky."

"Christmas time," she said and they smiled warmly into each other's eyes.

"That's an eternity!" they both said together, and they touched foreheads and laughed.

"A compromised woman you may be, my love," Christopher said, "but I will not have you a fallen woman. And you are in grave danger, believe me. Let us walk back to the house. Do you think the tea will still be warm in the pot?"

"We can find out," Rebecca said. "And I am just bursting to tell someone. The whole world, if possible."

He took her hand in a warm grip and turned her back in the direction of the house. "Let us go and tell the world," he said, smiling at her. But he did not immediately move. "But before the world is let in on the secret, love, one more kiss?"

Rebecca smiled and lifted her mouth to his.

About the Author

Raised and educated in Wales, Mary Balogh now lives in Kipling, Saskatchewan, Canada, with her husband, Robert, and her children, Jacqueline, Christopher, and Sian. She is a high school English teacher.

ROMANTIC INTERLUDES